ANGEL OF DESTRUCTION

The end of the war has not allowed beautiful but deadly Anna Fehrbach to retire. Working for the SS her principal antagonist was the Soviet Union, and to Joseph Stalin and his henchman Lavrenty Beria she remains the most wanted of all war criminals. Although under the aegis of the CIA, the Russians remain on her trail and elaborate plans are being laid for her capture and execution...

Christopher Nicole titles availble from Severn House Large Print

Angel Rising
Angel of Doom
Angel in Jeopardy
Angel of Vengeance
Angel in Read

ANGEL OF DESTRUCTION

An Anna Fehrbach Thriller

Christopher Nicole

Severn House Large Print
London & New York

This first large print edition published 2011
in Great Britain and the USA by
SEVERN HOUSE PUBLISHERS LTD of
9-15 High Street, Sutton, Surrey, SM1 1DF.
First world regular print edition published 2009 by
Severn House Publishers Ltd., London and New York.

British Library Cataloguing in Publication Data

Nicole, Christopher.
Angel of destruction.
1. Fehrbach, Anna (Fictitious character)--Fiction.
2. Women spies--Germany--Fiction. 3. Bahamas--Fiction.
4. Suspense fiction. 5. Large type books.
I. Title
823.9'14-dc22

ISBN-13: 978-0-7278-7981-3

Printed and bound in Great Britain by the
MPG Books Group, Bodmin, Cornwall.

I am become as death, the destroyer of worlds.

The Bhagavadgita

PROLOGUE

'It is such a lovely day,' Anna Fehrbach said. 'Would you like to swim with me?' Her voice was soft, with a delightful Irish lilt.

I was completely taken aback. Although over the last few weeks I had enjoyed a considerable mental intimacy with this remarkable woman, Anna Fehrbach, Countess von Widerstand, alias Mrs the Honourable Ballantine Bordman, alias Anna O'Brien, alias Anna O'Flaherty, alias Anna O'Donovan, alias Anna O'Rourke, alias Anna O'Reilly, alias Anna Fitzjohn, she had always maintained a physical aloofness between us, allowing herself nothing more than an occasional touch of my hand.

Now we sat on the naya of her home, high on the mountain known as Montgo, which rises above the little seaport and burgeoning tourist resort of Javea on the Spanish Costa Blanca. The house itself, cut six hundred feet up into the mountainside, was exquisite, the view, looking down on the Jalon Valley with its patchwork of multi-coloured fields, breathtaking.

Immediately beneath where we were sitting was the large pool, its water sparkling in the morning sunlight. But all of this beauty with which I was surrounded was eclipsed by the beauty seated beside me, sipping champagne as she smiled at me. Anna Fehrbach was eighty-nine years old! And yet so much remained of the young girl who had been called the most beautiful woman of her time, just as those who knew her secrets had called her the most deadly woman of any time. But after so many years, there were not many of those left; Anna had seen to that.

Having come across her name in a book I was researching on the Hitler war I had immediately been fascinated. References to her were scanty, again because most of the people who had known who and what she was were dead. She was a name here, a suspicion there, a whisper stealing through some of the darkest pages of recent history, who had disappeared without trace only a few years after the war had ended, while still in her prime and still pursuing her deadly purpose. It had seemed obvious that she must have died herself, murdered in some dark alley, finally overtaken by one of her many enemies. That is, supposing she had ever really lived, and not been a figment of frightened men's imaginations.

Inspired by the very idea of her, I had refused to admit that so evocative a personality could never have been, or that if she were now dead, there could be no trace of how and when and where it had happened. And so I had embarked on a hunt, whenever I could spare the time from earning a living, collecting every vestige of information I could discover about either her or the world in which she had lived, and fought ... and survived?

My search had received a huge boost when, in an old and tattered copy of the Tatler *glossy magazine, printed in early 1939, and depicting, amongst other celebrities at a race meeting in England, the Honourable Ballantine Bordman and his new and stunningly beautiful German bride, as had been her then persona; Anna was actually the daughter of an Irish journalist – which explained her brogue, certainly when speaking English – and an Austrian newspaper editor, born in Vienna in 1920. But by 1938, although she was only eighteen, the Nazis had already got hold of her, and quickly recognizing her enormous potential – in addition to her looks she had an IQ of 173 and was already a top athlete – had blackmailed her, by imprisoning her family as hostages for her cooperation, into working for them.*

The photo was a poor one, in black and white, taken from a distance, and somewhat blurred. But the tall, slender, so elegant figure in the sable coat and hat, from which her straight pale golden hair had drifted down to the small of her back, restrained only by a clasp on the nape of her neck had created an unforgettable image. That hair had alone made her stand out in a world of bobs and permanent waves.

And that alone had truly changed with age. It was now white and cut short. But the rest of her, the classic, slightly aquiline features, so poorly depicted in the photo, the so powerful but still compellingly shaped body, just under six feet tall, the long legs, the swelling bust, had hardly changed in seventy years. The only aspect of her not indicated by the photo, as she smiled charmingly at the man with whom she was speaking, was the ice-cold, lightning fast, and, when it was necessary, utterly ruthless brain, which had carried her, triumphantly, through so many potentially fatal situations, leaving behind her a trail of death and destruction ... when last we had spoken her body count had been ninety-four, and I knew that she had not yet completed her amazing story.

But from the beginning I had had no doubts that the legends of her deadly expertise with either gun, knife, or her bare hands were based on fact, and thus when my hunt had ended at the wrought-iron gates on the drive beneath the pool, and I had asked if I could see the reclusive widow who lived here, I equally could have had no doubt that I was taking my life in my hands.

I had been welcomed! I now knew that it had been a colossal stroke of good fortune, that I should appear at the very moment that Anna, for all her on-going good health, had been realizing that the end of her amazing life had to be in sight. The actually amazing part of that life had ended more than fifty years ago. Then circumstances had dictated that she should call a halt to her career: her two most long-standing and dangerous enemies were both dead, and so were too many of those she had counted as friends, and even lovers. Besides, by then she had accumulated the immense fortune that had enabled her to go where she chose, and live as she chose, with whom she chose.

So for fifty years she had disappeared from

that world stage across which she had flitted so tantalizingly. But now, just to vanish forever without trace into a remote Spanish grave with only her faithful companion Encarna to mourn her, would have made a nonsense of her life, and left her no more than an unsubstantiated legend. And then, while she had been brooding on this, even, she had confessed, contemplating writing her memoirs herself without any idea of what she would do with them when she was finished, who should turn up on her doorstep but an author-cum-journalist who had spent so much of his own life looking for her, almost like the answer to a prayer.

With a background such as hers, Anna was conditioned to suspicion of any itinerant stranger who might ring her bell. But after only a few minutes in my company, during which I had been uncomfortably aware that for all her age she yet possessed both the mental and physical ability to destroy me in seconds – even if she had only once revealed the pistol that was never far from her right hand – she had, with her acute powers of perception and understanding, been able to ascertain that I was no more than what I claimed, and warmed to me accordingly.

But yet, there had always been that suggestion of, this close but no closer. Until now! 'I would love to swim with you, Anna, but unfortunately—'

'You do not have a swim suit? Is that so important? I never wear one.'

Again I could not believe my ears. 'You mean—?'

Anna stood up. 'You have never struck me as being a prude. Or do you have some dreadful physical defect to be kept hidden?'

I could feel myself flushing. 'Well, no, but...'

She went to the head of the stairs and down to the pool level. 'This pool is absolutely private,' she said over her shoulder. 'It is above the level of the road beneath the house, and therefore cannot be overlooked from down there, and it is protected by the house itself from anywhere further up the mountain, and so cannot be overlooked from up there either.'

There was a table with a multi-coloured shade umbrella over it and two metal chairs. Anna took off her shirt and laid it on the table. Following her down the steps, I caught my breath. I had not known what to expect, what I dared expect of a woman who was eighty-nine years old. But she still wore no bra, and the breasts were still full, and if they sagged, it was only slightly, and were the more entrancing for that.

Now she released her belt and slipped her pants down to her ankles before stepping out of them. Her legs, so long, so slender, and yet so clearly strong, were no less breathtaking. And there, nestling into her groin on top of the silk knickers was the thin leather belt and the holstered Walther PPK automatic pistol that she had used to such deadly effect over the years. I had to ask, 'Do you always wear that?'

'It became a way of life. I put it on every morning when I dress.'

'Is it the same gun given you by Joe Andrews in 1946?'

'No. I told you, remember, that I lost that one in that mud-stained shoot-out in Brazil.'

'Four Russian operatives, all killed,' I recalled, 'with a single shot to the head.'

'Well,' she said, defensively, 'they had come to take me back to Moscow to stand trial for my attempt on the life of Stalin. Was I to walk meekly back into the Lubianka and then a hangman's noose? I had been there before. As for there being four of them, they made the usual mistake, even if they knew who I was, of supposing they were dealing only with a rather gorgeous and innocent young woman.'

She spoke in such a matter of fact, almost ingenuous, fashion of an incident that would have left most young women, whether gorgeous and innocent or not, in a traumatized state for the rest of their lives. But then that had been only one of a score of similar incidents, all with the same outcome. I remembered that she had often compared herself to a wartime fighter pilot, who dispassionately accepted being scrambled and required to fly into danger, almost daily, and who, equally dispassionately, shot down his enemies whenever they crossed his path ... and did so without remorse or regret.

'Anyway,' she added, 'There were only three single shots to the head. Owing to circumstances, I had to shoot the fourth man twice. But then I had to get rid of the gun. But I realized how useful a weapon it was. I mean, I preferred the Luger I had used in the SD, but that was difficult to conceal. This little thing, as you can see, fits into every nook and cranny. So I've used one

ever since.'

She took off the gun belt and laid it also on the table, then dropped the knickers. More entrancement, but I was already staring at the blue stain on the pale flesh, some inches above either the silk or the belt or the pale pubic hair. As she observed, 'That was where Hannah Gehrig shot me, remember?' she said. 'In 1939.'

'Seconds before you broke her neck.'

Anna gave one of her entrancing moues. 'If I had not done that, she would have shot me again.' She walked down the steps into the water, without, to my surprise, taking off any of her exquisite jewellery, the little gold bar earrings, dangling from gold clips, the gold crucifix hanging between her breasts – a reminder of her Catholic background and upbringing – the huge ruby solitaire on the forefinger of her right hand, not even the gold Rolex on her wrist, but this was obviously waterproof. I recalled that, the watch apart, the jewellery had been loaned to her by her Nazi masters to enhance the image they had wanted, that of a wealthy aristocrat, but being Anna, when the Third Reich had collapsed, she had made sure that the jewellery survived, along with herself.

I followed her into the water, watching her perfectly rounded buttocks moving gently against each other. Perhaps the most attractive thing about her was the complete absence of either self-consciousness or coquetry. 'May I ask...?'

'Of course you may. It is not a miracle, although of course I have been lucky. Every day

of my life that I have been able, that is, when I have not been travelling or under restraint, or –' she smiled as she turned to face me and touched the bullet mark – 'in hospital, I have exercised, quite severely. I do it still, every morning. Just as I practise with my pistol, several days a week. But apart from Hannah Gehrig's bullet, I have never received a more serious injury than a sprained ankle, and while I know that for all the care I take of my health I could easily have been struck down by or suffered a serious illness, I still have my appendix, and such things as diabetes or hypertension have passed me by, so far at least.' She gave one of her delightful girlish giggles. 'I even still have my tonsils.'

I supposed the fact that her blood pressure should never have got out of control, had to be the true miracle of her life, when one considered the events of that life.

'I sometimes feel,' she went on, 'that I can claim that perhaps my good health stems from the way I always kept myself so fit. But then I wonder if it is not because neither God nor the Devil are in a hurry to have to deal with my soul.'

'You have kept yourself fighting fit even though you are retired, have been retired, for so many years? I would have thought, after you escaped from Germany in 1946, with ten million dollars' worth of Nazi gold—'

'That I would be able immediately to turn my back on my past?' She began to swim, with slow, luxurious overarm strokes. I followed her, and we gained the far end, where she rested her arms

on the coronation, breathing as evenly as ever, nipples just touching the stone with every breath, while I was panting, not entirely with exertion. 'I knew then,' she said, 'that I had the physical means to retire. But to retire, and have to spend the rest of one's life running, or looking over one's shoulder, is hardly to enjoy that life. Even today, as you see, although it hardly seems necessary, I go armed. Lifelong habits are hard to break. And besides, do you know, I had got into a way of living. So I was a monster. But as long as I could justify, at least to myself, what I had to do, from time to time, what I was required to do, I had no real wish to end it. Besides, I still had too many enemies, men, and the odd woman, who wanted me dead. So...'

'When you say, things you were required to do, this was under the contract you still had with the CIA, right?'

'It wasn't a written document, if that is what you mean. But Joe Andrews, and that meant the CIA, had helped me get my money out of the Soviet Zone in Germany. I could not have done it without them, just as I could not have done it without Clive Bartley and MI6. Equally, I could not have survived the war without the support of both those organizations.'

'Even if the OSS once tried to have you assassinated?'

'They convinced me that was a mistake.' She swam back to the steps and left the water, which continued to roll down her back and legs. She towelled herself dry, and sat beneath the umbrella. Encarna, her maid and long-time

companion, although a lifetime younger than her mistress, had thoughtfully brought down the ice bucket and glasses, and Anna filled two of these as I sat opposite her, feeling a delicious warmth spreading through my body. 'So I realized that even if I had the money, I was not yet in a position to reject them. To have had both the CIA and the MGB out for my blood would have made life intolerable.'

'And as you say, you were doing what you had always done, throughout your adult life.'

Anna gazed at me, and as on the few previous occasions that I had dared even by implication to question her ethics, my warmth dissipated in a sudden chill.

'Yes,' she said. 'I continued to dispose of certain people who I was persuaded had no right to clutter up this earth and who could not be reached by conventional justice.'

'Forgive me,' I said. 'I find you so fascinating I cannot resist exploring every aspect of your personality.'

Her eyes softened. 'I will forgive you, Christopher, because, I suppose, being a woman, I am susceptible to flattery.'

'And all the time the Soviets were still breathing down your neck.'

Anna drank champagne. 'I was their Public Enemy Number One. Well, I suppose, I had killed more than fifty of their so-called best operatives.'

'And, despite all these distractions, did you ever get around to marrying Clive Bartley?'

Anna Fehrbach smiled.

PRELUDE TO AN EXECUTION

'So there it is.' Josef Stalin struck a match and lit his pipe, then puffed, but it was not a contented puff. It expressed frustration, which, to the master of all Russia and most of Eastern Europe, was an emotional rarity, and could easily lead to the utmost fury.

Not that he revealed any sign of this. His eyes remained sleepy, his huge moustache so shrouded his lips that even the pipe revealed no perceptible expression of discontent. But Lavrenty Beria, seated opposite him in his private office in the Kremlin, had known his master long enough, and closely enough, to be uneasy. He took off his pince-nez to polish them, thus leaving his huge, bland face which merged into his equally huge totally hairless head without a single point of reference. 'Are you sure we are not being premature, Josef?' he ventured.

'No. We are being made to look foolish. Molotov assured me that if we closed Berlin to all road and rail traffic the democracies would have to pull out and surrender their half of the city to us. So what has happened? They are flying in seven thousand tons of food and fuel every day. Every *day*, Lavrenty. They are displaying an air capacity that is light years beyond anything we could do in similar circumstances. And the world is watching, and laughing at our futility. Now, I am sure you have read this report that they are having meetings to form a vast alliance of all the Western nations to resist any aggression by us. Ha!'

'We could force the issue,' Beria suggested, cautiously. 'Before any such alliance can be formed. If we were to shoot down one of their aircraft, instead of merely buzzing them...'

'We would be at war. Again.'

'Well, now that we have the atom bomb as well—'

'Lavrenty, at this moment we do not have the physical resources to fight a war; we are still recovering from the last one. So we have the Bomb. We could devastate North America. But while we were doing that, they would be destroying Russia. Where would be the profit in that, for either side? And now the scientists are telling us that the fall-out from these bombs could contaminate the earth, the very air we breathe, for years, perhaps centuries. We would in effect be destroying the human race. Where would be the point in *that*?'

Beria preferred not to comment. He had never heard his boss, who he knew had personally commanded the death of more than ten million people during the purges of the 1930s, not to mention accepting the loss of perhaps double that number during the recent war, with apparent equanimity, express concern about the human race.

'So,' Stalin said. 'I have given orders for talks

to begin with the democracies with a view to ending the Berlin blockade.'

'But Josef, won't that be seen as a humiliating climb down?'

'A formula will be found. The West are as keen to end this crisis as we.'

'I was thinking of here at home.'

'The idea was flawed from the beginning. But it was Molotov's idea. He will have to go.'

'You mean...?' Beria was aghast. He did not like Molotov, because Vyacheslav Molotov was a difficult man to like. But they had been comrades for a good many years, and through some very uncertain times.

'No, I do not mean that I wish him executed,' Stalin said. 'He has been a faithful servant. But he has never been able to understand the Western mentality. He will be retired and replaced by Gromyko. Andrei has done a very good job in the United Nations, and he certainly knows, and understands, the nature of the beast with which we are dealing. But still...' He sighed, and laid down his pipe. 'It is a defeat. Our first, for a long time. I am growing old, Lavrenty.'

'You, Josef? Your brain is as sharp as ever.'

'The brain is the servant of the body,' Stalin said sombrely. 'I am seventy years old. That is, I have reached the end of my allotted span.'

'Age, by years, is a man-made invention,' Beria argued. 'A man is as old as he feels. And I would have said that the body is the servant of the brain.'

'That is because your body is still fully

functioning. There comes a time when one must face facts. When one needs to consider the events of one's life, whether one has been a success or a failure.'

'Well,' Beria said, 'You have the satisfaction of knowing that you are the greatest Russian of all time, perhaps the greatest man of all time. You have raised our motherland to heights of prosperity and international prestige not even dreamed about by the greatest of the tsars.'

Stalin regarded him for some seconds – there were limits to the most outrageous flattery – then said quietly, 'Yet I have had my failures.'

'You are allowing this Berlin fiasco to get you down. But as you rightly say, the fault is entirely Molotov's.'

'There have been others. One in particular.'

Beria held his breath. Every time he came to this office he dreaded this moment, but it had been some time since the subject had been raised. Simply because his boss had been so preoccupied with political matters since the end of the war. Now...

'Do you know,' Stalin said, 'the last time I saw her she was sitting in that chair, smiling at me. That was in June 1941, and she was just twenty-one years old. She was so young, but so calm, so poised, so inexpressively beautiful. Her voice was perfection, low and throaty. Her hair was like a shroud of fine-spun gold. Her eyes beck-oned, so blue, so deep. Her legs were things to keep a man awake at night. Do you know, Lavrenty, I actually invited her to come down to Yalta with me. And as she sipped tea and smiled at me, she was choosing how to kill me.' His voice suddenly became brittle. 'I have never trusted a woman since.'

Beria licked his lips. 'You are not the only man the Countess von Widerstand seduced by merely looking at him.'

'But not you, eh?'

'I, sir, have never had the privilege of meeting the Countess.'

'But you did once have her in your cells.'

'Yes, I did. But at that time I did not realize her importance, and left her to my underlings.'

'Who all got themselves killed,' Stalin mused. 'But you also signed the order for her release.'

'That, sir, will haunt me to my grave. I was completely taken in by that smooth-talking American scoundrel, Joseph Andrews, and at that time I *still* did not realize just who she was.'

'Well, I suppose we all make mistakes, although fortunately not all of our mistakes have had consequences quite so serious.'

Beria gulped, and again held his breath.

'That was nearly eight years ago,' Stalin mused. 'Eight years in which she has left a trail of destruction halfway round the world. How many of our operatives has she killed?'

'Ah ... I am not quite sure, sir.'

Stalin raised his eyebrows.

'I mean,' Beria hurried on, 'I think she has been responsible for the deaths of fifty-one of our people, but twenty-two of these were in that shoot-out in Germany in 1946, and Fehrbach had several people with her, so we do not know how many she killed, personally.'

'On her record, it was probably most of them. But as you say, she was certainly responsible for them. That was three years ago. So where is she now?'

'I do not know,' Beria confessed, miserably.

'Why not?'

'Well, Josef, as you may remember, she undertook that raid into our controlled territory in Germany to reclaim ten million dollars' worth of gold that she had concealed there during the last days of the Reich.'

'At which she was successful.' Stalin pointed out.

'Ah ... yes. And that is the problem. Possessing that much money enabled her to do anything she wished, go anywhere she wished. To disappear.'

'It is not possible to disappear, completely, in this day and age. Unless she is dead. And as we never succeeded in killing her it is unlikely that anyone else has managed to do so. But however many successes I may have had, I would regard my life as a complete failure were I to go to my grave without putting that devil's spawn in hers.'

'If we had the slightest lead—'

'Lavrenty, you are not thinking clearly. So she got away with ten million dollars, in gold bullion. That is not the sort of wealth even Anna Fehrbach can carry around, even in her infamous shoulder bag.'

'Well, of course we understand that, Josef. And we traced the gold, very rapidly. She and her associates had an aircraft waiting for them at Geneva, and they were flown to Paris, with the bullion. There they dealt with a very reputable banker, who converted the gold into currency and invested it, in the name of Resistance Holdings. You understand the significance of this?'

'Certainly. The German word for resistance is Widerstand, which is the spurious title given to Fehrbach by her SD employers to give the impression to the world, and especially her victims, that she was an aristocrat. Well, then, that was a start.'

'Unfortunately, it was also a finish. The original investment was then split up a hundred times, into smaller companies, scattered all over the world, and reinvested, again under a variety of names.'

'And you have been able to trace none of them?'

'We have traced several of them, but the names of the directors are all different, although apparently legitimate, all lawyers or bankers who, so far as we have been able to ascertain, are quite unaware of the identity of their principal. Nor, in view of the handsome fees they are paid, do they wish to. But there is no mention whatsoever of anyone answering to the name Fehrbach or Widerstand.'

'But the income from these investments must go somewhere for her to access?'

'Obviously. But as yet we have not been able to trace any of it. You must understand, Josef, that it is mostly channelled through American banks; with conditions the way they are, our people are labouring under a severe handicap when they attempt to follow up financial matters in the West. Since Churchill and Truman began spreading this atmosphere of hostility towards us, creating what their press is calling a 'Cold War', everything and everyone regarded as Soviet is being treated like pariahs. My agents tell me there is even a movement in the United States to outlaw Communism; this in a country which holds that free speech is an inalienable right. It would be contemptible, but it could also be catastrophic for those people we have infiltrated into the various government departments. And of course things like the Berlin Confrontation, which has been well publicized in the West, have exacerbated the situation.' He paused, indicating that what was happening was the fault of neither him personally nor the MGB.

'So your people are getting "cold feet",' Stalin remarked, with some satisfaction at his pun. 'Very good. Let us accept for the moment that your efforts to trace the money have proved negative. But there is another area you do not seem to have explored. Anna Fehrbach entered the Soviet Zone three years ago and removed a very large, and very heavy, amount of gold. Where, initially, did she remove this money to?'

'Well, she, and her gang, stole a truck, loaded it with the bullion, and drove it across a bridge into the American Sector.'

'Did we not have border guards on this bridge?'

'Well, of course, sir.'

'And they did nothing to prevent this happening?'

'They tried to stop it. And when it would not stop, they opened fire, but immediately fire was returned from the American side, and in the confusion the truck got across. You remember, Josef, we protested in the strongest possible terms, but the Americans claimed that it had been a misunderstanding, that their guards had assumed our people were shooting at them.'

'But they did not return the truck?'

'Oh, they did. A few days later. But it was quite empty.'

'How odd.'

Beria found a handkerchief to wipe his neck; his boss was not usually given to sarcasm. 'And, you may remember, sir, that there was a quid pro quo. Fehrbach's ten million was only a small percentage of the total Nazi reserves. Thanks to her, the Americans knew where the bulk of the bullion was hidden. And they were willing to share that knowledge, and the gold, if we did not press the matter.'

'So she was allowed to get away with her ill-gotten gains. But are there not other paths we can follow? You say that you discovered that Fehrbach and her gang flew out of Geneva a couple of days after her escape. Do you know how they did that? What airline did they use? It must have been booked well in advance.'

'We have no proof. But as it happens there was an RAF plane which had made an unexpected visit to Geneva the day before, and which flew out that very evening.'

'And you have not drawn any conclusions from these so coincidental events?'

'Well, obviously she had friends ... I mean, as she was the only one who knew where the bulk of the bullion was hidden—'

'Oh, come now, Lavrenty. A half share in a hundred tons of gold? That money was important to us. But the Americans claim to be the richest country in the world. That gold was peanuts to them. Yet they were willing to risk a diplomatic incident to get Fehrbach out of Germany before we could catch up with her. And the British were willing to lay on an aircraft to get her out of Switzerland before she could be traced there. We are not talking about friends, Lavrenty, we are talking about support at a very high level.'

'Well...'

'And why should the British and the Americans go to such lengths to protect a woman who is a wanted war criminal, who worked for the Nazis, who killed for them, for at least seven years? Is not the conclusion obvious?'

'You mean she had a lover, or more than one...'

Stalin gave him one of his devastating stares. 'I am quite sure she has lovers scattered all over the place. But men only go to such lengths to protect their mistresses in novels. The conclusion is obvious. She *works* for them. She works for MI6, and she almost certainly also works for the American OSS, or this new CIA they have created. It would be very interesting to know for how long she has worked for them, while masquerading as Himmler's personal assistant. I would say that it is a long time. You remember that in 1944 we presented irrefutable proof to the Americans that she was a Nazi agent, and they promised to eliminate her. And she is still here.'

'But ... if she was a double agent all of those years ago, and in the very heart of the Nazi establishment ... I mean to say, Himmler's personal assistant! ... She must be a quite exceptional woman.'

'We already know that, don't we?'

'But Josef, if she is working for MI6, or the CIA, or both, then we have lost her. These are two of the most secret organizations in the world.'

'Agreed. But they are not philanthropic institutions. They did not take those risks and go to all that trouble just to pat her on the back and say goodbye and good luck. She is still working for them.'

'I agree that is likely,' Beria conceded. 'But if so, I cannot see that we are any further ahead. Spies, by definition, work in secret, move in secret, live in secret.'

'Lavrenty, Anna Fehrbach is not a spy. She may have spied for her employers, whether they were German or British or American, from time to time. But her prime profession is that of assassin. Spies are two a penny. Assassins in her class are worth their weight in gold. Which is what she is to the Western governments. But Western, Christian, morality considers assassination a dirty word. Thus while everyone knows that it is practised, it must never be admitted, or brought into the open. Thus a shadowy figure like Fehrbach, whose very existence is known to only a handful of people, is invaluable. What you need to do is investigate every political assassination in the past three years committed by a lone operative, in which the assassin escaped. You will of course exclude those carried out by our people. Then you correlate that information, and you will obtain a pattern which will lead you to Fehrbach.'

Beria pulled his ear. 'That will be an immense task.'

'Nevertheless, it must be carried out, and the sooner the better. And it is not so immense. We located her in Scotland in 1946. She managed to escape us then, but we know that she then went, or was taken, to South America. But after what happened in Brazil, we also know that she is wanted by the police there. England, Europe is no longer safe for her. Neither is South America. She is running out of places to hide, save in North America, where, as I have said, there can be no doubt that she is protected by the United States Government.'

'You do understand, Josef, that if and when we do find her, it is liable to cost God knows how many more lives. I have sent four separate disposal units after her, never less than four of my best people at a time, and not one of them has ever returned to tell us what happened. She got out of Scotland by shooting four of my people. She killed four more in Brazil when they tried to kidnap her. When I think of what happened in Warsaw in 1944...'

'That was six, wasn't it? And another six in that catastrophic attempt to kidnap her in Washington in 1941. And then there was that fiasco outside Berlin in 1945.'

'That is exactly it,' Beria said. 'Whoever I send after her now will be virtually on a suicide mission.'

'That has been your recurring mistake.'

'Sir?'

'Anna Fehrbach can see one of our operatives coming a mile away, much less four or six of them, and as you have just said, she is a lethal machine who kills first and worries about the consequences or the reason later. That is supposing she worries about it at all. You need a different approach.'

Beria returned to polishing his pince nez, now less from apprehension than bewilderment.

'You need,' Stalin said, 'someone who either is capable of taking her out at a very long range, or who is capable of getting right up to her.'

'I thought...'

'That I wanted her alive, sitting in that chair, bound and helpless. I would like that, yes. But one must be realistic. If that is not to be, I want her dead.'

'I understand. But ... even supposing I can find her, where am I to find someone who will not immediately arouse her suspicions? Especially now all westerners are being encouraged to be hostile to us.'

'Have you never heard of an organization known as the Mafia?'

Beria frowned. 'I believe it is some kind of a criminal brotherhood.'

'That is very well put. It is certainly an organization that, like Fehrbach, deals in assassination, of anyone who opposes it, but, if the money is right, will carry out ... I think they call it a 'hit', on any selected target, with no questions asked, again, if the money is right. And, as I believe it has tentacles all over America, it may well be able to locate our target for us. The operative they will employ will be as American as jazz music, someone of a type Fehrbach has never dealt with before, and will have no reason to suspect. I wish you to contact these people. As I have said, they do not inquire too deeply into motive, but we will supply one. Do you still have that photograph of her taken in 1940?'

'Yes, I do. But, Josef, that was nine years ago.'

'I don't think she will have changed that much. Like all women of her type, she is too proud of her beauty to do that. So you will send an agent to find an appropriate Mafia ... I think they call them 'families'. He will give this family the photograph, tell them that she is an escaped Nazi war criminal named Anna Fehrbach, Countess von Widerstand – although I shouldn't think she will be using that name to live in America – whose penchant was killing Jews or sending them to Auschwitz – the Americans are being very supportive of the Jews right now – and that we are certain she is living somewhere in America, and that his principal wishes her dead. You have carte blanche to spend whatever is necessary to employ their people to carry out this hit, which will be for the good of all mankind.'

Beria stroked his chin. 'It is an idea.'

'It is an idea, Lavrenty, which I want carried

out and brought to a successful conclusion. We will, of course, require proof of her death.'

The woman behind the desk looked up, suspiciously. The only women who ever entered these doors worked on the premises; the House did have lesbian clients, but these always arranged a partner by telephone. And this woman ... she took in not only the striking features and the tall, obviously good figure, but also the quality of the clothes concealing it, the patterned summer frock with the new-style, flaring Dior skirt, and the light cloth coat which had never been taken off any peg. Nor had her somewhat large shoulder bag come off a roadside stall. While her tiny bar earrings and her wristwatch were clearly gold; any rings she might have been wearing were concealed beneath her kid gloves. Her hair was also totally concealed beneath a slouch hat, and her eyes by an unusual pair of dark glasses, with flared hinges rather like miniature wings, which she did not take off despite the somewhat gloomy foyer, but the general impression was that she was fair.

'You have business?' The woman spoke Spanish.

'I wish to see Senora Jaquetta.' The voice matched the physical picture, low and husky; she also spoke Spanish, but with a foreign accent.

'You have business?' the woman asked again.

'It is a personal matter.'

The woman continued to regard her for several

seconds. 'You have a name?'

'Anna O'Brien. I spoke with Senora Jaquetta on the telephone.'

The woman pressed the intercom on her desk. 'Senora?' Again she looked at Anna's gloves. 'A Senorita O'Brien is here, wishing to see you. Of course, senora.' She turned off the switch. 'You are to go up.' She sounded surprised.

'Thank you.' Anna turned to the double doors on her right, from behind which there was some sound, of laughter and clinking glasses.

'Not there,' the concierge said, and indicated the narrow flight of stairs behind her desk. 'It is on the left.'

'Thank you,' Anna said again, and went up the stairs, while the concierge watched her flawless, silk clad calves and high-heeled shoes.

At the top of the stairs there was a landing, off which there branched two corridors. That on the right led past several doorways, and as Anna glanced along it, one of these doors opened, and a man came out, straightening his tie. He checked at the sight of her, mouth open. Anna smiled at him. 'Your flies are still undone,' she pointed out, and went down the left hand corridor. Here there was a single door, and on this she knocked.

'It is open.'

Anna turned the knob and stepped into a spacious, high-ceilinged room, brilliantly lit by the huge chandelier, although the shutters over the large windows were closed to keep out the bright Mexican sunlight.

The woman behind this desk was heavy, in her early forties, Anna estimated, but from her general bone structure she could also estimate that she must once have been quite a beauty. She wore a somewhat shapeless dress and was laden with cheap jewellery; and her yellow hair was clearly dyed.

For her part, she was regarding Anna was less interest than awe. 'You, are Senorita O'Brien?'

'That is correct.' Anna took off her glasses, sat in the chair before the desk, uninvited, and crossed her knees. Then she pulled off her gloves, and Jaquetta stared at the huge ruby solitaire on the forefinger of her right hand; that had clearly never come out of a cracker.

She licked her lips. 'On the telephone you said—'

'That I would like to work for you.' Anna took off her hat and silky straight golden hair tumbled past her shoulders and down the back of the chair. 'Do you think I would be acceptable to your clients?'

Jaquetta gulped, and almost visibly pulled herself together. 'Senorita ... you do understand...?'

'That you operate a brothel?'

'Ah...'

'Or should I have said a house of ill repute?'

'Mine,' Jaquetta said proudly, 'is a house of pleasure.'

'Of course. I do apologize.'

'There is no better known house of pleasure in all Mexico City. And you wish to work in it? You? Our business is providing a service for the gentlemen, any gentlemen and any service they desire, who come to see us?'

'Of course.'

'And yet you wish to work here?'
'For one night.'
'Senorita?'
'Tonight.'
'I do not understand.'
'It is very simple, senora. There is a gentleman I wish to meet. But he is unapproachable, always surrounded by armed guards, never alone.'
'Ah. And you think this gentleman will come here, tonight?'
'No. He never comes here. But one of your women, goes to him, every night.'
Jaquetta drew a sharp breath. 'You are speaking of Senor Capillano.'
'You obviously know your principal clients, senora. Now, as I said, I understand that you supply Senor Capillano with company every night. I assume the arrangement for tonight has already been made, and the girl already selected and identified. I would like to take her place, just for tonight. This means that you will have to telephone Senor Capillano's secretary and tell him that the original young lady has been taken ill, but that you are, of course, supplying a replacement. You will then describe me so they will know who to expect.'
'All this is because you wish to meet him? Could you not just telephone him for an appointment? Or turn up at his hotel suite? I do not think any man the least interested in women would turn you away.'
'You say the sweetest things. Unfortunately, my information indicates that without an introduction from someone Senor Capillano knows

and trusts, I *would* be turned away. Is it not true that in view of his past he has a number of enemies?'

'I know nothing of Senor Capillano's immediate past, senorita, nor do I wish to. He comes to Mexico City from his hacienda in the mountains, perhaps twice a year. This is for business, and to ... indulge himself. I knew him years ago, before he became wealthy, and so he turned to me to supply the company he wishes when on these visits. However, as Roberto is both a friend and a valued client, I think I am entitled to know just what is your interest in him. As you say, he does have enemies. Fortunately, he also has friends.'

'And a great deal of money.'

'Money is very helpful in these circumstances.' Jaquetta waited.

Anna gazed at her with enormous, innocent blue eyes. She placed her shoulder bag on her lap, opened it, and took out her passport. 'My name is Anna O'Brien, and I am a citizen of Eire.' She held out the passport.

Jaquetta opened it, looked from the photograph to Anna's face and then back again. 'Born 21 May 1920,' she remarked. 'You are not yet twenty-nine years old.'

'Is there something wrong with that?'

'I was thinking how nice it must be to be not yet twenty-nine. And you do not even look that.'

'If it is any comfort to you, as you can see, I will be twenty-nine in a week's time. You have not told me if you will help me to meet Senor Capillano.'

'You have not told me why you are so anxious

to meet him.'

'It is confidential.'

'I have realized that. But if you do not confide in me, I cannot help you.'

'Well...' Anna appeared to consider while she came to a decision. 'I am gathering material for a book.'

'On Senor Capillano? Then I cannot help you.'

'I am no more interested in his business activities than are you, senora. This book is about the great lovers of history, and it has been suggested to me that Senor Capillano is one of the greatest.'

'Lovers?' Jaquetta was scornful. 'I do not think Roberto has ever loved anyone in his life. Save himself, of course. He is a great, what shall I say, sexual athlete, certainly.' She gazed at Anna from behind arched eyebrows.

'Is not being a great sexual athlete merely an aspect of being a great lover?'

Jaquetta continued to gaze at her for some seconds, then gave a snort which could just have been a short laugh. 'You have obviously lived a sheltered life, senorita. I do not think you know a great deal about love, and sex, and the forms it can take. Love suggests something soft, and beautiful.'

'Cannot sex be soft and beautiful?'

'Of course it can. But it can also be vicious. Roberto makes "love" as if he hates all womankind. As you have apparently discovered, when he is in Mexico City, he requires me to send him a girl every night. He has been here ten days, this time, and so far I have had to send one girl to hospital, and lay off another because the very suggestion of sex makes her scream.'

'But you continue to supply him.'

'Well,' Jaquetta said, defensively, 'He pays very well. And these girls are experienced sexual playthings. You ... I would say that you come from a well-to-do background. You are obviously well educated, refined, and, I would say, looking into your eyes, quite innocent of what the real world, Roberto Capillano's world, is like. He would take that lilywhite flesh of yours and turn it inside out. He would make you ashamed to be a woman. As for ever again touching yourself...'

'Well,' Anna said bravely. 'It would make a great passage for my book, wouldn't it?'

'I cannot believe you would risk that much, for a book.'

Anna opened her bag again. 'You say he pays well. How much, per girl, per night?'

'One thousand American dollars. And her expenses, if she has to receive hospital treatment afterwards.'

'Of which you take?'

'Well, half. That is the agreed percentage.'

'You are in a very profitable business.' Anna took out a wad of notes, secured by a rubber band, and laid it on the desk. 'Those are ten hundred dollar bills. That is to say, one thousand dollars.' She took out, one after the other, four more wads and laid them beside the first. 'I will pay you these five thousand dollars if you will send me to see Senor Capillano tonight. You may keep all of it, as well as the thousand he will pay you. And then I will disappear from your life, forever. But,' she added, 'I will send you a copy of my book, when it is published.'

Jaquetta gazed at the five packets of money lying on the desk, then at the bag, clearly wondering what else it might contain. 'You wish to pay me five thousand dollars so that you may be bullied, beaten, and very probably buggered?'

'Well,' Anna said, more bravely yet. 'An author must have experience, if she is going to write about life.'

Another long stare, then Jaquetta picked up the money.

INCIDENT IN MEXICO

Naked, Anna lay on her back on her bed, spread-eagled, arms and legs stretched to their widest extent, eyes open, staring at the ceiling. The hotel bedroom was air-conditioned, and her body was deliciously cool, after the heat of the street; at several thousand feet above sea level, the sun seemed to redouble its strength in the middle of the day.

It would not be hot outside tonight, once the sun had set. And inside? She was going to kill, for the ninety-eighth time. And then more, if all she had heard of Capillano being surrounded by bodyguards was true. Because she was a monster? Or because Fate, Destiny, perhaps even the Almighty, had set her feet upon a path, when she had been only seventeen years old?

Eleven years ago, she had been a serious-minded, devout schoolgirl, proud of the position she had achieved in her small circle, that she was the youngest ever head girl in her convent, that she was top of her form in most subjects, captain of the athletics team, daughter of loving and caring parents, and aware that her striking looks attracted attention wherever she went. She had attended confession every week, with only her pride for which to beg forgiveness. As she had no brothers, she had never known a boy, even as a casual acquaintance, and as her life had been so full, she had not even had any sinful thoughts to whisper to the priest.

And only six months later, having watched her parents and her sister marched off to gaol like common criminals, having expected the worst for herself without any idea of what that worst could be, she had found herself being subjected to the sexual humiliation of an SS training camp, of forced relationships with men who were nothing more than guinea pigs, for the benefit of her instructors, and finally, the never-to-be-forgotten day when she had been handed a pistol and told to kill.

Whatever had gone before, that day had been the watershed that had turned her from a bewildered schoolgirl, uncertain whether or not she was merely having a long nightmare, into what she now was, a woman who knew instantly what needed to be done, and who did it, without conscience or hesitation.

That day had not abated the nightmare, much less ended it. It had made her part of it, the creator of nightmares rather than their frightened victim. She could still ask herself why she had obeyed that first command. She had known, she had been told, within days of her own arrest, that if she would serve the Reich faithfully and well, she would survive, and so would her family, in close but not brutal confinement, hostages for her loyalty. At the age of just eighteen there had not seemed any alternative to acquiescence. There would have been none in similar circumstances today. But she had assumed, from her initial training, that her service would consist of seducing men to learn their secrets. Until the gun had actually been pressed into her hand, it had never occurred to her that she might also be required to kill them, if considered necessary by the Reich.

Perhaps she had been fortunate, that first day. Even the knowledge that refusal could involve the execution of her parents might not have been sufficient to overcome her moral and religious background. But she had been the second girl to be called forward. The first, the red-headed Karen – Anna had never learned her last name – had been unable to do it, had deliberately missed with all six of her shots. Karen had been stripped naked, there and then, and publicly flogged until she bled before a hundred jeering, leering men, and then sent to an SS brothel.

That fate was worse than to become a

murderess. If Fate had condemned her to hell, from which there could be no escape, it was surely preferable to be one of the devils!

Thus she had begun the career that had made her name a whispered terror throughout Germany, and, she now knew, most of the world, as she had operated in Moscow and Washington and a variety of other places, dealing in deadliness. Because her amazing speed of thought and reaction, her phenomenal skill, based on her immense powers of concentration, with a pistol, not less than with a knife or with the edge of her hand, all concealed beneath her outward appearance of blue-eyed, yellow-haired, long-legged innocence, had made her the most lethal woman in the world, and she had never yet encountered a man to match her.

But there had, after all, been a loophole of escape. It had appeared, quite fortuitously, when in a mood of angry outrage after being humiliatingly 'disciplined' by her then master, Reinhard Heydrich, for a breach of his rules, she had seduced the MI6 agent Clive Bartley, not because of any orders from above, but simply to restore her own battered ego. And found a man she could not only trust, but love. As she could not abandon Germany, and thus condemn her family to an unthinkable fate, she had done the next best thing, and agreed to work for him. From a double agent, spying and if necessary killing for the British as well as the Nazis, she had then become a triple agent with the entry of the Americans into the war, when they had discovered that this most wanted of Nazi operatives was actually employed by their British allies and thus that her enormous and terrifying skills were also available to them.

Superficially, the end had seemed to make it all worthwhile. Working for the Allies in the very heart of the Reich as both Hitler and Himmler, fascinated by her combination of innocent femininity and lethal ability had grown to trust her, she had been able to play her part in bringing down the Nazi regime, then with British help she had been able to get her parents out of Germany at the end of the war, and with American help she had been able to escape herself with a fortune in Nazi gold bullion. Thus, it had seemed, freedom at last. But that aid had come with a caveat, that she would continue to work for the CIA, in areas where even they could not reach, and in circumstances with which they, or the United States, could not afford to be involved or even associated. In these circumstances, MI6 had faded into the background, controlled as it now was by a government that was not only bent on shedding as many of the responsibilities, both moral and financial, of empire as they could as rapidly as possible, but also of the amoral requirements of exercising power.

Actually, it had not been so bad. She had been allowed to live wherever she chose, and had only been called upon twice in the past three years, before tonight, and those two missions had only involved three deaths. Only! It amused her to regard herself as America's secret weapon, to be used sparingly and only when absolutely necessary – a human atomic bomb, a uniquely destructive force, as Dr Goebbels had once described her. And in that regard she could at least be honest with herself, and reflect that after so many years she actually sought the excitement and the dangers of the chase and the execution, like the fighter pilot to whom she often compared herself, always with the confidence that his skill and superior equipment would prevail; she knew that during the recent war several German fighter aces had scored more than a hundred kills, mainly on the Russian front. If she was up there with the stars, she also knew that not one of those men had survived the war. But their records were immortal.

Thus that this promised to be as dangerous an assignment as she had ever undertaken, was merely stimulating, not frightening. She looked at her watch. Six o'clock. It was time to move.

She had a bath, put on a dressing gown, and ordered a light early supper. 'I am expecting a car to pick me up at eight o'clock,' she told the floor waiter. 'Will you ask the desk to call me when it arrives? I shall be in my room.'

'Of course, Senorita O'Brien.' The Irish beauty had now been resident in the hotel for a week, and he felt he knew her quite well ... even if he would dearly have liked to know her better.

'Thank you.' She ate, sparingly – even her stomach could be tense before a hit – and had a single glass of wine, while going over in her mind what might lie ahead. Her plans were all made and already part implemented. After leaving Jaquetta, she had returned here, transferred her remaining money to her evening bag, and repacked a complete change of clothing in her shoulder bag. These had been carefully selected before she began the assignment, and would assist in transforming her from a beautiful and glamorous woman into an itinerant hippie. To these she had added her spare passports, retaining only her Irish one, which she also placed in her evening bag, and her three pairs of sunglasses; she had learned from experience that things like sun glasses and jewellery were what people noticed as much as facial features.

Then she had taken a taxi to the railway station, hired a left luggage box – for this service a section of the station was open all night – and left the bag there. Thus her escape route was under way, and as she would leave the hotel that night without either of her suitcases they could have no doubt that she was coming back and not doing a runner. The rest of her clothes, regrettably, would have to be written off ... but she had had to do this often enough in the past, and their cost would go on her expenses: she might be a multi-millionairess, but nowadays she believed in being paid for her services, handsomely. When she remembered the years she had worked for the Nazi SD and British MI without being paid at all, simply because for the one she had had no choice and for the other she wanted to, she had to smile.

But the immediate situation was more dangerous than usual because she had been unable properly to reconnoitre her ground and the probable conditions in which she would be operating. Over the past week she had surveyed, from the street, the hotel in which Capillano maintained his suite, but had not risked actually entering the building, as she wished no one to recognize her when she appeared tonight.

And although, once she had accepted her money, Jaquetta had given her a briefing as to what to expect, she had not wanted to ask any probing and thus possibly suspicious questions. Thus she only knew that the suite was on the third floor, that there were always at least three guards in attendance as well as a secretary, and that she would be searched before being admitted to the great man's presence.

When she remembered the elaborate security with which both Hitler and Himmler had been surrounded, this was less than par for the course. But what she did not know was the exact lay-out of the suite, how many, if any, suites were on the same floor, the situation of the elevators, or how many hotel staff were allotted to each floor, or how inquisitive they were. But she had long ago realized that nothing in life, or for that matter, death, was ever perfect. She would have to play it by ear; that too she had had to do often enough before.

Seven o'clock. She pushed the trolley into the hall, locked the door, and dressed. She rolled on her stockings and fastened her suspender belt, added her knickers. Then she checked the magazine of her Walther. This tiny pistol – it fitted neatly into her hand – contained only five bullets, and there were likely to be at least five people in the apartment. Thus she might need a spare magazine. This she usually carried in her shoulder bag, but lacking that and in evening dress – as apparently was required by Capillano – and knowing that her handbag was liable to be opened, there was not a lot of easily accessible space available.

She strapped on the thin, narrow belt, which fitted snugly round her waist, resting on her hips, settled the holster into her groin. The belt had a pocket for a silencer, but as she did not think she was going to have the time to screw it into place she had stowed this also in her shoulder bag; the point two-two made very little noise in any event. Then she opened her first-aid pack – this also would have to be written off – took out a roll of plaster, placed the spare magazine on the inside of her left thigh, under the knickers and where the thigh joined the groin, and taped it into place. This involved trapping several wisps of her somewhat luxuriant pale pubic hair – which she had always been too proud to trim – which meant that removing the magazine in haste was going to be painful, but if that was the worst she would have to suffer tonight she would be laughing.

From the wardrobe she selected a high-necked green sheath dress with an elaborate sash; she wasn't planning on doing any running. This buttoned up the back, but as with all her working clothes there was also a vent, fastened with a zip, on the right side of her waist, large enough for her to slip her hand in and draw the pistol or even to reach the spare magazine.. She worked the zip several times to make sure it was absolutely free, then stood in front of the full-length mirror to smooth the gown and make sure there was no unsightly and suspicious bulge. But the pistol always fitted perfectly between her hip and her groin, and was in any event partly shrouded by the sash, the tail of which she now made sure hung in exactly the right place. She smiled as she recalled that she had worn a gown almost exactly matching this to go out to dinner with the Nazi colony in Brazil, in 1946 ... and had wound up rolling in the mud while fighting for her life. She could only hope that tonight was not going to be as dramatic.

Satisfied, she sat before her dressing mirror, applied make-up, and put her hair up, remembering the meticulous care with which her German maid, Birgit, had done this. Poor Birgit, she thought. The foolish woman had elected to remain in Germany instead of fleeing with her mistress in March 1945; Anna had no idea if she had survived, and if she had, what were her present circumstances.

She added her jewellery, surveyed herself in the mirror, and grimaced; as she lacked Birgit's talents as a hairdresser, it was by no means perfect. But actually the slight suggestion of untidiness, the odd escaping wisps of hair, went perfectly with the face and the expression, which even after ten years of murder and mayhem remained that of a slightly bewildered angel.

Satisfied, she sat in an armchair and waited, keeping absolutely still, hands resting on the arms of the chair, fingers spread and motionless, always aware of the pistol resting against her groin and the magazine on the inside of her thigh. This was a routine she had practised for all of those ten years, and which had never let her down. She was concentrating, at once turning her nerves and emotions into a solid block of ice, and at the same time preparing her brain and her muscles for instant, irrevocable, and absolutely ruthless violence when the time came.

The phone rang. 'Your car is here, Senorita O'Brien.'

'Thank you. I will be right down.'

She picked up her evening handbag, looked round the room. She had spent a very comfortable week here. But from this moment it, Mexico City, the entire country, was barred to her. There were an increasing number of countries to which that applied.

There was no need for a cape on a warm night. She went down in the lift, smiled at the clerk behind the desk as she handed him her key, and then at the uniformed driver, who touched his cap. 'Senorita! It is a great pleasure.'

'And for me, I hope.'

She got into the back of the car. It was only a short drive, through crowded, brilliantly lit streets, and then they were stopping outside another hotel, this one somewhat more imposing than her own modest establishment.

The chauffeur opened the door for her and she got out. 'Tell me ... ah ... I'm terribly sorry, but I do not know your name.'

'It is Rodrigo, senorita.'

'What a nice name. What happens when I am ready to leave, Rodrigo? Do you wait for me?'

'Well, no. I would very much like to do that, senorita. But it is impossible to say how long you will be.'

'I will be back within an hour.'

'An hour? That cannot be possible.'

'Why cannot it be possible?'

'Well, senorita, the patron has paid a great deal of money for your company. He will not be satisfied with an hour.'

'Rodrigo, do you not think that I can completely satisfy any man in an hour?'

He gulped, and she rested her hand on his arm, giving it a gentle squeeze. 'And when I return, well, the whole night is there in front of us, is it not. And Rodrigo, it will not cost *you* a centimo.'

'Oh, senorita.'

'Wait for me over there,' Anna said, and entered the foyer.

She went to the reception desk. 'I am to see Senor Capillano.'

The clerk surveyed her with glowing eyes. 'Oh, yes, senorita.' He looked at his pad. 'Senorita O'Brien.'

'That is correct.'

'You are from Senora Jaquetta.'

'That is also correct.'

'Forgive me, senorita. Security, you understand. Use elevator number three; it goes directly to the third floor.'

'And does it return the same way?'

'Of course.'

'How terribly convenient.'

'I will just telephone to let them know you are coming. It is the door opposite the elevator.'

'Thank you.'

Anna went to the lift, rode up. The time for thinking, planning, was past. Now there could only be execution.

The corridor was empty. The entire set-up might have been created especially for her convenience. Although as she stepped from the lift the door opposite opened and a man emerged. He wore a dinner jacket, looked ordinary enough, and not in the least hostile, but the slight fullness of the left shoulder of his jacket indicated to Anna's practised eye that he was armed. 'Senorita O'Brien?'

'That is my name.'

'Well! I think you will please the patron.'

He indicated the doorway, and she stepped into a comfortable lobby beyond which there was a sitting room. It was reminiscent of so many hotel suites in her past, most of them associated with violence.

There were two more men in there, also wearing tuxedos, and also, she saw at a glance, armed. The man who had greeted her closed the doors behind her. 'Senors,' he said proudly. 'Senorita O'Brien.'

Anna smiled at them, and they walked around her, as if she were a thoroughbred horse at an auction. Well, compared with these, she supposed she was.

'You understand that you must be searched, senorita?'

Anna shrugged. 'If that is what you are required to do.'

'So we must ask you to stand still.'

'Am I not doing that?' She wondered if she going to have to go into action immediately. She hoped not. She liked symmetry, the carrying out of her assignment in its proper order, just as she also liked to make absolutely sure her objective deserved to die. And a normal, routine search, a passing of the hands over the body, would not reveal either what lay against her groin or between her legs.

One of the men stood in front of her, the other two behind her. She gazed into the eyes of the first man. You may have less than half an hour to live, she thought, and smiled at him.

She felt fingers on her back, unbuttoning her gown. As she had supposed would be the case, the 'search' was actually a means of satisfying their desire, even if hardly all of it. The man at her buttons grunted as he realized she was wearing no visible underclothes. Then she felt his fingers on her flesh. As she had anticipated, with her gown loose from her shoulders, they immediately moved to either side, sliding under her armpits to come in front and cup her breasts; if he had noticed the side vent it did not appear to interest him. Behaviour like this made it easier to kill him, but she asked, in her most dulcet tone, 'If you will tell me what you are looking for, senor, I may be able to tell you where it is.'

He kissed her ear while plucking at her nipples. 'You have sophistication. The patron will like that.'

The crunch was approaching. If he intended to go lower ... but at that moment the inner door opened. 'Up to your tricks, as usual, eh, Carlos?'

The hands fell away, while Anna surveyed the newcomer. He was a little man, bald but with a pencil moustache, and like the others, impeccably dressed in a dinner suit; she reckoned that, unlike them, he was not carrying a gun – at least in a shoulder holster. 'I am Esteban,' he explained. 'And I must ask you to forgive Carlos. He is a great gatherer of crumbs from the table.'

'He has cold fingers,' Anna complained.

'You hear that, Carlos? You are a failure, even with your hands. The patron is waiting, Senorita O'Brien.'

'Do you think Carlos could do me up?'

'Do you think that is necessary?'

'I like to be properly dressed,' she explained. 'At least for an introduction.'

'Of course. You heard the lady, Carlos.'

The fingers were back, this time nervously scrabbling from button to button.

'Thank you,' Anna said, and went forward. 'And you are?'

'I am the patron's private secretary,' Esteban said.

'Well, I am pleased to make your acquaintance.' She held out her hand.

He squeezed the gloved fingers, raised them to his lips. 'You are a singularly self-possessed young lady.'

'I have been in this business a very long time,' Anna said, with absolute truthfulness.

'And yet you look as if you were born yesterday. You are enchanting.'

Anna made a moue. The last man who had described her as enchanting had been Adolf Hitler. She rather liked this little fellow. But her motto had always been, business before pleasure ... or friendship.

He was holding the door for her. She stepped into a large bedroom, on two levels. The rear, upper level, reached by a single step of the floor, was nearly all bed. The lower contained a group of armchairs around a low glass-topped table, with a well-stocked sideboard against one wall and a large desk against the other.

Roberto Capillano stood in front of this, also wearing evening dress. He was not very tall, but very heavily built. His hair was thick and black, brushed straight back from his forehead, with a carefully delineated centre parting. His features were pronounced, and strong, but there was no immediate evidence of either excessive dissipation or viciousness. His eyes were black, his smile pleasant. If Anna had not been told of what he was guilty, and would undoubtedly be again if given the opportunity, she thought she might even have liked him as well. But like his bodyguards, there was that fullness at the left shoulder. She was relieved at that; she hated having to kill unarmed targets.

He advanced with outstretched arms, held her shoulders 'Do you know,' he said. 'Jaquetta told me she had something very special for me, to replace Martina, and I did not believe her. But you...' His hands slipped down her arms to hold her gloves, rather, she remembered, as the

Fuehrer had liked to do.

'You say the sweetest things, senor,' she said.

'Now tell me what that boor Carlos was up to?'

'He said he was searching me. But he was actually feeling my tits.'

'And you do not like having your tits felt?'

'I enjoy it. If they are felt by the right person.'

'You are delightful. Thank you, Esteban. I shall not need you again.'

'Senor. Senorita.' The secretary withdrew through the door, and closed it.

'Now we shall not be disturbed,' Capillano said.

'Not even if I scream for help?'

'Not even if *I* scream for help,' he assured her. 'Are you going to scream for help?'

'Am I going to need to?'

His eyes narrowed for a moment, then he smiled. 'You have a quick wit as well as a beautiful face, and I am sure, a beautiful body. Let me see your hair.'

Anna reached up and pulled out the pins, laying them on the coffee table. Her hair fell past her ears and tumbled down her back, assisted to lie straight by a quick shake of her head.

'What perfection,' Capillano remarked. 'Champagne?'

'Thank you.' She sat in one of the chairs, crossed her right leg over her left to leave the pistol fully accessible, and laid her handbag on the table. Then she took off her gloves, and while he was preoccupied, slipped the zip on her vent down, covering it with her arm.

The champagne was already open, and waiting in its ice bucket. Capillano filled two glasses, gave her one, and sat opposite her. 'How is it that I have not seen you before?'

'I am new.'

'All the way from Ireland?'

'I found it convenient to leave Great Britain. But I need to earn a living.'

'I would have thought someone like you could do better than Jaquetta's. Your health.' He drank. 'That is a very unusual watch. I have never seen one like it before. Is it Irish?'

'It is German.'

'German? It looks like solid gold.'

'It is solid gold. It is a Junghans.'

'You have been to Germany?'

'I lived there for some years. During the war.' He stared at her, so she added, 'The watch was a gift from my lover, Reinhard Heydrich. Have you heard of him? At one time he was quite well known.'

This time the stare was hostile, as he began to suspect that she was teasing him, as of course she was ... while sticking strictly to the truth. At last he said, 'Carlos was pretending to search you. Did he look into your bag?'

'He preferred my tits.'

'The man is a lecherous cretin. Do you mind if I look into the bag?'

'Of course I do not mind. But ... you may not like what you find.'

Again he regarded her for some seconds, then leaned forward, picked up the bag, and opened it. Anna slipped her hand inside her gown.

Capillano took out first her lipstick and compact, her comb, then her small vial of perfume, sniffed it. 'This is very nice.'

'It is Adoration.'

'Ah. I thought I recognized the scent when you came in.' He opened the passport. 'The photograph does not do you credit. But then, passport photos never do.' He held up the key. 'This is the key to a night storage box.'

'That is absolutely correct.'

'What is in this box?'

'I would say that is my business.'

Yet again he stared at her, then emptied the ten wads of notes on to the table, thumbed one of them. 'Ten American hundred dollar bills. And ten packets. Do you habitually walk around with ten thousand dollars in your purse?'

'One should always carry some small change, for things like taxis.' Now she was deliberately baiting him, willing him to lose his temper and make the first move.

He took a final look into the bag, and found another bundle of notes. 'What are these?'

'Those are Bahamian twenty-pound notes.'

These he riffled in turn. 'There are fifteen of them. That is three hundred pounds. Over a thousand dollars.'

'Well—'

'You need taxi money. Do you live in the Bahamas?'

'When I can spare the time, yes. Have you never been there?'

'No.'

'You should try them. They are very peaceful.'

'So, you walk around with more than eleven thousand dollars in your handbag. And you say you needed work.'

Anna shrugged. 'Not even eleven thousand dollars lasts forever.'

He laid the bag beside the notes on the table, while Anna sipped champagne, holding the glass in her left hand. 'I think you must be the most beautiful woman I have ever seen,' he remarked.

'There you go again, flattering me.'

'But you are also the most deceitful woman who has ever had the temerity to visit me. You are clearly well groomed and well educated. You live in the Bahamas, and you carry a small fortune in your purse. You use the most expensive perfume in the world. And that ring you are wearing is worth twenty grand if it is worth a penny. I would not care to estimate the value of the watch. And you are masquerading as a common prostitute?'

'A girl must have her secrets.'

'I do not like deceitful women. But I do like beating beautiful women. Strip, and kneel, with your arms on the chair.'

Anna placed her glass on the table. 'Before I do that,' she said. 'I would like to ask a question.'

'Yes. I am going to have sex with you. After I have heard you squeal with pain.'

'You make the sweetest suggestions. But that was not the question. Is it true that you once had a tenement building in Chicago burned down because someone who owed you money was sheltering inside?'

Again his eyes narrowed. 'How do you know about that?'

'And is it true that there were eighteen women and children in that building, all of whom were burned to death, because you had had your thugs shatter all the nearby water hydrants? I am assuming that the thugs in question included your people in the other room.'

'Almost you make me think that you work for the FBI. Of course they are my people. They do what I tell them to.'

'You haven't answered the first question, Roberto.'

He shrugged. 'I lost my temper.'

'And did you also lose your temper when you threw your wife out of the twenty-first storey window in your New York apartment? A clever lawyer got you off that crime by claiming that she fell rather than was pushed, but for the murder of all those innocents you were arrested and condemned to the electric chair. And managed to escape from Death Row. They are still trying to discover how you did that.'

He pointed. 'You *do* work for the FBI. And they have sent you, a mere chit of a girl, to arrest me? Well, my dear young lady, you seem to have forgotten that the FBI have no jurisdiction in Mexico. So when I am finished with you, and they find your body, if anyone is able to identify it, no one will be able to do a damned thing about it.'

'It sounds so exciting,' Anna said. 'But actually, you are mistaken.' She was still willing him to make the first move, but he was not responding, such was his confidence. It was time to end it. 'I do not work for the FBI, and therefore, I have not come to arrest you. I have come to carry out the death sentence that was passed on you six months ago, and should have been executed by now.'

He stared at her, and then at the pistol that had suddenly appeared in her hand, pointing at him. 'You ... who are you? *What* are you?'

'Do you know,' Anna said, 'I often ask myself that very question. My only clue is that someone once described me as an angel from Hell. Isn't that sweet? Because Hell is exactly where I am sending you, now.'

At last he moved, reaching beneath his jacket, but he was far too late: Anna levelled the Walther and shot him between the eyes.

She remained sitting still for several seconds, waiting, the gun still levelled. But Capillano had fallen back against the chair and was totally inert. She had not really doubted that he would have died instantly; even a point two-two bullet, fired at six feet range, will tear its target apart, and while the entry wound was not large, the exit wound in the back of Capillano's head, as she ascertained when she got up to stand over him, had left a mess of blood and brains scattered across the chair and the floor.

Blood was seeping down his face and dripping from his chin, staining his shirt. Anna holstered her pistol, the warmth from the barrel penetrating the silk of her knickers into her groin, closed the zip, then, carefully making sure her hand did not get stained, she rested two fingers on his neck for several seconds, ascertaining there was not the slightest trace of a pulse. Then she pulled on her gloves, and again carefully, opened the jacket, put her hand inside, and withdrew a Browning nine-millimetre automatic pistol. That was what she might have asked for.

She checked the magazine; it contained eight cartridges and there was one in the breech. She looked into his side pockets, but these were empty. She glanced around the rest of the room, selected the desk against the wall opposite the sideboard, and sat at it, resting the pistol on the blotting pad before starting to open the drawers. In the third she found the silencer she wanted, and screwed it into place.

She stood up, surveyed the dead man once again. Ninety-eight, she thought. But as she could not afford to leave anyone behind her to raise the alarm, he was about to be joined by four more; by his own admission, they were all guilty men.

She used her handkerchief, and carefully cleaned the glass she had been holding, then repacked her handbag, adding the discarded hairpins, held it in her left hand, went to the door, drew a deep breath, opened it and started shooting. The four men were seated at a table playing cards; the first she shot through the head as he turned to look at her, the second also took a bullet in the head as he raised it. The third, Carlos, reached his feet and had half drawn his pistol when he too went down, his brains scattered across the floor.

Esteban had fallen to his knees on the far side of the table, hands held to his head. 'Please,' he gasped, as Anna moved forward to stand above him. 'I am not armed.'

'I am sorry about this,' Anna said. 'I think you could be quite a decent man. So tell me this: how long have you worked for Senor Capillano?'

'I have been his private secretary for twenty years.'

'So you know all of his dealings during that time. And approved them, I suppose.'

'Yes, yes. I know all of his secrets. Ask me any questions, and I will tell you.' Then he asked, somewhat ingenuously, 'Is he dead?'

'Yes,' Anna said, 'He is dead. And you have answered all of my questions and proved my initial assumption incorrect.' She shot him through the head. Number one hundred and two, she thought. She laid the pistol on the table on top of the scattered cards, looked around the room; there was no trace of her presence anywhere, save for the whiff of perfume. But that would fade during the night.

She went to the mirror above the mantelpiece, surveyed herself. She looked exactly as she had done when entering the suite, save that her hair was now loose. Satisfied, she let herself out, listened to the latch clicking shut behind her, and took the elevator to the lobby. It was a quarter to nine, and the place was quite active. If it was inevitable that she should attract glances, no one seemed to be very interested in what she was doing, and she kept on the far side of the foyer from the reception desk, which was, in any event, coping with several customers.

She went through the doors from the air conditioning into the sudden warmth of the night; although with the sun gone, and at this altitude the temperature had dropped considerably from the afternoon, it was by no means uncomfortable. She crossed the road to the waiting car, tapped on the window. Rodrigo, who had seemed to be asleep, jerked upright. 'Senorita? But—'

'I told you I would not be long,' Anna reminded him. She went round the car and got into the front beside him.

'Senor Capillano let you go so soon?'

'It took only a few minutes for him to lose all interest in me.'

'But that is bad. What are you going to tell Senora Jaquetta?'

'I don't think it is my business to tell her anything. If Senor Capillano wishes to complain, then let him do it himself. I thought we were going to spend the night together.'

'Oh, senorita...'

'But first, there is something I must do. Take me to the Central Station.'

'You wish to leave Mexico City? Leave me? But you cannot do that. There are no trains at this hour.'

'I know that, Rodrigo. And I promised to spend the night with you, remember? But there is something I have to pick up from a left luggage locker.'

He seemed content with that, drove her to the station. 'You will come back,' he said, anxiously, as she got out.

'Of course I am coming back. You are my transport. I will be five minutes.'

She went inside, opened the locker and removed the shoulder bag, left the box open with the key in the lock, returned to the car.

'Now,' Rodrigo said, 'we go to your hotel, eh?'

'I don't think we should do that,' Anna said. 'I think we should go for a drive in the country.'

'A drive in the country?'

'It is a lovely night, and look, the moon is just rising. Let us go north, find a lonely road, and then we can stop, and ... get to know each other better.'

'This is not good, senorita. Lonely roads ... they are full of bandidos. I would not like you to be raped. I would not like to be raped, either,' he added.

'I give you my word that no one is going to rape either of us,' Anna said.

He didn't seem entirely convinced, but took the Calz de Guadeloupe through the suburb of that name. The various suburbs continued for a good distance, still full of people and lights. 'It will be some time before we find a lonely road,' he said.

'The night is young. Look, there is an open gas station. Pull in and fill your tank. Then it doesn't matter how long we have to drive. What is the capacity of your tank?'

'It holds thirty gallons, senorita.'

'And what do you expect to get for a gallon?'

'On an open road in the country? Oh ... we

should get twenty-five kilometres.'

'Well then, you see, when you have filled up, we can travel seven hundred and fifty kilometres.'

'But we have to come back.'

'Rodrigo, if you spend your life worrying about every little thing, you will give yourself grey hairs. Or even a heart attack. You must learn to take life as it comes.'

Clearly trying to work out what she meant, he nonetheless pulled into the gas station and got out to fill the tank. Anna took the opportunity to unzip her side vent, just in case, and then to take three of the packets of money from her purse; these she folded into her left hand. She was still on a high, as she always was after fulfilling a commission, and she knew it would not settle for several hours. But it could be alleviated, and fortunately, Rodrigo was quite an attractive man. Just as long as she did not allow her bubbling libido to interfere with the clarity of her thinking.

Rodrigo paid for the fuel, returned, and they drove off. 'Now,' Anna said, 'let us relax and have an enjoyable drive.'

'There are less houses now,' he said. 'Soon we will find this lonely road, eh? Senorita, I am on fire for you.'

'Well, you should be,' Anna said. 'But I have been thinking, about what you said. You are right, it may be too dangerous to stop.'

'I do not understand, senorita. If we do not stop, how—'

'Let us go to somewhere safe. Somewhere ... I

know, let's go to Matamoros.'
'Matamoros?'
'You do know where Matamoros is?'
'Yes, senorita. I know where it is. It is at the mouth of the Rio Grande River, just before it enters the Gulf of Mexico.'
'And the Rio Grande is the border between Mexico and the United States, isn't that right? The town of Brownsville is on the other side. Right?'
'Yes, senorita. But ... you wish to go to Matamoros?'
'That is what I said.'
'But senorita, it is more than six hundred kilometres.'
'No, we've done about eighty. So it's only about five hundred and fifty from here. And you have a full tank'
'That is still not less than nine hours driving.'
'That will be ideal. It is only just past ten o'clock. So we will reach the river at seven tomorrow morning. Just when everyone is waking up.'
'You promised to spend the night with me.'
'Is that not what I am doing?'
He considered this, and she went on. 'I do not wish you to take your eyes off the road, but take your right hand off the wheel and put it in my left.'
He obeyed.
'What do you feel?'
'You are holding some crisp paper.'
'You are absolutely right. It is a wad of American hundred dollar bills. There are thirty of

them. Do you know how much that is?'

'Ah...'

Anna sighed. 'It is three thousand dollars. This I am going to give to you to drive me to Matamoros.' She stuffed the notes into the side pocket of his jacket. 'I would say that is a good night's work. Wouldn't you?'

'Oh, senorita.'

'And,' Anna went on, 'if you promise to keep your eyes on the road and both hands on the wheel, I will give you a bonus.' She unbuttoned his flies and slipped her hand inside.

PARADISE

'I think,' Anna said, 'that you're nodding off.'

The car had just swerved violently, and now it swerved again as Rodrigo brought it back under control. 'I have been driving for so long. What time is it?'

'Four o'clock. You have only been driving for seven hours.'

'Seven hours! I have never driven for seven hours at a time in my life. And those mountain roads...'

'But the mountains are now behind us.' They had just completed the passes on the Sierra Madre Orientale and were descending again, past houses and hamlets, all apparently firmly asleep. She wondered if anyone had as yet tried to enter Capillano's suite. But there was no reason for them to have done so, nor should there be a reason before possibly breakfast this morning, by which time she would be across the border. 'And you are increasing your experiences.'

'Perhaps, if you were to give me another bonus...?'

'Perhaps later. Look there!' Through a gap in the trees that lined the road, she could see the waning moon streaming across the water. 'Isn't that romantic?'

'Romantic,' Rodrigo groaned.

'Listen, let us go down there and break our journey.'

'It would be better to go to Monterey. It is not far from here, and I have a cousin living there. He will let us have a room.'

'It would be more romantic to find a beach and have a swim.'

'I do not have a bathing costume.'

'Well, now,' she said, 'neither have I.'

This idea seemed to activate him, and he began driving faster, following a succession of roads, continuing to descend until they could actually hear the sea, and turning down a lane, found themselves overlooking a beach, just as the sun rose out of the east.

'Isn't that magnificent?' Anna asked.

'Oh, yes, senorita. Oh, yes.'

She got out of the car and stretched, then retrieved her shoulder bag from the back seat and walked through the trees to the beach, hearing him behind her. She took off her shoes and felt the sand beneath her stockings, taking deep breaths of the utterly fresh air.

'It is good to be alive on a day like this,' Rodrigo suggested.

'Absolutely,' Anna agreed. 'Would you like to unbutton my gown?'

'Oh, senorita!'

She felt his hands on her back. His fingers were less knowledgeable than Carlos's, and it took him longer, but she waited patiently until she could shrug the gown from her shoulders and past her hips, gathering it as it reached her ankles to stop it falling to the sand. She draped it on a convenient bush, keeping her back to him.

'Oh, senorita,' Rodrigo said. 'May I ... you are so beautiful.'

'You say the sweetest things,' Anna said. 'Of course you may touch me.'

The adrenaline had by now stopped flowing at the furious rate it had been when she had left the hotel, but she still felt that, supposing circumstances were different, he could grow on her. He was attractively endowed, and his touch was gentle. If the main reason that he was still here was that she had needed a chauffeur – as her German masters had not thought it necessary for her to learn to drive, she had only held a licence for the past three years and had driven very little in that time – it was also because she liked him, and she hated taking innocent lives; merely to have turned him loose and stolen the car, even if he had been bound and gagged, would have risked having the Mexican police on her trail sooner than was necessary. But now she reckoned she was within five miles of the river.

He was still standing behind her, and slid his hands under her armpits, much as Carlos had done, to cup her breasts; she felt him tremble against her. But then his hands continued downwards, across her stomach, while he nuzzled her neck, before he seemed to freeze as his fingers touched her belt and the pistol.

'Senorita?'

Anna stepped away from him and turned.

He gaped at her. 'That is a gun!'

'Something no girl should be without, wouldn't you say? Don't look so alarmed; I'm not going to shoot *you*.'

He gulped, but could not take his eyes from her body.

'I tell you what,' she said. 'If you turn round, I will give you a surprise.'

He obeyed, appearing to be almost mesmerized by her beauty combined with her charisma combined with the fact that she was armed; obviously he was wondering if she had been armed when having sex with Capillano. Anna stepped up to him, took a long breath, and swung her arm, as she had learned at the SS training school eleven years before, striking him on the neck just above the shoulder with the edge of her hand. This was intended to be a lethal blow, if delivered with the full weight of the body behind it, as it was aimed at the carotid artery, the principal conveyer of blood to the brain; if that flow was interrupted for any length of time death would follow. But she had deliberately not put all her weight into this swing, so that Rodrigo merely lost consciousness. His knees gave way and he collapsed on to the sand.

He would only be out for a few seconds. Anna knelt beside him, pulled off his tie, rolled him on his face and bound his wrists together. Then she pulled off his belt and secured his ankles as well, just as he began to stir.

Neither of those bonds would last very long; he was quite a powerful man. She tore her evening gown into strips, while he blinked at her, trying to focus. 'Senorita,' he muttered. 'You hit me. What are you doing? I do not understand.'

'I wouldn't even try, if I were you,' Anna recommended, and completed the destruction of the gown, leaving her with several lengths of quite strong material, as well as her sash. 'Open wide.'

He obeyed, still goggling at her. She passed a length of material round his mouth and drew it tight. Another length she passed round his body, and one round his thighs, and then took off her stockings to add yet another layer of binding. The last strip of cloth she passed round his eyes, so that he could not see what she was going to do next, and thus be unable to describe what clothes she would be wearing when she left him.

She understood that she was being utterly unprofessional. The correct thing for her to do in these circumstances was to kill him. Abandoned on this lonely beach it might be days before his body was found, and while the Mexico City police, once they had interviewed Jaquetta, would certainly deduce that she had made off with the taxi, they would have no idea where she had gone and thus where to start looking for her. But he was absolutely innocent, and rather charming ... and all she really needed was a few hours.

'There you go,' she said, and took her spare clothes from her shoulder bag, dressing herself in the denim pants, the crushed and untidy check shirt, the rather grubby jerkin, and the lace-up canvas ankle boots she had placed there earlier. She tied up her hair in a bandanna so that it was totally concealed, put on a pair of sunglasses that were entirely undistinguished save for the enormous lenses, which obscured even her eyebrows, and stuck a strip of chewing gum into her mouth. She placed all of her jewellery, including her watch, in the bag, replacing the Junghans with a tinny ten-dollar variety she had picked up in Miami, added her gloves and shoes, but left her pistol and the spare magazine in place.

Satisfied, she turned back to Rodrigo. 'Please don't look so morose,' she said. 'In my experience, if you work real hard, you should be able to free yourself in about three hours. In any event, I will send you help. Perhaps in less than that. Your car will be in Matamoros, and I reckon that is only about an hour's walk from here. I will leave the key under the front seat floor mat. You should look at it this way. You have had a nice drive in the country, a stimulating sexual experience, and you have picked up three thousand dollars into the bargain. I think you are a very lucky man. Adios.'

She got into the car, and after some experimentation started it up. Despite her inexperience

– she had only driven by herself on about half a dozen occasions – she knew what was necessary, and early in the morning the road was deserted. As she had anticipated, Matamoros was only five miles away from where they had stopped, and she was in the suburbs in fifteen minutes. She parked the car at the kerb, put the key under the mat as promised, slung her shoulder bag, and walked towards the river, flowing westward to where it would enter the Gulf of Mexico, some thirty miles away.

The town was just waking up, and there were some whistles from early-rising youths, but she had no trouble with the border guards, who surveyed her with the invariable masculine pleasure, even if with her hair concealed and her legs in pants she was far from at her best, checked her US passport, which was in the name of Anna O'Donovan – a play on the name of her previous US employer, Wild Bill Donovan, dreamed up by her current CIA controller, Joe Andrews – and waved her on to the first ferry.

The US immigration was a little more punctilious, but her passport was unarguable. However...'No transport, Miss O'Donovan?'

'Ah guess not.' She spoke in a drawl and took off her glasses to flutter her eyelashes at him, while chewing vigorously.

'So how did you get to Matamoros?'

'Ah thumbed a ride.'

'From where?'

'Mexico City.'

'Jesus! That's a long way. You don't reckon that was, well, kind of asking for trouble?'

'The guy who gave me the ride was a real gent.'

He gazed at her for some moments, clearly wondering how accommodating she had felt it necessary to be, then remarked, 'Lucky,' without specifying whether he was referring to her or her gentleman friend. 'But if you were coming home, how come you didn't catch a plane or a train, instead of risking the road?'

'Ma asshole boy friend threw me out,' Anna explained. 'And Ah had only a few bucks.' She returned his gaze, eyes enormous.

'I'd say he was a dope.' He stamped her passport.

Fifteen minutes later she was on a bus for San Antonio. She took a taxi to the airport, found a flight to Miami leaving in an hour. Having booked her seat, she had a substantial brunch – it was a long time since her light supper – waited until ten minutes before departure, and then went to a phone booth and put a call through to the Matamoros police station. 'It may interest you to know,' she said in Spanish, 'that on a beach five miles south of you, there is a man, bound and gagged. I would like you to go there and release him.'

'Senorita? Your name, please.'

'The man will tell you that, when you free him.'

'Where are you calling from?'

'I am in Monterey. But I am about to leave. Good morning.'

She hung up, joined the boarding queue. They would undoubtedly put a trace on the call, and discover it was long distance international. They might even be able to trace it to a call box at San Antonio airport, and eventually discover that a woman roughly answering her description had taken a flight to Miami. But all she had to do was reach there and she would be virtually home, and as always after the completion of an assignment, she wanted to lead her pursuers a dance. It was all part of the lethal game that was her life.

At two o'clock Anna was at Miami International, which in addition to the various flight desks and satellites was a huge shopping emporium. She went to one of the pharmacies within the terminal building and bought herself a toothbrush and some paste. Next she went to the Bahamas Airways check-in desk and booked a seat on the late flight to Nassau, using her reserve passport, in the name of Fitzjohn, this being the name under which she was known in the Bahamas.

Flying home from a mission was outside her usual practice; normally she went to her CIA contact in the city and used his radio to call the cay and have her boat come across to pick her up, thus avoiding any risk of identification. But it would take them a good eighteen hours to get here, and she didn't feel she could wait that long: experience had taught her that while many of her own successes had depended on her patience, her willingness to wait for the opposition to make a mistake, the biggest mistake that *she* could make would be ever to assume that the opposition would get it wrong, or not, in fact, get it all right. Thus she had to assume that the Mexican police, with American help, would probably be able to track her as far as here – certainly after they had traced the phone call to San Antonio Airport; she had been warned by the CIA that all police forces would be instructed to give maximum cooperation in the search for the perpetrator of what was going to be a crime of worldwide sensation; much as Washington wanted Capillano to pay for his crimes there was equally no way they could afford to be in any way involved in such arbitrary justice, carried out without a by-your-leave in a nearby and friendly country. Which was exactly why they had employed her.

So although there was only two hours to her flight, there was still work to be done, which included confusing the issue as much as possible. If both Jaquetta and Rodrigo would be able to describe the long-haired blonde with the expensive jewellery who had visited Capillano's suite and then hijacked the taxi for the ride to the border, she would have disappeared after leaving the beach. However, American immigration, given an approximate timing, would have been able to deduce that the somewhat scruffy young woman stepping off the ferry and said long-haired blonde were one and the same, thus it would be the scruffy blonde they would be looking for at Miami. Therefore, the best thing she could do was let them find her.

She went to the Airport Hotel, which was also a part of the terminal building, and booked a room for the night, using the name Eliza Doolittle. The reception clerk looked doubtful as he surveyed the untidy young woman carrying only a shoulder bag, so she smiled brightly and said, 'Ah guess you'd like me to pay up front?'

Now he looked embarrassed. 'Well...'

'How about a hundred?' She peeled off the note and laid it on the counter, allowing him a glimpse of the other nine notes in the wad.

'Well, of course, madam. I wouldn't like you to think—'

'You're doing your job,' Anna pointed out. 'If it runs over that, Ah'll settle up in the morning.'

'Of course, madam,' he beamed.

She went up to her room, locked the door, removed the bandanna and then undressed, making a face as she tore off the spare magazine, and had a long shower, which she sadly needed. She then strapped on her pistol, stowing the spare magazine in her spare handbag, a utilitarian piece of fake leather, as she was no longer in any danger of being searched, transferred the contents of her evening bag, the money, the three passports, her lipstick, comb and perfume, and her jewellery, restored her bandanna, put on her big dark glasses, looked sadly at her shoulder bag and evening purse, which like her gear in Mexico City, would have to be abandoned, together with the evening shoes, then opened each one to tear out the manufacturer's tab which indicated that they had been bought in Nassau. These she added to her handbag and went downstairs, the bag slung on her arm, smiling at the reception clerk, who would have to note that she had left her luggage, such as it was, in her room. 'What time is dinner served in your restaurant?' she asked.

'This is an airport hotel, ma'am. You can have a hot meal any time of the day or night.'

'Say, that's great. Do Ah need to book?'

'No, ma'am. It's a big restaurant. They'll fit you in.'

'Thank you. And breakfast?'

'Well, you can go to the restaurant if you want. But we'll serve it in your room, if you prefer. What time's your flight?'

'It's for New York. Ah think, ten o'clock.'

'Then you can have a lie in. Give us a call on room service when you're ready, and we'll send it up. You can have a continental, or a full. The full,' he added winningly, 'comes with English muffins.'

'That sounds great. Ah'll do that.'

She flashed him another smile and disappeared into the crowd of people outside the doors, walking casually until she was out of sight of the desk, then visited one of the several boutiques scattered about the building. Here she bought a new summer dress in pale blue with a plunging neckline, a straw hat with a matching pale-blue ribbon, a new pair of shoes, a clean pair of knickers as well as a pale-blue retaining band for her hair, and a new stylish handbag. She changed in the privacy of the fitting cubicle, and combed out her hair before attaching the band; then she added her watch and jewellery, changed her glasses for her winged Italian model, and pulled on her gloves. Her passports, toiletries and money she transferred to the new bag, together with her spare magazine.

She had obtained a large carrier bag from the desk when she had paid for the goods, and in this she placed her discarded clothes and shoes and handbag, then left the cubicle, smiled brightly at the woman on the desk, and vanished into the throng. She would certainly be remembered here, but unless the search for her was made very public, no one should ask them to do that. A few minutes later she had dumped the bag in a large waste bin as she walked by, joined the queue for the Departure Lounge, and an hour later was disembarking into the heat of Oakes Field, just over the hill from Nassau.

She took a taxi into the city, to the Royal Victoria Hotel, the oldest and most venerable of Bahamian hotels, which had stood since the days of the American Civil War, when Nassau had been the centre of the blockade runners who had taken guns and ammunition into the Confederate ports of Charleston and Wilmington, under the cannon of the Federal navy, and brought out the raw cotton which had paid for them. The trade had been so lucrative that it was said one could see the skippers in the Royal Vic ballroom lighting their cigars with hundred-dollar bills.

As this was the hotel she always used when passing through Nassau, Anna was both known and welcome. 'Miss Fitzjohn,' said the maitre d', who happened to be at the reception desk. 'Good to see you, ma'am. Good to see you. You checking in?'

'That's right.'

He turned the book towards her. 'How many nights?'
'Just the one, this time, I'm afraid.' She signed the book.
He peered over the counter. 'No luggage?'
'I'm just passing through. So, would you do one or two things for me?'
'Any time, ma'am.'
'Well, first thing, would you book me a table for dinner? I've been travelling all day, and I'm ravenous.'
'Sure thing.'
'Early. I didn't sleep very well last night and I want my bed.'
'Seven o'clock?'
Which was less than half an hour away. 'That will be perfect. Tell the chef I want fillet steak medium rare, and I'll have a bottle of Chateau Batailley.'
'Yes, ma'am.'
'Then would you make a radio call to the cay and tell Tommy I want to be collected, tomorrow morning?'
'You got it.'
'And lastly, I'd like to send a wire.'
He pushed the block of forms towards her and she wrote, rapidly, and pushed it back. He counted the words aloud. 'Mr Joseph Andrews, 6666 Langley Virginia. Jiggety jog. Anna.'
He raised his head, questioningly.
'It completes a nursery rhyme,' Anna explained. 'Home again, home again, jiggety jog.'

Anna was more exhausted than she had realized.

She was in bed by ten, and slept without moving until seven the next morning. It was not just the fact that she had not closed her eyes for thirty-six hours, more it was the events of that day and a half; as she was finishing her wine at dinner, she was reflecting that only twenty-four hours before, she had been leaving her hotel to visit Capillano.

But as always, when she awoke her brain was absolutely clear; she was prepared, as she had to be, to face the facts of who she was, what she had done, and what was necessary for her own survival ... until she was summoned again? It was always like this. If she had killed a hundred times, with remorseless professionalism, no one, not even Clive Bartley, and certainly not Joe Andrews, any more than her Nazi bosses, had any idea of the emotional cost of those executions. Even Clive, she suspected, if she did not question his combination of desire and affection, out of which real respect and love might well grow, considered that within that cocoon of charm and sophistication and charisma there lurked some terrifying force which she could summon into action by a simple act of will. The horrifying fact was that he, and they, were quite right. What none of them understood was the enormous effort required to summon that force ... or the emotional desert it left behind it.

A desert which had to be subjected to the cold light of realism. Her present position came first. But she could not fault it. Presumably by now the shambles in the Mexican hotel suite would have been discovered, and the entire city, perhaps the entire country, would be buzzing. But she did not suppose even a mass murder, as it would be considered rather than a mass execution, in Mexico City, of so high profile a man as Roberto Capillano, would make the *Nassau Guardian*. She felt no remorse. They had been guilty men, enemies of all mankind, and she had carried out their execution with all the speed and efficiency that had earned her her reputation, even if only a handful of people in the world knew of her existence, much less that reputation.

She went over the evening in her mind, not that she considered she had made any mistakes. As she had reckoned earlier, Jaquetta and Rodrigo would have been able to describe the Irishwoman named Anna O'Brien who had visited Capillano on the evening he had been killed, and Rodrigo would be able to tell them that she was armed and that she had been in a hurry to get out of the country. That he would be able to do that would be considered, certainly by Joe Andrews, and no doubt even by Clive, as an absurd and unnecessary and almost criminal act of generosity on her part; had she hit Rodrigo hard enough to kill him, she would have left no track to follow.

What her employers did not understand was that she was *not* a cold-blooded murderess. She was an executioner, who dealt the ultimate sanction to people whose guilt was proven and who could not be reached by conventional means. Rodrigo had been guilty of nothing. To have killed him simply to make her getaway secure would have lowered her to the level of

Capillano himself.

In any event, being able to discover that Senorita O'Brien had made herself scarce and fled the country, even if she had also been armed with a small pistol, as four of the dead men had been killed by the Browning did not necessarily indicate that she had carried out the killings; if she had been an inadvertent witness to what had happened, she might well have determined that her best course was to get as far away as possible as rapidly as possible. But the Mexican police would certainly want to interview her, and possessing her description they would undoubtedly trace her movements. But lacking a photograph, and with conflicting descriptions, persuading people to remember her would be difficult; wearing her hippie gear she had melded as much into the background as it was possible for someone like her to do. There would then be only a name, and the suggestion, supplied by the staff at the Airport Hotel, that she had been on her way to New York.

Satisfied, she got up, had a shower, dressed, strapping on her pistol, although she could not imagine herself ever needing to use it in Nassau – lacking her shoulder bag and with her new handbag stuffed with money and passports and toiletries and her spare magazine, there was simply nowhere else to carry it – put on her jewellery and ordered breakfast. She felt totally rested, rejuvenated, and ready to enjoy her private paradise. She was drinking her second cup of coffee when the phone rang. 'Tommy Rawlings is here for you, Miss Fitzjohn.'

'Thank you. Tell him I'll be right down.'
'And there's a telegram for you. Shall I send it up?'
'Why not read it to me?'
'Yes, ma'am. It says, "Good girl. I love you. Joe."'
'Isn't that sweet?'
'Yes, ma'am.'
'I'm on my way.'
She hung up, put on her hat and winged glasses, picked up her handbag, and went down to the lobby, where she paid her bill in cash.
'Welcome home, Miss Anna.'
'Tommy!' She shook hands with the large black man wearing a yachting cap.
'It sure is good to have you back.' He had now worked for her for over two years, and still regarded her with a mixture of admiration and apprehension. He knew nothing about her background, or about what she did when she mysteriously disappeared for a fortnight at a time; even on those occasions she had required him to crew her to Miami, and either wait for her or return for her when called, he was quite prepared to respect her whims. Nor did he have any idea of her worth, although having been with her since she had bought the cay he had to know she was pretty wealthy; it was her sheer aura even more than her beauty that left him, as it left most men, feeling that he was in the presence of a goddess. Kali, she thought; the Hindu Goddess of Death.
'I've only been gone two weeks,' she reminded him.
'Seemed like an eternity, ma'am.'

'You say the sweetest things. Well, I hope it's going to be an eternity before I have to travel again.'

'No baggage, ma'am?'

'I lost it along the way. Thank you, Charles.' She smiled at the waiting maitre d', and slipped a twenty-pound note into his palm. 'See you again soon.' She accompanied Tommy down the steps to the waiting taxi, got into the back seat beside him. 'All well on the cay?'

'No problem, ma'am. That Jupiter near caught a ray a couple of days gone.'

'Oh, good lord! He didn't get hit by the tail?'

'No, ma'am. He missed, and the fish was so scared he swam away too quick.'

'Thank God for that. Boat at the dock?'

'Yes, ma'am.'

'Take us to Rawson Square, will you please,' she told the driver.

'Yes, ma'am.'

A few minutes later they were disembarking beneath the statue of Queen Victoria.

Anna paid the driver. 'Now, Tommy, I have a couple of things to do. You wait for me on the boat. I'll be about half an hour.'

'No problem, ma'am.'

Anna walked along Bay Street, as always attracting the attention of just about everyone she passed; Anna Fitzjohn in distinctive dark glasses and a summer dress which flared in the wind, with her golden hair floating out from under her straw hat was a sight sufficient to stop traffic anywhere.

She went first to the bank, ignored the various

tellers' cages in favour of the open counter, and smiled at the accountant.

'Miss Fitzjohn! Good to see you.'

'Nice to see you, Mr Newton. I'm terribly sorry, but I seem to have forgotten my cheque-book on the cay. Could you cash a counter cheque for me?'

'Of course. How much would you like?'

She still had five thousand of the original twenty thousand dollars with which she had begun her trip, but that money – picked up from the CIA agent in Miami on her way to Mexico – was not something anyone in this bank should know about; the Bahamas, as a British colony, were within the sterling area and thus subject to the very strict exchange control rules governing that area. There was also the three hundred pounds. But she didn't intend to leave the cay again for some time, and she liked to be ready for any emergency. So she said, 'I'm a little low. I think a thousand will do.'

Newton looked pained. He well knew, from the balance in her account as much as from the large deposits that were regularly paid in to that account that to Anna Fitzjohn a thousand pounds was the equivalent of ten pounds to his average customer – he had absolutely no idea where her capital had arisen or where it was invested, or indeed, where she herself had come from – but the idea of a somewhat insouciant young woman walking the streets of Nassau with a thousand pounds in her purse was extremely disturbing.

Anna was well aware of what was going through his mind, and with her wicked sense of humour could not help wondering what his reaction, and that of his staff, would be should she faint and have to be removed to the rest room for resuscitation and the pistol strapped round her thighs be uncovered. 'Half in tens and half in twenties,' she said brightly.

He swallowed. 'Of course, Miss Fitzjohn,' he said, and hurried off.

When Anna left the bank, her handbag stuffed with the additional seventy-five notes, she went to her favourite boutique. 'Do you remember that lovely big shoulder bag you sold me last year?' she asked the manageress. 'The one with the thick leather strap?'

'Of course, Miss Fitzjohn.'

'Can you match it?'

'I should think so. But ... those bags are supposed to last forever. Well, for a very long time. If the material has proved defective in any way...'

'No, no,' Anna said. 'The material is fine, so far as I know. But I lost it. The bag.'

The woman stared at her.

'I must have put it down somewhere,' Anna explained. 'And forgotten it there. And now I can't remember where it was.'

Another pained expression. Again Anna could tell exactly what was going through her mind: this dumb blonde, for all her good looks, shouldn't be allowed out without a minder. But she said, 'I'll just get the bag, ma'am.'

With the bag, even if presently empty save for her purse, resting reassuringly on her hip, Anna made her way to the dock where Tommy was waiting, seated patiently on the upper steering position and reading the *Guardian*. She stood for a moment admiring the Chris-Craft motor cruiser. She had never been on something like this until just under two years before. Then, with the assistance and advice of a CIA agent who knew about boats, she had bought this at a Miami boatyard. Jimmy Flynn had also crewed her across to Fair Cay, a matter of some two hundred and fifty miles.

By the time they had got there, she had overcome her initial hostility to the sea; the last time she had been on a ship it had been torpedoed! But with Jimmy's encouragement she had been helming herself, and fallen madly in love. Forty-two feet long, driven by two powerful diesel engines which gave her twelve knots cruising and fuel tanks with a range of seven hundred miles, and with comfortable accommodation for six, she was the ultimate freedom; at sea, while one had to understand the weather, and the tides and currents, and how to read a chart and navigate – which she found fascinating – there were no street signs, no policemen or pedestrians, and above all, no possible enemies lurking round street corners; the enemies were all beneath the surface, and all one had to do was keep on top of the water. With its well-equipped galley and full water tanks, it was a world of its own, where only one rule mattered: hers.

She had called it *Fair Girl*.

Anna took off her high heels and stepped on board. Tommy stood up 'OK, ma'am?'

'Couldn't be better.' She went into the saloon, which was also the lower steering position, and down the short companionway into the aft, master, cabin. Here she always kept several changes of clothes, so she stripped, removing her suspender belt and stockings as well as her pistol belt, stowed them in one of the lockers, put on a shirt and slacks, thrust her toes into canvas shoes, tied her hair in a bandanna, and returned to the bridge. 'Eleven o'clock. We'll be home for a slightly late lunch.'

She half turned the two ignition keys, waited until the glowing lights on the facia faded to tell her that the heat starts had kicked in, then completed the turn; both engines burst into life. Tommy took in the mooring warps, and the little ship moved away from the dock, watched by a considerable crowd of spectators, both on account of the beauty of the craft and of the helmswoman.

Now an expert, Anna steered the cruiser between the various wharves and moored craft into the wide expanse of the harbour itself, turning east, with Hog Island on her left hand. Sparsely inhabited, even, nowadays, by the hogs that had given it its name, it possessed, on its northern side, a magnificent beach, a very popular destination with Bahamians on a Sunday morning. As it could only be reached by boat, there were various suggestions that the harbour should be bridged, but that was an enormous proposition for a not very wealthy community; Anna doubted that it would ever happen.

The normal entrance to the harbour was at the west end, where there was a lighthouse and a broad, deep-water channel, although the bigger ships still required the use of a pilot. The eastern end was narrow, shallow and encumbered with reefs, but Anna, with her photographic memory and immense powers of concentration knew it like the back of her hand, and they were soon through and in open water, following, some five miles off shore, the chain of islands stretching to the north-east.

Fair Cay was some forty miles away from New Providence, and they had not been under way for more than an hour before she could see it on the horizon. The sea around them was empty, so she switched on the auto pilot and went down to the saloon to use the radio; the radios on the cay were always on stand by, but not closely monitored, and she had to call several times to raise a response.

'Fair Cay! Is that you, Anna?'

'It's me, Mama. We're out of Nassau and should be with you just after two.'

'Have you eaten?'

'Not since breakfast. What's for lunch?'

'Grouper steaks.'

'Couldn't be better. You go ahead and have yours; I'll eat when I get in.'

'All right. Anna...' Even if she had no idea where her daughter had been and what she had been doing, Jane Fehrbach knew enough about Anna's background to be unable to keep the anxiety out of her voice.

'I'm here, Mama. All in one piece. See you in

a couple of hours.'

She returned to the bridge, reclaimed the helm, and studied the island, growing larger by the minute. A slow glow of exultation spread through her body. Fair Cay was the first thing of value she had ever legitimately owned; her jewellery had been 'retained' from her Nazi masters when she had escaped. Just over a mile long, the cay had originally belonged to a wealthy American recluse, who, like this more recent wealthy Irish recluse, had turned it into a permanent home. When Anna had selected the Bahamas as her refuge – close enough to her employers to suit them, and yet capable of being utterly remote – she had hunted through all the many possible sites before choosing this one, renaming it Fair Cay, which, while reasonably sensible to most people, was, like the name of her boat, actually a play on her real name, Fehrbach ... but this was known only to herself and her parents.

Now she could make out both the ripple of surf on the reef that entirely surrounded the cay, and the main house, which was two-storied and rose above the trees, and the radio mast; the little dock was on the eastern side, sheltered by the other islands in the chain which enclosed a large area of relatively shallow water; here the reef was closer than anywhere else, within three hundred yards of the dock, which was gained by a single narrow passage between the coral heads, but this also was like a front drive to Anna, and just after two they were nosing alongside the stone breakwater, where there waited another boat, an open twenty-five-foot runabout. This belonged to her staff, a gift from Anna; they lived on the island during the week, but went back to their home island of Eleuthera, a large bank on the northern horizon – it was over a hundred miles long – every weekend.

Although the main house had been comfortable enough when she had first come here, she had spent a quarter of a million dollars on making improvements, not only to the house, but on building a cottage for Tommy and his wife Desiree, and another for the three other black men, the 'boys', who looked after the garden and the farm; the island was self-sufficient in vegetables and tropical fruit, and she kept a large poultry flock: the boys also caught all the fish she required, leaving only fresh meat, drinks, whether soft or alcoholic, and such things as milk and household items to be obtained from the nearest inhabited island, Spanish Wells, just off North Eleuthera. These items she left to her mother, who went up there with Tommy three times a week.

She had also installed a saltwater swimming pool, right up against the house and therefore absolutely private. This was not such an absurdity as it might have seemed on a Bahamian island. There was certainly a splendid beach on the north-west side, fronting the lagoon created by the reef, a quarter of a mile from the shore, but it was exposed to every passing boat. Anna liked to bathe in the nude, and although she had no objection in principle to being overlooked, she had no desire to draw any attention to herself by causing the least breath of scandal in gossip-hungry Nassau.

The boat secured, they plugged in the electric cable to the shore supply that Anna had had laid on to the dock; this maintained constant power to the fridge as well as keeping the batteries always topped up – at sea the fridge ran off battery power, when the engines did the job of charging. Then they walked up the path towards the trees surrounding the house, listening now to the growl of the generator that was the sole source of power for the island, including, apart from the boat, the houses' electric light, and such essentials as the huge chest freezer for food storage and the water pumps, both for fresh from the cistern and salt from the sea; apart from the pool, all the toilets used salt water.

As they left the dock they were greeted by a baying sound, and the two huge Dogos came charging down the path. Anna had selected Dogos as her pet-cum-guard dogs because of their twin characteristics of complete and faithful loyalty to their owner, and unbridled ferocity towards anyone else. The eight permanent inhabitants of the island were their friends; anyone else was an enemy, unless they happened to be accompanied by their mistress and told what not to do. The known fact that the fearsome creatures were resident on the island effectively protected it from any trespassers, just as the fact that they would accept no food except from one of the Fehrbachs or one of the Rawlings meant that they could not be fed poisoned meat.

Anna braced herself for the charge, ruffling the huge white heads and having her hands licked again and again. 'Juno! Sweetheart! Jupiter, you old devil! Tommy tells me you've been chasing stingrays. You are a naughty fellow.'

Jupiter, if he could not understand her words, could certainly understand the tone of censure, and hung his head accordingly. Anna gave him another stroke and led both animals up to the house, and to the two people standing there, waiting for her.

It always gave her a glow of warmth to see them, even after a day's shopping trip to Nassau. When Johann and Jane Fehrbach had been arrested in Vienna in 1938, and their elder daughter had been taken away from them, they had feared the worst. When their guards had triumphantly told them that their Annaliese, the sweetest and most docile of their children, was now working for the Nazis, they had realized they had not understood how bad the worst could be.

Thus for seven years they had endured their relatively humane captivity, their lives distorted by shame and indeed loathing, compounded by tragedy, as their younger child, Katherine, fed up with imprisonment, had voluntarily joined the Reich and progressed, like her sister, into the ranks of the SD. But not being an Anna, Katherine had not survived.

Then had come the day when Anna had been able to extricate them from their Polish prison camp. Her immediate plan to get them out of Germany had failed, but she had been able to reveal to them that she was actually an Allied agent. Their relief and suddenly renewed love for her had been almost overwhelming, and only a few months later she *had* been able to rescue them from the collapsing chaos of the Third Reich to the safety of England.

Yet the mental scars of their ordeal had remained, accentuated by the fact that at that time she had been unable to be with them, except occasionally. But when, three years ago, she had achieved her last triumph over the by then defunct Reich, once she had chosen her spot, she had removed them here to be with her for the rest of their lives.

In the utter peace and tranquillity of Fair Cay they had bloomed like dying flowers suddenly given light and water. Johann, now nearing sixty, kept himself busy writing, as he had done all his life; whether or not his books would ever be published was of no importance; putting words, thoughts on paper was all he lived for, and after a lifetime of suffering the restrictions and indeed dangers of living under a dictatorship, either before or after the Anschluss of 1938, was a dream come true.

That he now knew his daughter's profession was no longer a barrier between them; whatever her methods, he knew she was on the side of right. But he also knew that whenever she left the cay for more than a brief visit to Nassau, she was taking her life in her hands. His greeting was a long, loving hug.

Jane Fehrbach was less stoic. Anna had never been sure from which of her parents she had inherited her exceptional mental powers, the superior intelligence and the devastating speed of thought that were the secrets of her success, but she felt it was more likely to have been her mother.

As a brilliant and enthusiastic young investigative reporter, Jane Haggerty had, in 1919, persuaded her newspaper, a leading London daily, to send her to Vienna to report on the horrendous rumours coming out of the capital of the erstwhile Habsburg Empire. Conditions had in fact been worse than she had ever suspected. With no access to the sea and Europe still largely under blockade, with the countries with which she was surrounded in a turmoil of revolution and financial collapse, and stripped of her once vast food-producing hinterland by the decisions taken at Versailles, Austria, and Vienna in particular, had been perhaps the most terrible example of a cut flower in history, trapped in its elaborate, beautiful vase, with no sustenance, withering day by day. Every day more and more people had starved to death, while the reports of crimes as ghastly as cannibalism were rife.

Jane had not returned to London. She had stayed to do what she could, and in doing so had fallen in love with the handsome young newspaperman who had helped her in her investigations. In May of the following year she had given birth to their first child, and marriage, and a grasp of happiness, had followed. But seven years in a Nazi prison had taken its toll. How beautiful she had been in her youth could be confirmed by a single glance at her daughter, and the perfect bone structure remained. But although she was some years short of sixty, the flesh was lined and the magnificent blue eyes too often dulled, while the once glorious and abundant golden hair was white and worn short.

But the eyes could light up again as she looked at Anna, and held her close. 'Every time you go away...' she said into her ear.

'You know that I am going to come back.' Still holding her arms, Jane moved back to stare at her. 'I know,' Anna said. 'Sheer hubris. But Mama ... it is hubris that makes me what I am.'

'The most deadly woman in the world.'

Anna kissed her. 'One should always try to be the best, at something.' She held her hand as they walked into the house. 'Desiree!'

'Miss Anna!' Desiree Rawlings was a very large black woman, matching her husband for size. Anna had no idea whether she in any way justified her name in bed, but she was an excellent housekeeper and an even better cook; Anna left all domestic arrangements to her and Jane.

She embraced her. 'I believe you have something nice for me to eat.'

'Yes, ma'am. Yesterday them boys did catch one big grouper. Thirty-five pounds.'

'Lead me to it. Then you'd better take some home to feed Tommy; he must be just as hungry as I am.'

Jane settled her at the head of the dining table before a plate of steaming fish, with tomatoes and avocado pear on the side, and a glass of her favourite Puligny Montrachet.

'Any mail?'

'Oh, yes. Tommy brought it over last week.' Jane placed the two letters beside her plate.

Anna put down her fork and picked up the first envelope. 'Stattler.' She slit the envelope. 'He's coming down next month.'

'There's nothing wrong?' Johann, seated beside her, knew that Paul Stattler was Anna's accountant, appointed by the CIA, and indeed, a member of that organization.

'Just his bi-annual report.' She laid it down and picked up the next, heartbeat quickening as she recognized the handwriting. She tore the envelope open, scanned the brief note. 'Clive's going to be here for my birthday.'

'I'm so glad. Will you be marrying him, this time?'

Anna made a moue. 'We'll have to ask him, won't we?' She laid down the letter. 'It's so *good* to be home.'

As a rule, when on the cay, Anna had a siesta. But after a fortnight's absence she wanted to make sure all was well, even if her parents and Tommy had been verbally reassuring. So after she had finished her meal and had a leisurely cup of coffee, she went up to her bedroom, changed into a pair of shorts and a clean shirt, and replaced her bandanna with a sun hat, watched sceptically by Isis, her large black cat, who spent most of her time asleep in Anna's king-size double bed, and did not appear to have noticed that her mistress had been away at all, although she began a loud purr when she was picked up for a hug and a kiss.

Both floors were fronted by verandas and Anna first of all walked round these, still carrying the cat, looking down on the pool and the small garden surrounding the lawn – neither flowers nor good grass took very kindly to either the Bahamian sun or the rather thin soil, which was liable to gather in pockets on the coral rock rather than be spread evenly and to any great depths over a wide area.

But they all looked in good order, as did the rest of the house as, having restored Isis to bed, she wandered through it, checking as she always did the screening, which, while it kept off the mosquitoes, needed constant coating with proofing to repel the tiny but voracious sandflies, known locally, for obvious reasons as no-see-ums, that came to life at dusk. Then she visited the radio room in which were situated both the huge green Sailor HF set, and the smaller, also green, VHF for calls to and from the boat and Nassau. Both crackled reassuringly.

Beside the radio room was the study-cum-library, her favourite room, one which, like the cay itself, she had always dreamed of owning. Apart from her desk and her accounts, two of the walls were floor to ceiling bookshelves. There were few novels; her own life was too full of drama and emotional trauma for her to be very interested in fictional experience. So apart from the complete *Encyclopaedia Britannica* and up-to-date copies of the various *Fodor's Guides* – essential in her business – most of her books were history and biography and philosophy, subjects she read with the attention of a student; as the nuns had assured her that with her brains she would certainly gain a university place, it amused her to suppose that but for the Anschluss and what had followed, she could well have wound up a schoolmistress.

But the library was also the home, neatly stowed on its rack, of her Remington riot gun, a police weapon given her by Joe Andrews. Pump action, its seven-shot magazine would take either scatter shot or two-inch long solid cartridges, known as deer shots, which had a range of several hundred yards. Should she ever have to defend the cay, this would be a far more efficacious weapon than her little Walther.

She went outside and down the steps, snapping her fingers to summon the dogs, who came bounding up to walk beside her and dart into the bushes after rustling lizards. She went first of all to the powerhouse. Here she had two twenty-five-kilowatt generators, which were used in rotation so that Tommy could service them and change the oil as necessary. This was where she had made one of the major changes, removing the overhead cables to the houses and the dock, and the cistern, and having them buried. It had been a major and expensive operation, as they had had in places to burrow through rock, and the cistern was very nearly a mile away, but it also meant that the power supply was safe from being brought down by strong winds, or falling trees. And although she had the utmost confidence in both Tommy's diligence and his skills, she could not stop herself checking the oil and water levels; her survival had always depended on being a perfectionist.

Beside the generator shed was the huge oil storage tank which held five thousand gallons. Having this refilled by tanker from Nassau was her biggest single housekeeping item; but the sight gauge was showing three-quarters full. Close by were the several large filters that purified the water pumped up from the reservoir; how necessary they were could be seen at a glance from the amount of green and brown slime that clung to their sides, despite the fact that they were cleaned every week.

The house, situated on the south-western end of the island, was surrounded by coconut and casuarina trees, swaying in the afternoon breeze, and effectively isolating it from the rest of the cay. The casuarinas grew to a great height, and their always moving branches set up a constant soughing, louder than the surf on the beach, but at the same time utterly soothing. Their needles, however, hard little serrated cones, constantly dropping and littering the paths, were murder to bare feet.

The path led through the trees, and she followed this past the two staff houses into the fruit grove, feeling pleasantly warm rather than hot; at half past four the sun was just beginning to droop into the western sky. Here there were masses of bushes from which hung oranges and grapefruits, sheltered by the huge sapodilla trees, also laden with fruit, as were the no less massive mangoes. Beyond were the lime and lemon trees, after which were the avocados and bananas. These were so profligate that there was no way they could all be eaten, and Anna was in the habit of allowing the boys regularly to take the surplus up to Eleuthera for sale in the markets there.

Beyond the trees was the vegetable garden, where Elias, the head gardener, was somewhat sombrely surveying his rows of tomato plants while his two juniors squatted, chopping at weeds with their long, razor-sharp knives.

'Good afternoon, Elias,' she said, brightly. 'How's it going?'

The sight of her seemed to cheer him up. 'Good afternoon, borse. Man, is good to have you home. You seeing them bugs? They eating up all them plants.'

Anna smiled at the two boys, then squatted herself to peer at the damage, which was considerable. Every tomato on the lower branches whose weight had it resting on the ground had been reduced to a pulpy, oozing mess. She knew absolutely nothing about agriculture, was as a rule content to let Elias manage the garden as long as he produced a constant supply of fruit and vegetables for the table, but she didn't need to call on her genius to discern what was wrong. 'They're only eating the tomatoes that are lying on the ground.'

'That's a fact, borse. That is what they do.'

Anna took off her glasses to peer at the tomatoes hanging on the higher stalks; these were, without exception, round, full and succulent, their skins unbroken. 'Why aren't they eating these?'

'Well, borse, they don't get up that high, you

see.' His tone indicated, one couldn't expect a white woman to understand the nitty gritty of gardening.

'Well, then,' Anna said, patiently, 'wouldn't it be possible to tie up the lower stalks so that the fruit don't droop on to the ground?'

Elias tilted his battered fedora forward to scratch the back of his head. 'I ain't never heard of nobody ever doing that, borse.'

'Well, I think it's worth trying. Cut off all this rotten stuff. Put it on the dump, and burn it with the other rubbish. Then get some string and tie up the lower stalks so they don't touch the ground.'

'If that's what you want us do, borse.' His tone was redolent of doubt.

'Yes,' Anna said. 'That is what I want you to do.'

'You heard the borse,' Elias announced.

The two boys immediately changed their positions and fell to.

'Now tell me,' Anna said. 'How's the water?'

'Well, borse, we could do with some rain, and that's a fact.'

'Hm.'

She continued her walk, through brush now, followed by Elias, the dogs still rooting around to either side, but staying close to her as they passed the hen run. As there were no predators on the island – save the dogs themselves – this was unfenced and they were immediately surrounded by clucking hens and the strutting cock. The dogs had been carefully trained never to touch the chickens; as a result the fowls treated them with contempt, and the dogs had come to regard the poultry as sinister creatures, to be avoided wherever possible, except when in the protective company of their mistress.

'Are they laying?' Anna asked.

'Oh, yes, borse. Every day we got plenty eggs.'

'Can't be bad.' She was now very nearly at the eastern end of the cay, where the catchment was situated. This was the sole source of fresh water on the island, and here there was a huge concrete surface, raised into a slight slope by packed earth. It faced south-west, where the rain clouds mostly came from, but would trap rain from any direction. At its foot was the cistern, a huge concrete reservoir, roofed but open to the water cascading down the slope, although fenced to prevent the chickens from either committing suicide or fouling the contents.

Catchment and cistern had been constructed by the previous owner, but Anna had doubled the size of the cistern from sixty to a hundred and twenty thousand gallons; although Bahamian rainfall was fairly consistent, there was the occasional dry spell, such as they were presently experiencing, that could last up to a fortnight. Anna standing beside the pump, which purred constantly, could see that the tank was only half full.

'We're OK for another few weeks,' she shouted above the hum. And sniffed. 'There's no chlorine.'

'Well, borse,' Elias shouted back. 'We running low, and that's a fact.'

'Listen, you put in every drop you have, tomorrow morning; I have a guest arriving next week, and I don't want him to get a funny tummy. I'm going in to Nassau to meet him and I'll bring back a fresh supply.'

'You got it, borse.'

'Well, everything seems to be under control. Well done, Elias.'

'Thank you, borse.' He glowed.

Anna and the dogs made their way back along the path. It was *so* good to be home. Her own private paradise!

THE INTRUDERS

Amy Barstow stood hesitantly in the doorway of Clive Bartley's office. 'Mr Baxter ... ah...'

'You really don't have to announce me, Miss Barstow,' Billy Baxter said, stepping past her with some difficulty; Amy was inclined to be overweight. 'Just close the door.'

Clive had risen in some haste; it was extremely unusual for his boss to come downstairs to see him, usually it was the other way around. 'Slumming?'

Baxter sat down in the chair before the desk, and Clive also sat, uncomfortably aware that the chief had something on his mind. The two men had known each other and worked together at MI6 for a dozen years, and for all their occasional difference of opinion on how some matters of possible danger to national security should be handled, they had the highest respect for each other's abilities and capabilities.

Physically they could not have been less alike. Clive Bartley was six feet two inches tall, built like a second row forward, with attractively rugged features, his dark hair just beginning to streak with grey; this was a result of the exigencies of his job, as he was only in his middle forties. Baxter was several inches shorter and slightly built, with sharp features and deceptively disinterested eyes; his untidy sandy hair was now mostly, if less obviously, grey: this was because all problems concerning MI6 eventually wound up on his desk. That he was not always as calm as he liked to pretend was revealed by his sweater, which he wore on the hottest day, and in which were embedded generations of tobacco, spilled from the pipe to which he was wont to turn when under stress.

As Clive did not smoke, he was relieved that Billy did not appear to have brought his pipe with him, but ominously, he was carrying some sheets of paper; there was a crisis somewhere in the world that needed attending. Now he remarked, 'I see that you're down for a week's leave.'

'It's due.'

'I'm not disputing that. Would I be right in assuming that you are spending your vacation in the Bahamas?'

'You would be right, yes,' Clive said, carefully.

'When are you going to marry the girl?'
'Ah!'
'Don't tell me she's gone off the boil?'
'Anna has not gone off the boil. At least, as regards me.'
'You mean *you've* gone off the boil? For a beautiful multi-millionairess who has the hots for you? I always knew you were a twit, but I had no idea you were that much of a twit.'
'One should be careful about making assertions without being in possession of the facts,' Clive said mildly. 'You happen to have been married, I assume happily, for twenty years, within the parameters of your job, your society, your friends, your hobbies, your family. Therefore you are quite unable to understand other situations. Did you ever read the story about the couple shipwrecked on a desert island?'
'You mean *The Blue Lagoon?* Yes, I've read that. A long time ago.'
'I do not mean *The Blue Lagoon*. That was about two kids, growing up together, discovering what life, and each other, was all about. I am thinking of the one about the couple on their honeymoon. She was beautiful and charming, he was handsome and charming. They had everything in common, the same interests, the same ideals. And the ship they were on was wrecked, and they were alone on this island, for ten years. When they were rescued, they couldn't stand the sight of each other.'
'Philosophy, at ten o'clock in the morning, has never been my scene,' Baxter pointed out.
'But don't you see, Billy? I have spent damn

near my entire working life in this department, first in the field as an agent, recently in this office controlling agents.'

'Amongst them, Anna.'

'Quite. But circumstances have conspired to force Anna to disappear, in order to stay alive. Only a handful of people know where she is, or can be allowed to know where she is. As a completely anonymous, if wealthy, beachcomber she leaves her island not more than once a fortnight for a quick trip to Nassau for supplies, then pulls up the drawbridge again.'

'You mean, she's getting bored.'

'I don't think so. After the life she's been forced to live for the past ten years, she's in paradise. She has her island, she has her parents with her, she has her dogs and her cat and her faithful retainers ... and if I were to marry her, she'd have her favourite man.'

'It seems to me that you are describing a fate worse than death, which most men would happily die to achieve, even if briefly.'

'Billy, if I married Anna, I would have to retire from MI6. Right?'

'Well ... yes, if you intended to live with her on a permanent basis.'

'I seem to have missed something here. Isn't that what husbands normally do with their wives? More than that. I would become a kept man, a parasite, living off Anna's millions. It isn't me.'

'You could write your memoirs. No, I suppose you couldn't; I'd have to slap a D-notice on you. We all have our problems. However, indirectly, that is what I'm here to discuss. Anna *is* retired, right?'

'This government we're presently suffering insisted on it.'

'Absolutely. And as you say, she never leaves her island except for brief trips to Nassau, right?'

Clive frowned. 'Just what are you driving at?'

Baxter waved his sheets of paper. 'Just a report I received today from our Mexico office.'

'And that's important to me?' Clive asked. 'My field of operation is Europe.'

'Absolutely. However, it seems that a couple of days ago, a chap named Roberto Capillano was shot dead in his hotel suite in Mexico City. That ring any sort of bell?'

'Ah ... Capillano. Isn't he top of the FBI most wanted list?'

'The correct word is "was".'

'Well, I would say, jolly good riddance. A gangland killing?'

'A professional hit, certainly. Our people say, from what they have learned from the Mexican police, that he was killed by a single bullet to the head from a point two-two pistol, probably a Walther PPK.'

Clive's frown was back.

'Capillano was of course well protected,' Billy went on. 'He had three armed bodyguards, together with a secretary. All of these were also killed with single shots to the head, although the assassin seems to have switched weapons and used a Browning nine-millimetre automatic. This gun appears to have belonged to Capillano, and may have been used because the assassin lacked a Luger. Does any of *this* ring a bell?'

'Oh, my God, my God, my God,' Clive said. 'But wait a minute, Billy. This is purely circumstantial, based on what we know of Anna's methods. There is nothing concrete to implicate her.'

'I haven't finished,' Baxter pointed out, and referred to his papers. 'The Mexican police have no clues as to the perpetrator of this dreadful crime, their words, but it was clearly a highly professional job. There is not a trace of a fingerprint anywhere apart from those of the people living in the suite. There were two champagne glasses on the table in the room where Capillano died; one bore his prints, the other had been wiped clean. That is the only indication that anyone was there apart from his people. As I recall, just for example, when that fellow Johannsson was found dead in his apartment in Stockholm in 1944, suffering from a single bullet wound in the head, there was also not a fingerprint or a suggestion that anyone had been there. However, unlike the Swedish police, the Mexicans have a lead; they are looking for a young woman using the name of Anna O'Brien.'

'Oh, Jesus Christ,' Clive said.

'This woman,' Baxter continued, inexorably, 'is described as a strikingly good-looking blonde prostitute.'

'Prostitute?'

'That's what they say. Employed on a temporary basis by one of Mexico City's leading madames, someone named Jaquetta. This Jaquetta claims to know nothing about O'Brien, simply that she suddenly appeared and asked for employment, as a whore. Well, according to Jaquetta, while she reckoned there was something odd about her, as she was absolutely dripping expensive jewellery, not unreasonably she felt she was just too good to refuse. In this capacity, the young lady seems to have visited Capillano on the night in question, stayed with him for just over half an hour, and left him just about the time of the massacre of him and his friends. You'll note that the police are not accusing her of carrying out the crime. At least, yet. I suppose they find it impossible to believe that a pretty girl would, or in fact *could*, shoot five armed men dead with five shots. However, they do know that she made herself scarce, hijacking a taxi to drive her four hundred miles to Matamoros. Outside of the town she left the driver bound and gagged on a lonely beach. She then drove into Matamoros itself ... I know Anna was taking driving lessons when she had to leave Scotland in a hurry, but did she ever get a licence?'

'She got a licence.' Clive's voice was redolent of gloom. 'In America.'

'Not,' Baxter said, 'that when you have just killed five men and wish to remove yourself from their proximity the absence of a driving licence is likely to stop you driving a car. Anyway, she drove into the town, took the ferry across the Rio Grande to Brownsville, using, they have been able to ascertain, a passport in the name of Anna O'Donovan.'

He paused, but Clive was holding his head in his hands.

'This was an American passport,' Baxter said. 'So she had no problem entering the States. She then seems to have gone to San Antonio, as there is a record of a woman that same day and using the name O'Donovan boarding a flight to Miami. The incredible thing is that having got clear away, she telephoned the Mexico police to tell them where the taxi driver could be found. Has she completely lost her marbles, or does she have a death wish?'

Clive sighed as he looked up. 'It's the way Anna is.'

'You mean she rations herself. Only five murders a day, or a night, or whatever?'

'They were not murders, Billy. They were executions. Anna does not commit murder. As far as she was concerned, this taxi driver was an innocent bystander; to have killed him *would* have been murder.'

'It's a point of view. The real point is that she was now leaving a trail as wide as a four-lane highway. At least, up to a point. At Miami she checked in at the Airport Hotel ... and simply disappeared. She had only a single piece of luggage, a large shoulder bag –' he paused to look at a stricken Clive – 'and this was found by a chambermaid the next morning, apparently with all possible identification removed. There was nothing else. Now, do you think we are still talking about circumstantial evidence?'

'But—'

'I agree entirely. The number of buts is monumental. But only one concerns me: was she working on her own, or is she being employed? If so, by whom? She's supposed to be ours.'

Clive seemed to wake up. 'She is not ours, Billy. Not any more. She *was* ours. But when we pulled in our horns in 1946, she was left out on a limb. We stuck her up in that so-called safe house in Scotland while the government decided what to do with her, and they took so long over it that the Reds were able to trace her.'

'So she shot four of them dead, I suppose that was because there were only four of them available to shoot, and departed, leaving a monumental diplomatic mess behind her.'

'She left with the aid of Joe Andrews and the CIA.'

'Correct. And then worked for them in South America, briefly, leaving another trail of murder and mayhem. She said she took on that assignment because they promised that if she helped them get Martin Bormann they would help her get her money out of Germany. We agreed to go along with that on condition she then agreed to retire and disappear. But she doesn't seem to have done that. So?'

'I would say,' Clive said thoughtfully, 'that she had a different agreement with the Yanks.'

'You mean with Andrews.'

'Well...'

'With whom, if I remember correctly, she had been, how shall I put it, associated, in the past.'

'He saved her life,' Clive said miserably. 'In Russia, in 1941.'

'And she's a girl whose gratitude knows

no end.'

'All right, Billy, you've made your point and ruined my day. But what the hell do you propose to do about it? So she has just murdered, she would say executed, five thugs. I suppose old habits die hard.'

'In the past two years, you have spent four holidays in the Bahamas, and you knew nothing about these, shall we say, extra- curricular activities? I am assuming this Mexico business is not the first.'

'No, I did not know anything about what she's been doing with her time. She has always appeared totally normal and contented.'

'A vampire can appear totally normal and contented as long as he, or she, gets his regular ration of blood. So, now that you do know about it, what are *you* going to do about it?'

'What can I do about it? She is no longer ours to command.'

'Oh, yes?'

'Billy, we retired her, told her to get out of the UK, and to stay out. She has done that. We didn't specify what she was to do with her retirement. Anna was never one to lie on a beach.'

'May I remind you that no matter what she may be doing on her beach, said beach is situated in a British colony, and is therefore subject to British law?'

'And may I point out that so far as we know she has broken no British laws? If she killed those blokes, it was in Mexico.'

'And when they track her down and demand her extradition?'

'You are supposing they can do that. I mean, track her down. Apart from doing the right thing about the taxi driver she seems to have covered her tracks pretty well. You are also assuming that they'll really want to go after her. Capillano may have had a lot of friends in high places to stand between him and extradition to the States, but they were friends simply because he kept their palms well greased. That doesn't alter the fact that he seems to have been the nastiest creature to walk this earth since Jack the Ripper. And maybe I'm being hard on the Ripper. I'd bet all his "friends", and definitely the police, while obliged to go through the motions, are saying to themselves, good riddance.'

Baxter snorted. 'You make an unconvincing advocate. So do you think she's set herself up as some kind of supreme judge and jury, the ultimate international vigilante, dedicated to wiping out all the baddies she can locate? If that's the case, we simply have to do something about it; some of those undesirables are living in England.'

'As I said just now, almost certainly she's working for the CIA.'

'You mean Andrews. And you still think she's yours for the taking, whenever you can summon the guts to do it?'

'God, I don't know. Don't you think it keeps me awake at night? Look, I'm seeing her in a few days' time. I'll see if I can sort things out.'

'I'm coming with you.'

'What? Now, Billy, strong-arm tactics won't work with Anna. The only thing you're likely to achieve is joining the bullet in the head club.'

Baxter grinned, an unusual event. 'Well, if that happens, we'd at least have her for committing murder on British soil. But I'll have you to protect me, won't I?'

'But why do you want to come? She's not likely to listen to you if she won't listen to me.'

'Do you know,' Billy said, remembering. 'It's three years since I last saw Anna. Maybe I just need to get my hormones moving again, in the right direction. The point is, Clive, although it seems to have escaped you, if by any chance you are wrong, and the Mexican police are serious about trying to get hold of her, and there is a risk of her being returned to Mexico City to face their methods of interrogation, and she decides to talk her way out of trouble, or simply to go out with a publicity bang, she could blow a big hole in the credibility of this government, and the US Administration, and international relations all over the world. The merest suggestion of some of the jobs she has carried out for us, and the Americans, would fill the front pages for months. So you see, if there were any risk of that happening, we would have to take the young lady out ourselves to prevent it. And when I say we, I mean you, as you are the only member of this organization who has both the ability to get up close to her, and who also has the ability to do the job. So we need to have a serious chat with her. You with me?'

Clive gulped.

'Besides,' Billy went on, 'there is something I wish to talk to her about.'

'What thing?'

'You'll have to ask her. After I've talked with her.'

'Well, if I may give you a word of advice, leave your pipe behind. Anna does not allow smoking on her island.'

Don Giovanni Ravanelli was a very big man. Naturally tall and heavy, he had added to his size by a lifetime of overeating. The result was, now that he was in his sixties, constant indigestion that, despite a steady consumption of Rennie's, left him with a jaundiced view of life and unable properly to enjoy the wealth that years of being boss of the Ravanelli Family had brought him, and often caused him to exercise the power of his position with angry ruthlessness.

All his employees were afraid of him, and so was his actual family, with the exception of his son Luis, who being an only son and thus certain to succeed his papa in the course of time – and perhaps not all that much time if the old man refused to change his habits – took him in his stride, as it were. Thirty-one years old, married and with a family of his own, Luis had, with Don Giovanni in front of him as a bad example, always kept himself well in hand. He neither ate nor drank to excess, spent an hour every morning in the gym, and as a result had a well-balanced figure to go with his strongly aquiline features and his sleek black hair. Always immaculately dressed, he was most often seen in a tuxedo attending one of Chicago's nightclubs – in most of which his father had an interest –

surrounded by his four bodyguards and always with a beautiful woman, not necessarily his wife, on his arm.

This morning he wore a perfectly cut three-piece grey suit, with a carefully knotted quiet blue tie, a red carnation in his buttonhole, and smiled across the huge desk at his father's expression. 'You got the burn?' he asked, solicitously.

'Fucking razor blades,' Don Giovanni growled. 'And it ain't nothing to do with breakfast.' He tapped the newspaper lying on his desk. 'You seen this sheet?'

'You mean about Roberto buying it? I reckon he had it coming. He was a shitting asshole.'

'So who do you reckon did it?'

Luis shrugged. 'Those women and kids he burned up must have had fathers, husbands, brothers, maybe even adult sons.'

'This was a top-class professional hit. For Christ's sake, five bullets, five dead men? Shit! And they were good. That guy Carlos Dias was the best. I tried to get him on my payroll one time. And he never even got his gun out of its holster.'

'So, maybe it wasn't a gifted amateur. They have hit men in Mexico as well, you know. Although I'd still go for someone from up here.'

His father gazed at him for several seconds. 'What about the broad?'

'The key, eh? Having set it up, and apparently hanging around to make sure their eyes weren't on the ball, she flees back home. That's what makes me think the job originated here rather than Mexico. But I don't think she's going to do anyone much good. She's got her feet in concrete by now.'

'What makes you think she set it up?'

'Well, that's pretty obvious, Pa. This Jaquetta says Capillano hires a girl for the night, every night. So this girl turns up and asks for the assignment. So she goes in at eight and leaves half an hour later. Half an hour, not the whole night. And the moment she leaves, presumably after letting the hit man, or hit squad in, boom boom.'

'That's what you think happened.'

'That's what the police say happened. Who are we to argue with the cops?'

Again Don Giovanni considered for some seconds. Then he opened his desk drawer and took out a rather tattered photograph, held it out. 'What do you think?'

Luis studied it. 'Wow! Somebody you know? She sure is someone *I'd* like to know.'

'You wouldn't sit in on the meeting I had with that guy Botten a couple of weeks ago.'

'Hell, Pa, he was a Red. I can smell those guys a mile away.' A Veteran, Luis had finished the war as a captain in the infantry, and was a patriot to his bootlaces ... as long as patriotism did not interfere with the Family business.

'Maybe. But he was offering ten thousand dollars for a hit.'

'Ten ... a hit on whom? The president?'

'That dame. He gave me the photo.'

Luis was still holding the photograph. Now he looked at it again. 'Ten thousand dollars ... he was putting you on. This is just a kid.'

'That was taken a few years back. Nine to be precise. Although apparently she hasn't changed too much. And it seems she was worth a lot of money, dead, even then.'

Luis was still studying the photo. 'Just where was this taken? Those buildings in the background don't look like anything I've ever seen, at least in this country. That church, with all those onion domes...'

'That's St Basil's Cathedral. She's standing in Red Square, in Moscow. That high wall on her left is the Kremlin.'

'Holy shit! You mean she's on the run from the Reds? And you want to go along with them?'

'They want her because she's a war criminal, a Nazi, who's a killer, and who escaped capture when they fell apart. Amongst other things she spent the war rounding up Jews and either bumping them off herself, or handing them over to the Gestapo for the gas chambers.'

Luis continued to stare at the photograph. 'This guy Botten tell you this?'

'That's right.'

'And you believe him?'

'Ten thousand dollars says he could be right.'

Luis tapped the cardboard. 'A face like that couldn't harm a fly.'

'There were guys in the old days who made the same sort of misjudgement about Lucretia Borgia. And all they got was a slab in the morgue.'

'I still don't believe a word of it. But even if it's true, what the hell are we supposed to do about it. The war ended four years ago. If she's still alive, she could be anywhere in the world.'

'These guys seem to feel that she is alive, and somewhere on this side of the Atlantic.'

'For Jesus' sake, Pa, somewhere from Labrador to Cape Horn, right? Anyway, if she is here, she's probably married with six kids.'

'Ten thousand dollars.'

The two men gazed at each other. And Don Giovanni opened his desk drawer to find his packet of Rennies.

'You're not supposed to take more than twenty of those a day,' Luis remarked. 'You'll give yourself ulcers.'

'I already have ulcers,' Don Giovanni pointed out. 'If this dame is the vicious murderess Botten's principals think she is, she ain't got six kids. She's never had the time.'

'But he couldn't prove that.'

'Ten thousand dollars still says he could be right.'

'For Christ's sake Pa, do we need ten thousand of probably Russian money?'

'Maybe we don't, right now. But with this guy Kefauver and his Crime Commission breathing fire and smoke, it could come in handy. Anyway, I took the money.'

Luis gazed at his father for several seconds. He knew the Family's code of honour. 'And you genuinely think she did the job on Roberto. The Mexican police aren't claiming that she's anything more than a witness.'

'They don't know what we know.'

'I still don't see how we have a hope in hell of

finding her.'

'The trouble with the modern generation,' Don Giovanni commented, mildly, 'is that they, you, have lost the power to think. They like everything spelled out for them. So let me spell it out for you. I've had Benjy look into this and get some details: he has an in with the Mexico City police. So, according to the chauffeur, this O'Brien, who fits in with the long-haired blonde in that picture, hijacked his car and forced him at gunpoint to drive her to Matamoros, with the intention of crossing to Brownsville. She told him she was going to do this.'

'Why?'

'To get out of Mexico, of course.'

'I mean, why did she tell the taxi driver what she was aiming to do. According to you, she'd just killed five men, right? And you say it wasn't the first time, right? One more life ain't going to make a damn bit of difference to her, right? So she needed transport to get to the border, fair enough. But why didn't she just have this guy drive her out of town on to a lonely road, put a bullet through his head, roll him into a ditch, and take off with the car?'

Don Giovanni considered. 'How the hell do I know what goes on inside a dame's brain? I never met one who thinks like a human being. Maybe, as this was obviously a contract killing, she only kills for money, and this guy wasn't on her list.'

Luis blew a raspberry.

'The point is,' his father went on, 'we know from this Senora Jaquetta, that O'Brien was travelling on an Irish passport. But according to US Immigration at Brownsville, there is no record of anyone answering that name or description entering the country on the date in question.'

'So she either didn't cross, which would be a good reason for her to tell the driver that she *was* crossing, or she used some kind of disguise and a false passport. Either way, that was it. She's gone.'

'Not that far. You won't believe this, but that same morning the Matamoros police received a telephone call from San Antonio Airport, from a broad with an Irish accent, telling them where to find the driver.'

Luis looked at the photo again. 'She has to be nuts. But she don't look nuts.'

'The Mexican police were able to trace that call, so they went back to Brownsville, again, with time and date, and this time they came up with a hippie type Irish girl, probably blonde although they couldn't be sure as she had her hair concealed, with an American passport in the name of O'Donovan. Using that they were able to discover that this dame boarded a flight that same morning, San Antonio to Miami.'

'So she's organized. And in Miami she disappeared, right?'

'Right. So she flew San Antonio–Miami. Tell me where she went after that.'

Luis shrugged. 'The obvious place would be somewhere in Florida. She either hired a car or had one waiting for her, and went home.'

'No she didn't. They checked Miami out, and

while they drew a blank with the airlines, using both the description and name O'Donovan, the clerk at the desk at the Airport Hotel had a customer that day, a hippie-type using the name Eliza Doolittle.'

'You're putting me on.'

'Fact. It didn't register with this guy. But he remembered her because she paid for the night in advance, told him she was flying out the next morning to New York, and then half an hour later just walked out, apparently looking for a meal, and leaving her gear, such as it was, in her room; she never came back for it.'

'So she was trying to muddy her trail. But obviously she never intended to catch that flight. She's in Miami. Or somewhere in Florida.'

'So you tell me why, if she simply had to catch a cab to her home, she bothered to check in to the hotel at all, and pay for the room? If she had a car waiting for her, or intended to hire one, why didn't she just use it? The hotel provided an extra link in her trail, so why take the risk?'

'Because,' Luis said patiently, 'She was laying that extra trail.'

'Think. God damn it. She's running for her life, mind. If she was merely heading for home in Miami, why try to pretend she was going on?'

'Like I said, because she knew they'd be able to find out which flight she was on. So she tried to throw them off her track.'

'But she must've known, after the way she walked out of that hotel, that they'd figure she wasn't taking that flight to New York. Then they'd start looking locally. And they'd find her, eventually. If she was there. Just as she must've had a pretty good idea they'd find her wherever she went in this country. This is a high profile hit.'

Luis considered, frowning. Then snapped his fingers. 'She was leaving the country.'

'Bright boy!'

'Going back to Ireland.'

'Dumb boy.'

'Eh?'

'If she wanted to go to Ireland, and she's in a hurry, mind, why go to Miami first? San Antonio is a big international airport. She could probably have got a flight from there. But even if she felt she had to get further east, it'd be for another big international, say for another really big one, like Atlanta or Idlewild, where she'd get a trans-Atlantic flight much quicker than from Miami, it'd be too much of a risk, after that phone call. She was using the name O'Donovan, and she'd know the cops would latch on to that, PDQ. It's maybe four hours from San Antonio to New York, then a wait for a flight, then maybe eight hours to Shannon. Once they picked up that booking, they'd have the Garda waiting for her as she stepped off the plane. Anyway, Botten said that if she was in Europe, or went back there, they'd be able to take care of her themselves. She must've known that.'

'So where would she go from Miami, internationally? If not to Europe? South America? Cuba? Cuba! That's the most likely.'

'I've been looking at some schedules. She could have caught a flight to Havana from San

Antonio. She had to go to Miami because only from Miami could she get the flight she wanted, to the Bahamas. There's a local airline operating out of there. Otherwise she'd have had to go to Atlanta or New York, and they only operate one flight to Nassau a day. By the time she got there, she'd have missed it.'

'Yeah, but say, if the cops could track her to Miami surely they could track her to a one-horse town like Nassau.'

'How? They tracked her to Miami because they had a name. They also had a description, but the way she could change her appearance it wasn't too accurate, and there are one hell of a lot of good-looking blondes wandering about. It was the name on the passport that mattered. O'Donovan.'

'But if she flew out, it'd have to be on a ticket register at some airline desk in Miami. Don't you suppose the cops checked that out?'

'Of course they did. I told you that. But like I said, they only had a name and a rough description. She must have had a third passport.'

'In a name we know nothing about. I'm pretty goddamed sure it wasn't Doolittle.'

'*We* don't need a name. We have that photograph. And this is a dish not too many men would forget.'

Luis studied the photo once again. 'Nine years. I still think she could've changed.'

'Not that much. Unless she's had her face pushed in, and both Jaquetta and this driver say she was a looker. Now I don't want your people asking questions around Miami International.

She's still hot, and we don't want to have the cops getting interested in what we're doing. We're going to act on my hunch. You have someone go across to Nassau and show that photo around the shops, hotels, banks ... the Bahamas don't have too many blonde visitors. If she's there, she won't be bothering with no disguises, and someone will remember her.'

'She might have moved on again.'

'OK, so she's moved on. But if she was there, even for a day or two, we'll have a lead we can follow. Nassau is a mainly black community. A dame like this would stick out like a beacon.'

Another study of the photo. 'You know what, Pa? There ain't too much going on around here right this minute, and I've never been to the Bahamas. I'll handle this one myself.'

'You just want to get your hands on those tits. You telling Lisa about this?'

'Lisa,' Luis said, 'Doesn't want to know what we do, or have to do, in the business. She told me so.'

'But I bet she don't want to be a widow, either.'

'This chick? Don't make me laugh.'

'Look, according to this guy Botten, this *chick* kills, with gun, knife or her bare hands. And she's fast, so fast that her victims don't know what's hit them till they're dead.'

'Botten says.'

'Maybe. But it seems to be a fact that a couple of days ago she did for five guys, and they were the best in the business. Like I said, Carlos Dias was a top gun. According to Benjy, his hand was round the butt of his weapon, so he knew what was happening, but he never got it out of the holster. Anyway, you can't go right now. We have the Family AGM coming up next week, and I want you here for that. Now I'm getting on, some of these guys are getting a little uppity. You may have to knock a few heads together.'

'No problem. OK, Pa, I'll have Lorna take a preliminary look. Send a snake to catch a snake, eh?'

'Yeah, that's a good idea. But you tell her to take a back-up and don't take no risks. She has to treat it as a major job and plan it that way. She also wants to bear in mind that we don't have any clout in the Bahamas, and that British law acts kind of quicker than ours. They don't go in for too many appeals. If they get her for murder, she could be standing on the trap with a cloth over her head before our lawyers could spring her.'

'I'll remember that. What's the old saying? Softly, softly catchee monkey? But you know, Pa ... if this dame is as good as all this, maybe instead of doing her we should get her working for us. You can always give Botten back his dough and say we couldn't find her.'

'That,' Don Giovanni said, severely, 'would be to break a contract. Oh, there is just one thing more. If Lorna were to get close enough to do the job, Botten's principals want proof of death.'

'How the hell are we supposed to provide that?'

Don Giovanni pulled his nose. 'They want her head.'

Luis stared at him. 'You have to be kidding me.'

'That's what the man said. Seems it's an old European custom. Kind of went out of fashion a few hundred years ago, but these guys would like to revive it.'

Luis looked at the photograph. 'That head? *Shit!*'

'What's eating you?' his father inquired. 'She'll be dead when they cut it off.'

As was her usual custom, Anna was awake at dawn. And this was a special day: Friday, 20 May.

She stroked Isis, who responded with her usual loud purr, got out of bed, and went down to the pool for her swim. Normally she exercised first – a large room in the house had been fitted as an elaborate gymnasium and short shooting range, a copy of the SS one in which she had trained in Berlin – but today she had too much to do. She swam several lengths, hair piled on top of her head, joined by the dogs who swam beside her, then had a freshwater shower, while Jupiter and Juno shook vigorously. Then she rinsed the dogs clean of salt, returned to her bedroom, and dressed, in pants and loose shirt; she would change into shore-going clothes when she got to Nassau. As she could not possibly have any need for her shoulder bag in Nassau – in any event her pistol and spare magazine were both on board the Chris-Craft – she selected a straw shopping bag in which she placed her jewellery and kid gloves and a straw hat before going down to breakfast with her parents.

'Excited?' Jane asked.

'My bed gets very lonely, from time to time.'

'Do you think, this visit...?'

'We'll have to wait and see.'

'I know we all owe this man our lives,' Johann said, 'And I know he's your favourite man. But you're quite sure he's not just stringing you along?'

Anna refused to take offence. 'He's genuine, Daddy. It's just that with me having to lie low and stay out of the UK, for him to join me permanently, cut himself off from the surroundings he's lived in all of his life, would be an immense step, both physically and psychologically.'

'And he knows that you'll always be here, waiting for him.'

'Yes, he does.' She squeezed her father's hand. 'If I wasn't a patient woman, none of us would be here now.' She finished her coffee.

'What time are you leaving?' Jane asked.

'Nine. The flight is due in about two, so if I get to Nassau by twelve I'll have time for lunch.' She looked at her watch. 'Eight thirty.' She kissed them both. 'See you for dinner.'

As she left the room, her parents exchanged glances. They had seen her in action, more than once, appreciated and admired, even if they could not entirely understand, the ice-cold way in which she went about her business, and indeed, all life, apparently. So they could both tell, from her restlessness, that today she was agitated.

Anna went on to the porch, carrying her hat

and bag, put on her dark glasses, and whistled. Immediately the dogs came bounding round the house, still shaking water. 'No hugs,' she warned. 'You're still wet.' They padded at her heels as she walked down to the dock, where Tommy was polishing the bright-work on the boat. 'Good morning, Tommy. All set?'

'All set, Miss Anna.'

'I'll be with you in a moment.'

A snap of the fingers, and the dogs followed her along the path to the two cottages, and Desiree, having served breakfast at the house, sweeping her front porch. 'You were going to give me a list for Nassau.'

'Yes, ma'am.' Desiree went into the house and returned a moment later with a small sheet of paper. Anna glanced at it and then folded it into her bag. 'I'll give it to Tommy. And as I told you, there'll be a guest for dinner and the next few days.'

'Yes, ma'am. But you said not to make up the spare room, right?'

'That's right, Desiree. I'll see you this evening.'

'You stay here with Desiree,' she told the dogs, and joined Tommy on the dock. It was five to nine, and he already had disconnected the electrics and had the engines running, growling quietly to themselves. Anna went up to the bridge. 'Let's go.'

He cast off the warps, stepped on board, and the boat glided away from the dock. Tommy took in the fenders while Anna made herself comfortable on the steering bench, guided the boat through the reef, and then opened the throttle to her cruising speed of twelve knots, feeling as she did so a glow of the most utter contentment. This, she thought, was what she had wanted all of her life ... and when she came back this afternoon, Clive would be beside her!

They tied up in Nassau just after twelve. Anna went below, changed into the frock she had bought in Miami, replaced her bandanna with her straw hat, leaving her hair loose save for a clip on her neck, put on her Italian dark glasses, pulled on her gloves, picked up her high-heeled shoes and went on deck. 'Here's Desiree's list, Tommy,' she said. 'And I want you to go to the Lumber Company and order four five-gallon drums of chlorine. Have them delivered by half past two. While you're there, get a couple of bottles of algaecide and some tablets for the pool. Tell them to put it on the account. And have some lunch. I'm going to do the same, then I'm going out to Oakes Field to meet the London flight. I'll be back on board by three.'

'You got it, ma'am. I thought I might top up on fuel at the same time.'

'Why not? Just be back here by three.' She walked into Rawson Square and hailed a taxi for the Royal Victoria Hotel.

'Miss Fitzjohn!' Charles the maitre d' was as ever delighted to see her. 'It is so good to have you back so soon. But of course, you are meeting someone.'

Anna took off her glasses. 'How did you know that?'

'Well, the lady was here yesterday, ma'am.'

Anna considered. 'You'll have to fill me in on this, Charles. A lady was here, yesterday, looking for me?'

'Yes, ma'am.'

'And she asked for me, by name?'

Charles looked embarrassed. 'Well ... not exactly, ma'am. As I understand it, she went to reception, and showed them a photograph.'

'A photograph?!' Anna's brain started to buzz. The only photographs of her that existed, so far as she knew, were in the possession of herself, Clive, or Joe Andrews. 'What exactly did she say, do you remember?'

'She said she was supposed to meet you, and did we recognize you. Well, naturally, James said of course, that is Miss Fitzjohn.'

'And she said,' Anna instantly deduced, 'that's her, Miss Fitzjohn. And James said...?'

'Well, ma'am, he said, Miss Fitzjohn comes in here often. I mean, ma'am, you're our favourite guest.'

'You say the sweetest things.' Anna wondered how many hotels the woman had tried before reaching here. Or had she begun with the banks? Her bank certainly knew where she stayed when she was in Nassau, and would have suggested she try here. But they also might have let slip her name. A woman!

'Did we do the wrong thing, ma'am?' Charles was anxious.

'No, no. This woman ... can you tell me what she looked like?'

'Hi, you, James,' Charles commanded. 'Come

over here.'

The clerk emerged from behind the reception desk. 'Tell Miss Fitzjohn about this woman who said she was to meet her here.'

'Yes, sir, Mr Charles.'

'That's what she said, was it?' Anna asked. 'That she was to meet me here.'

'Yes, ma'am.'

'So describe her to me.'

'Well, ma'am, she was a white lady. But ... well ... not like you.'

'You mean she had dark hair.'

'Yes, ma'am. Black hair.'

'Was she tall, or short?'

'Well, ma'am...' James was a little man. 'She was kind of tall. Not so tall as you, mind.'

'Did she have a good figure?'

'It looked good to me, ma'am.' He gave his superior an anxious glance to make sure he wasn't stepping out of line. 'But not so good as yours, mind.'

'You are a true gentleman, James. How was she dressed?'

'Well, she was wearing a blouse, loose like, and a pair of them ... ah...' he looked at Anna's hips. 'What they call ... ah...'

'I think he means stretch pants,' Charles suggested.

'That is the very thing. They fit kind of ... well—'

'Tight.' It was Anna's turn to interpret. 'That was how you were able to tell she had a good figure, right? Did she also have a pretty face?'

'Well...'

Anna realized that his idea of what might be pretty was almost certainly different to hers. 'I mean, did she have any striking features? Her eyes.'

'Well, I ain't knowing that, ma'am. She was wearing them, ah...' He looked at Anna's dark glasses, which were dangling from her fingers.

'Of course. Now this hair, was it long or short?'

'I think it must be long, ma'am.'

'You think?'

'Well, she was wearing one of them kerchief things on her head, but some hair did escape down she neck.'

'Very good. Now James, how did she speak?'

'Ma'am?'

'Her voice. Her accent. Was she a Bahamian?'

'No, ma'am.'

'You mean she was foreign? Or English?'

'I don't think so, ma'am. I think she was an American.'

Anna wasn't immediately sure whether that was better or worse than she had feared. With the pound sterling pegged at just over four dollars the Bahamas was far too expensive for the average American pocket, at least when compared with Florida, thus the possible implications of who this woman was or was working for had suddenly doubled.

'Thank you for your help, James.' She slipped a ten-pound note into his hand and he gave a brief bow and hurried off.

'You don't know this woman,' Charles suggested, more anxious than ever.

'No, Charles, I'm afraid I do not know this woman.'

'Then we *have* done the wrong thing.' Now he was obviously worried.

'Of course you have not done the wrong thing. James was asked a perfectly innocent question, which he answered. There can be nothing wrong with that. Now, can you squeeze me in for lunch?'

He exuded relief; clearly he had supposed he was about to lose her as a customer. 'Of course, ma'am. You will always be accommodated here.'

'Thank you, Charles.' She considered, but her stomach was no longer in the mood for her favourite fillet steak. 'I will just have a conch salad.'

'Of course, ma'am. And a bottle of ... ah ... Montrachet?'

'Not today, thank you, Charles. Just a glass of house white, medium dry. I'm meeting a plane at two o'clock.'

'Of course, ma'am.'

He waved away the waiters and served her himself, clearly thinking while doing so. 'If you do not know this woman, ma'am,' he ventured. 'Then obviously you were not intending to meet her here.'

'Obviously.'

'What would you like me to do when she comes back?'

If she comes back, Anna thought. Here. If she had begun her search equipped with only a photograph and a possibility that her target might be living in the Bahamas, she now had a name and a certainty. With those, she would be able to discover that there was a woman named Anna Fitzjohn who owned an island named Fair Cay, and also exactly where the cay was to be found. She would be doing that now.

Suddenly she had an urgent desire to be back on the cay as rapidly as possible. But she didn't suppose that an extra couple of hours would make a lot of difference; it was already half past twelve.

'If she comes back,' she said. 'I think you will be entitled to ask for her name, and an address where she can be contacted. Tell her that I was indeed expecting her, and would so like to see her.' Those were her two stocks in trade, at once confusing the enemy and suggesting a picture of total naivety.

Now Charles was also confused. 'I will do that, Miss Fitzjohn. Enjoy your meal.'

He had to be joking. It was a long time since she had been so agitated. If she was quite prepared to accept the risks of her profession, when engaged in that profession, and even perhaps enjoyed them, she had, over the past few years, increasingly looked forward to, and appreciated, those periods of quiescence, and more important, absolute safety, which she had been promised and had so desperately sought. Even the year she had been required to spend in the bleakness of the Scottish Highlands at the end of the war had been, in retrospect, a momentary paradise.

Of course a great deal had been wrong. She

had been separated from her parents, except for rare visits, and separated from Clive, also except for rare visits. Her only continuous company had been Mrs Bridie, her housekeeper-cum-minder-cum-, as the poor woman had supposed, body-guard. Yet for all her discontent, compounded by the uncertainty as to her future, as with the shooting stopped the British Government had clearly not been able to make up their minds what to do with an agent for whom shooting had become a way of life, she had been *safe*. The Government had guaranteed that.

Until the day that first Joe Andrews and then four MGB agents had come knocking on her door ... and the shooting had started all over again. She had made sure Joe had survived, for all their considerable past differences: he had once been commanded to have her eliminated when his American bosses had felt she was too hot to handle any longer. But he had also once saved her life, and he had promised to take care of her future ... if she would put her trust in the CIA.

That promise had come with a price tag, but as MI6 had proved quite incapable of protecting her, she had not felt that she had a choice. And her three years working for the Americans had not only enabled her to regain the fortune she had been forced to abandon in Germany, but had brought her to this paradise, with the family for whom she had fought throughout the war and the pets she had always wanted, and a lifestyle of which she had always dreamed ... and absolute security. Until today.

She chewed, slowly and thoughtfully, taking an occasional sip of wine. What had she done wrong in escaping from Mexico City? She went over it again, step by step, and could not fault it. She had always known that after that telephone call the police would be able to trace her as far as Miami International. But with no guaranteed name to go on, and no name at all after she had left the hotel, and with only several conflicting descriptions – she was well aware of the difference she could make to her age and appearance by wearing her hair up or down, by switching her various distinctive sunglasses, and most of all, of being to most men a charismatic dream-like memory rather than a distinctive human being – she had not seen how they could proceed. Without something indisputable to present to potential witnesses. Such as a photograph!

Where, in the name of God or the Devil, had this woman got hold of a photograph? And why? From what Charles and James had told her, she did not sound like a Mexican plainclothes policewoman. But whoever she was, wherever she had come from, she was a threat to paradise. Anna finished her meal, got up and went to the desk, summoning Charles to join her. 'Lovely meal, Charles.' She wrote a cheque to cover it and the tip.

'We will see you again, Miss Fitzjohn?' He was still anxious.

'Of course you will. When I am hoping you may have some information for me. But until then, will you send another wire for me?'

'But of course, madam.' He pulled the block

towards him. 'To the gentleman in Virginia?'

'What a good memory you have. Yes. Just three words: help, urgent. Anna.'

Charles wrote, and raised his head. 'It's not on account of that woman, is it?'

Anna slipped two ten pound notes across the counter. 'That woman, Charles, is a secret between you and me. And James, to be sure. Let's keep it that way. See you soon.' She put on her glasses.

THE PROPOSITION

Anna took a taxi to the airport, arriving just before two. 'Presuming the flight is on time,' she told the driver, 'I'd like you to wait.'

'Yes, ma'am, I going do that, sure,' he agreed.

She went upstairs to the bar, which had a balcony overlooking the runway. As always when a London flight was due in, the bar was crowded, and as always when Anna entered a room, taking off her hat and glasses as she did so, her hair floating past her shoulders, all conversation stopped and heads turned. 'I'll have a Planters' Punch,' she told the eager barman, and as there was no unoccupied table remained at the counter, sipping through her straw.

'I'm sure we've met before,' a man suggested, standing beside her.

Anna regarded him. 'There's an oldie.'

He had sleek black hair, wore a small moustache, and clearly fancied himself. Thus he decided to ignore her snub. 'I would take it as an honour if you would let me buy you another drink.'

'I'm sure you would,' Anna agreed. 'Consider that it was an honour. Unfortunately, I would not, and I do not wish another drink.'

She left him looking dumbfounded and went on to the balcony, replacing her glasses; the huge Britannia was just landing. A few minutes later the passengers were filing down the steps. Heart beating pleasantly quickly, she studied them. Clive, taller than most, was easily discernible, but then she frowned at the man immediately in front of him. What in the name of God was Baxter doing here?

She made her way through the throng and down the stairs to wait outside the door to the Customs area. They were out fairly quickly; both had only a single suitcase, although Baxter also carried an attaché case.

'Anna!' Clive took her in his arms for a hug and a kiss. 'Life begins again.'

'You say the sweetest things.' Anna released him. 'Why Mr Baxter, *what* a pleasant surprise. Don't tell me you've come to see *me*?'

'Ah...' Billy looked at Clive, somewhat anxiously.

Both men had known Anna long enough to remember that her phrase, 'You say the sweetest things,' was double-edged and quite often used when she was about to dispose of the speaker. 'Well, he needs a holiday,' Clive explained.

'And when I told him what a lovely place you have here...' He also paused, anxiously: she was not looking the least mollified.

'Well, that is absolutely charming of you,' Anna said. 'And of course you are welcome. But where is Mrs Baxter? Doesn't she need a holiday too?'

'Mildred doesn't like flying,' Billy explained.

'Do you know, I didn't either, once. But I hope you like boating.'

'Ah...'

She studied him. In contrast to Clive's lightweight suit and open collar, he was wearing a business suit and tie, the material far too heavy for the sub-tropical heat, and a bowler hat. At least he had discarded his usual ever-present sweater, and was not actually carrying an umbrella. 'I'm afraid that if you don't, you will have to swim, and it's forty miles, with lots of unfriendly fish. I have a taxi waiting.' She led them to the car. 'I assume they fed you on the plane?'

'Several times,' Clive said. 'It was a nine-hour flight.'

'And of course it's now seven o'clock, stomach time, for you. I'm afraid it's a three-hour trip to the cay.'

'Three hours?' Baxter muttered.

'But you're welcome to sleep all the way.'

'Sleep on what?'

'My dear Billy,' Clive said, 'you will be travelling on a luxury cabin cruiser.'

'You mean this boat has a cabin?'

'A few,' Anna acknowledged. 'I think you

should sit in front, Mr Baxter.'

He obeyed. She got into the back and Clive sat beside her.

'Rawson Square Dock,' Anna said.

'No problem, ma'am.'

The car moved off, and Clive squeezed Anna's glove. She turned her head. 'I'm terribly sorry,' he mouthed, 'what was I to do?'

She looked at him for several seconds, then squeezed his hand back.

Ten minutes later they were at the Square.

'My God, but it's hot,' Baxter remarked as he got out of the car.

'What did you expect in the middle of the afternoon?' Anna asked. 'I would take off your jacket, if I were you.' She paid the driver, and led the two men down to the dock, Clive carrying both suitcases, although Baxter, his jacket folded over his arm, but retaining his tie, carried the attaché case. Now he peered at *Fair Girl*. 'Good heavens! Is this yours?'

'Every inch. You remember Tommy, Clive.'

'I do indeed.' Clive shook hands with the big black man, waiting at the foot of the steps.

'And this is Mr Baxter.'

'Welcome, Mr Baxter.'

Billy hesitated and then shook hands. 'And you are Miss Fitzjohn's boatman?'

Tommy looked at Anna.

'Tommy,' she said, 'is my right-hand man. And my friend. Now, gentlemen, will you please take off your shoes.' She stood on one leg to remove her own high heels. 'Would you put these cases in the saloon, Tommy?'

'You got it, ma'am.' Tommy stepped on board, a case in each hand.

'You want me to take off my shoes, here?' Billy asked. There were the usual spectators to watch Anna departing.

Anna regarded his black city shoes with disfavour. 'My decks don't take kindly to clodhoppers. I'll bet those heels are steel rimmed.'

'Well, of course.'

'So, please.'

Billy looked at Clive, but he had already removed his shoes.

'But what am I to wear?'

'You can take off your socks as well, if you wish. Don't you have any soft shoes?'

'I don't use them.'

'Well, I'm sure we'll be able to find you a pair of flip-flops on the cay. Now, we really should get on.'

Billy sighed, and stooped to unlace his shoes.

'You'd better give me that case.'

'That case does not leave my side.'

'Good lord! You mean you've brought the Crown Jewels with you? I can hardly wait to see them. You'd better help him on board, Clive. If he goes into the drink he'll lose the lot. You can use the fore cabin for anything you wish, Mr Baxter.'

'Fore cabin,' he muttered, still busy unlacing.

'It's the one at the narrow end. It has two bunks and its own heads.'

'Heads?'

'Toilet,' Clive explained.

Anna left them to it, carried her shoes on board, regarded with satisfaction the four large drums of chlorine, the smell tingling her nostrils, and went down to the aft cabin to change her clothes, put on her deck shoes and tie her hair in a bandanna. She heard a sound and turned; Clive was standing in the doorway. 'As I said, I am most terribly sorry.'

'Perhaps you'd like to tell me what he's doing here?'

'I wish I knew. He suddenly announced that he was coming. I believe he wants to have a serious discussion with you.'

'And he's still your boss.' Anna stood against him, put her arms round his neck for a long, slow kiss.

Clive continued to hold her close. 'I think it's something to do with Mexico City.'

Anna pulled her head back. 'What has Mexico City got to do with him? Or with me?'

'My dearest girl, anyone reading even the sketchy report that we received, and has ever had the slightest acquaintance with you, would know that you were involved. Five men, five shots to the head, no trace of anyone's presence, apart from the corpses? You may as well have written, Anna Fehrbach was here, in blood on the wall.'

Anna gazed at him for several seconds, then released him. 'You think I should change my technique and start shooting them in the body? That is seldom immediately fatal, and far more painful for the target.'

'I know, you're all heart.'

'I try to be as efficient as possible.'

'And this business ... well, the report describes you as a prostitute.'

'Anyone who knows my methods, darling, should also know that I do whatever I have to do, to get the job done. Don't tell me you're jealous?'

'Well Roberto Capillano?'

'Relax. He never touched me. He never had the time. Clive, what happened in Mexico City was a job of work, and has nothing to do with Britain, or the British Government.'

'It could have, if it were traced back to you.'

'That's not possible.' But it could be happening, she thought.

Clive had worked with her for ten years, and caught the quick flicker of expression. 'I think you have something to tell me.'

'Perhaps later. Let's move.'

She went up to the bridge, started the engines. That brought Billy out of the cabin. He had taken off his socks but still wore his tie, and absurdly, had rolled his pants up to his knees as if about to go wading on Blackpool beach, especially as he was still wearing his hat. But that was probably a good idea, if it stayed on; at three o'clock the sun was at its hottest.

He stood on the after deck to watch Tommy taking in the fenders as the boat glided away from the dock. 'Who's driving this thing?'

'The boss always helms,' Tommy explained.

'The boss?' Billy looked up to the flying bridge, where Anna was seated on the bench, Clive beside her.

'You're welcome to come up, Mr Baxter,' Anna called. 'It's quite safe,' she assured him. 'Although it would be a good idea to hold on, certainly when using the ladder.'

He came up slowly, collapsed on to the bench beside Clive, taking deep breaths, while Anna threaded her way through the moorings. 'You really know how to handle this thing?'

'Billy,' Clive said, 'You are liable to wind up swimming, whether you feel like it or not.'

'Just asking. What about all those dials and switches? Do you understand them all?'

'If I didn't, we could be in trouble.'

He gazed left and right as they emerged into the harbour, and Anna as usual turned east. 'I must say,' he remarked. 'This is a lovely spot. So peaceful, unhurried.'

'It's had its moments,' Anna reminded him. 'Every generation or so, something happens to bring it to life. Then it slips back again.'

'It could happen again, quite soon,' Clive suggested.

'How do you figure that? Or are the Americans bringing back Prohibition?'

'I don't think they're that stupid. But have you never wondered why a place this beautiful and only a few miles from the mainland isn't an American playground, like Miami?'

'Simply because the dollar doesn't go as far here as it does on the mainland.'

'Spot on. But what do you think would happen if the pound were to collapse?'

'Is that likely?'

'British finances are in such a state it well

could.'

'I would have thought,' Baxter remarked. 'That with your millions, international finance would be important to you.'

'My millions,' Anna replied, 'are in the hands of my accountants. I let them worry about international finance.'

'You must have enormous faith in them.'

'I do.'

'Perhaps you could tell me their name?'

'Will you tell me the name of yours?'

'My dear girl, on my salary, I do my own accounts.'

'Then it won't do you any good to know the name of mine.' They were now through the narrows and out into the open sea. Anna pushed the throttles forward to increase speed, checked her course, and made sure there were no other boats in the vicinity. Then she engaged the autopilot. 'I'll be back in a few minutes.'

'Eh?'

'I just need to call the cay and tell them we've an extra guest.'

'You have a radio on the cay?' Billy asked.

'Of course I do. Two, HF and VHF. The HF has a range of four thousand miles, so you see, Mr Baxter, next time you feel the need of a chat, you can call me up instead of coming all this way. I'll give you the wavelength.'

'But who's going to steer the boat?'

'His name is George.' She swung her legs over the seat and slid down the ladder.

'Some woman,' Billy remarked. 'Is she always as spiky as this?'

'She can be, when she's upset. Didn't you notice that when you saw her that time in Stockholm? You told me that she opened the door of her hotel room for you with a gun in her hand?'

'Well, yes. But circumstances were different. She thought I might be a villain.'

'Ah,' Clive commented.

They docked just after six, with the sun hovering above the western horizon, and the light beginning to fade into the brief tropical twilight.

Baxter emerged from the fore cabin, having resumed his socks and carrying his shoes in his hand, as well, of course, as his attaché case. 'That was most enjoyable, Anna. I do congratulate you on your handling of the boat.'

'Why, thank you, Mr Baxter.' Anna had also been below to pick up her hat and gloves and handbag, and also carried her shoes in her hand. 'Now, please don't leave the boat until I tell you it's safe to do so.'

'Eh?'

Anna pointed at the two huge white shapes galloping down the path to the dock.

'My God! What are those?'

'My Dogos.'

'Eh?'

'Argentinian hunting dogs.' Clive had joined them. 'Just about the fiercest canines in existence.'

'Don't panic.' Anna stepped ashore. 'They only eat people when I tell them to. But they're still only two years old and are inclined to be frisky.'

The dogs surrounded her, licking her hands, having their heads rubbed. 'Now listen very carefully,' she said. 'These gentlemen are my friends. Actually, I should think they remember you, Clive. They have long memories. You come first.'

'Good luck,' Billy muttered, as Clive stepped ashore, and stood beside Anna.

'Hello, old fellows,' he said.

The dogs gurgled.

'Stroke their heads,' Anna commanded. 'See, they do remember you.'

Jupiter was licking his hand.

'Now, Mr Baxter.'

Visibly holding his breath, Billy stepped ashore, carrying his briefcase and his shoes in front of him like shields.

'Friend,' Anna said again. 'This is Jupiter, and this is Juno. Stroke their heads.'

Tentatively, Billy put down his shoes and extended his hand, and was rewarded with a low growl.

'No, no,' Anna said. 'They can smell fear, and hostility. Be positive. They're your friends, remember?'

Billy took a deep breath and gave Jupiter a vigorous stroke. This time his reward was to have his hand licked.

'There,' Anna said. 'That wasn't so bad, was it? Now, you'd better put your shoes on for the walk up to the house.'

Clive was already doing so.

'You want these drums taken up now, Miss Anna?' Tommy asked, having connected the shore supply.

'They can wait until tomorrow morning. But you'd better take the groceries up. Pass the cases over, first.'

Clive and Billy took delivery of their suitcases.

'What are in those drums, anyway?' Billy asked. 'It's a very strong smell.'

'Chlorine,' Anna told him. 'For purifying our water supply. It is strong stuff, yes; a drop on your clothing will go right through it.'

'And you put it in your fresh water?'

'It's essential. Don't worry, only the faintest taste gets through the filters, and that's preferable to bugs.'

They followed her up the path towards the lights, Billy looking left and right into the gathering gloom. 'Strange,' he commented. 'The wind feels quite light, yet it sounds almost like a gale.'

'That's the casuarina trees. The slightest breeze sets them rustling. Mind Isis.'

'Eh?' He stared at the large black lump that was sitting in the centre of the path. 'My God! What's that?'

'My cat. Isis. She was the most powerful of all the Egyptian goddesses, called the Great Enchantress. Even Anubis, the god of the dead, was subject to her decisions. I think that's rather appropriate, don't you?'

As Billy was not up on Egyptian mythology, that failed to register. But he said, 'I'm allergic to cats.'

Anna had already picked Isis up for a cuddle; the sound of purring rose above even that of the casuarinas. 'Then I suggest you keep your bedroom door closed at all times. She does like to nestle in beds, whether they are occupied or not.' She carried Isis up the steps and placed her on the veranda floor, embraced her mother and father.

'You remember Clive.'

'Of course. Welcome back, Clive.' Johann shook hands and Jane presented her cheek for a kiss.

'And this is Mr Baxter. You should remember him as well.'

'Certainly,' Jane said. 'We met when we first got to England.' She extended her hand. 'Welcome to Fair Cay, Mr Baxter.'

He clasped her fingers. 'My pleasure, Mrs Fehrbach. Mr Fehrbach. Some set-up you have here.'

'It's Anna's,' Johann said proudly. 'The place and the set-up.'

'I'll show you up to your rooms,' Anna said. 'Papa...?'

He nodded. 'I'll open the champagne.'

'He's in a bit of a whirl,' Clive explained, somewhat hesitantly carrying his suitcase into Anna's bedroom, as indicated.

'So he should be.' She had managed a quick word with her mother, and been reassured that, at least so far as Jane had noticed, there had been no visitors and no suspicious craft in the vicinity of the cay, either.

He placed the suitcase on the floor, and she was in his arms. 'It seems to get longer every time.'

He kissed her forehead, her ears, her eyes, her nose and her chin, before settling on her mouth for some moments, while his hands roamed over her back, from her shoulders down to her buttocks. She was doing some roaming of her own, content to remain where she was until he said, 'As I get some more grey hairs every time I think of you...'

She released him, went to the dressing table to take off her bandanna and run a comb through her hair. 'You know the deal.'

'Does it last forever?'

'I hope not. I'm working on it. But you know, it's not a matter of snapping my fingers. Even if I could drop the CIA, with all the financial restrictions that are in place, transferring funds is not the easiest thing in the world. So all my money is in their hands as well, because they can do things with it that I can't, without risking prosecution.'

He considered. 'Does this sterling crisis bother you?'

'Not really. I don't think I have much invested in the sterling area. But I suppose that in itself is an irregularity.'

'You don't *think*? Don't you have any control over your capital at all?'

'Of course I do. My accountant is coming down in a couple of weeks for our twice-yearly get together. If there is anything I want or require over the norm he sees that I get it.' She gave one of her wicked smiles. 'He also pays me what I'm owed by the US Government. Right this minute they owe me quite a lot.'

'You mean, for this Mexican job.'

'Well...'

He held her hands. 'Anna, you do realize that one day you are going to make a mistake. And in your business...'

'One mistake will be the end. It's up to me to put off making it until the very last minute.' Another smile. 'Because that will *be*, the very last minute. For me.'

He sighed. 'You are incorrigible. Do you honestly not care whether you live or die? Do you honestly not fear death?'

'I care, Clive. I care that I should be the most efficient in the world at my job. As long as I am that, I'm safe. As for fearing death, when I start doing that, I'm done.'

'And this problem you have. I know you have something on your mind. That doesn't worry you?'

'Yes, it worries me. But not for myself. For my parents, my people here, my pets. My island. They are all I have in the world. All I want in the world.' She kissed him. 'Apart from you, of course. Anyway, the problem will be taken care of. I hope.'

'By the CIA?'

'They're calling the shots, right now.' She went to the door. 'There's Veuve Clicquot waiting downstairs, and I can guarantee you a superb dinner.'

After the meal, she spent ten minutes in the radio room, having locked the door so that she could not be interrupted. But nothing came through, and she had to accept that she was being over-anxious; she had sent her telegram after one that afternoon. Even nine hours was hardly time for Joe to have considered the matter and come to a conclusion as to what to do about it, especially as she had been unable to specify in the wire just what she needed help with; the problem with the radio link was that it had not been considered necessary for her to have a call sign of her own, only for her American masters to be able to call her to set up a meeting, and a contract, where and when she was required.

But this situation had not arisen before. She had not been lying to Clive when she had told him that she was not personally afraid of any adversary; she had no doubt she could handle any situation that might arise. But the thought of there being any danger to her loved ones was distressing. And even if she could avoid that, if there was any trouble on the cay, especially if it involved shooting, it would certainly get back to Nassau and have the police investigating; the thought that this idyllic lifestyle she had set up for herself, and her mother and father, could be ended, or even interfered with, was even more distressing.

She sighed, and closed down the set. There was no point in brooding when she could do nothing to alleviate the situation. So, forget about it until tomorrow. In the meantime ... Clive was sitting on the bed, naked, stroking Isis. 'You don't look a happy bunny,' he remarked.

'I'm happy here with you,' she reminded him, and went into the bathroom to remove her make-up and clean her teeth. 'Nothing else matters.' She undressed. 'Would you mind using the other side of the bed, Isis? Just for the next couple of hours.'

The cat obediently made a nest for herself on the other pillow. Anna pushed Clive on to his back and sat astride his thighs. 'I need an awful lot of loving tonight.' She felt him rising between her legs, and leaned forward to kiss him, hair drooping to either side of her face.

When she awoke, as always at first light, he was still fast asleep, which did not surprise her as they had climaxed together three times; she had actually had five orgasms but she reckoned the night had taken more out of him.

And during the night, they had also celebrated her birthday. That meant it was just over eleven years since she had first been commanded to take a life. Had there ever been a young girl named Annaliese Fehrbach before then? Or had the Countess von Widerstand sprung, fully formed and ferociously fatal to her enemies, from the pit of Hell?

She decided to let Clive sleep, along with Isis, who had also necessarily had a disturbed night, about which she had complained bitterly, and without bothering to dress, went down to the gym and worked out vigorously for half an hour. The whole house was still asleep, so she decided to leave her usual shooting practice until later; she was, in any event, running short of cartridges, which were supplied for her, in bulk, by her CIA contact in Miami, as and when necessary. She thought the moment they could unload Baxter and solve the strange lady problem, it would be fun to take Clive across for a night on the town and pick up what she needed.

Feeling absolutely rejuvenated and full of energy, she went down to the pool, being joined by the dogs, who slept on the veranda, and the three of them swam up and down a few times. She was at the far end when a familiar voice said, 'Am I interrupting?'

She turned on to her back. Billy was, as always, dressed as if for a London office, even wearing a tie, although not his jacket. 'Why, Mr Baxter,' she said. 'Of course you're not interrupting. Did you sleep well?'

'Like a log.'

'Then come on in.'

'Ah...' As she was on her back, moving her arms and legs to keep afloat, it was slowly dawning on him that she was naked. 'I really don't think ... I mean, I do beg your pardon. I had no idea ... I'll come back later, shall I?'

She turned over and stroked her way towards him. 'Don't tell me you've come to the Bahamas without a swim suit? But it doesn't really matter. I never wear one.'

'The thing is,' he said, 'I really would like to have a word with you, in private. Perhaps when you're ah...'

'There's no time like the present.' Having got him firmly on the defensive, she intended to keep him there, and having reached the steps, walked up them, water streaming from her hair, dripping from her nipples and pubes, rolling down her legs. 'Mind yourself.'

'Eh?' Already retreating as if expecting an imminent assault, he was overtaken by a cascade of water as the two dogs, having followed her, emerged from the pool and shook themselves.

'There you go,' Anna said. 'It is far better to be naked around here.'

'I must change,' he spluttered.

'You'll dry,' Anna pointed out. 'And if you wish to speak with me in private, now is your best time.'

'Haven't you got a towel?'

'I'll dry as well, given time.'

He gulped; the sun was already high enough to be warming the air, but it remained sufficiently cool to keep her nipples proud. Cautiously he lowered himself into a chair on the other side of the table. This was wet, but then, so were his pants.

Anna stood beneath the fresh water shower and rinsed her hair, then snapped her fingers to be joined by the dogs, who were thoroughly washed with shampoo. 'Must get the salt off,' she explained, 'or they get sores.'

Billy watched her in fascination; he was not interested in the dogs. Satisfied, Anna let them go, then sat opposite him, crossing her legs and squeezing water from her hair. The dogs were now rolling in the grass. 'I understand that today is your birthday.'

'How sweet of you to remember.'

'So ... many happy returns.'

'Thank you.'

'Twenty-nine, is it?'

'You mean you're still keeping a file on me?'

'It goes with the job. This is quite a place you have here,' he remarked.

'It is my dream come true. And I know that you, MI6, played a part in getting me here. I'm grateful, believe me.'

'Well, we are very happy to see you settled. To know that you have turned your back on the dreadful business of killing to order.'

'Billy ... you don't mind if I call you Billy, do you? I mean, since you retired me, you are no longer my boss or employer, and I feel, as you're here on my island, we should drop both formality and, if you'll pardon the expression, bullshit.' She gazed at him from enormous eyes.

He flushed, and endeavoured to regain his ground, trying to keep his eyes on her face. 'I have always had the highest regard for you, Anna, and have always had your best interests at heart.'

'Is that why you sent me on at least one suicide mission?'

Again he flushed. 'I ... well ... believe me, those weren't my decisions. I was obeying orders. Under protest.'

'Do you know, I do believe you. But then, I always was a soft touch for a sob story.'

'I'd like to think that we could be friends.'

'You mean after, and despite, what you are trying to work yourself up to say. Tell you what: why not say it, and then we can talk about being friends.'

'You are a singularly direct young woman.'
'It helps.'
He drew a deep breath. 'This Mexican business...'
'Has absolutely nothing to do with you, or MI6.'
'It could have, if you were ever to be arrested, or even connected, with the crime.'
'I beg your pardon.'
'All right, all right. I beg *your* pardon. An execution, was it? All five men were equally guilty.'
'As a matter of fact, they were. But had they lived, they could have prevented my escape.'
'The ultimate crime.'
'Billy, you're not doing too well in the friendship stakes. But just to put your mind at rest, there is absolutely no risk of the Mexican police tracing me to here.' I hope and pray, she thought.
'You're probably right. But, suppose, that as the only thing they have on you is an Irish passport, they ask for help from both the Garda and Scotland Yard—'
'Neither of whom are aware of my existence, so far as I know. And as my Irish passport is forged, they can't carry that any further either. I simply do not exist.'
'Again, you are probably right. But once an inquiry is made, they're obliged to do all they can, look wherever they can for an answer. This was a highly professional and quite ruthless, ah, execution.'
'Why, Billy, you say the sweetest things.'
'So, they might well feel we could have some

idea of whom this international assassin might be.'

'Do I detect a touch of the iron fist inside the velvet glove? Don't you protect your operatives, active or retired, no matter what?'

'I certainly would like to do so. But I am, as I am sure you know, only a cog in a vast machine. We are loyal to our employees as long as they are loyal to us. But I am sure you would agree that if one of our people suddenly turned into a homicidal maniac, well, we would be duty bound to do something about it. Even if it meant ending this paradise you have here.'

'I think *you* need to bear in mind that you are at this moment resident on the homicidal maniac's island, where her word is law.'

'The office knows where I am.'

'Of course. But there isn't a lot they could do if you were, for instance, to fall overboard from my boat while out fishing, and drowned.'

'I'm a strong swimmer.'

'Ah, but you see, you'd hit your head in going over, and before we could get you back on board ... these things do happen, quite regularly. Especially with people who know nothing about boats and the sea.'

He gazed at her. 'You're serious, aren't you?'

'I'm only as serious as you are, Billy. But we both have our duties in life. Yours is to King and Country. Mine is to me and mine. Threaten mine and you threaten me. You should remember that the Third Reich made that mistake.'

'You, young lady, are suffering an extreme case of hubris.'

'I know,' she agreed. 'It keeps me alive.'

He licked his lips, leaned forward. 'Anna, we're on your side, believe me.'

'Convince me.'

'Anna, you may have no doubt of your ability to protect yourself, and your family, but you're in an extremely vulnerable position. We know you are working with the Yanks. That is your decision, and I have no doubt that they will protect you as far as they can. But they can't protect you on British soil, without risking an international incident. Only we can do that.'

'Only you're not prepared to.'

'Yes, we are. If you'll play ball with us.'

'Sorry, Billy, I'm not prepared to stop working for the CIA. I can't.'

'We accept that. But I say again, on British soil, only we can protect you, when you are found out, as you must be eventually.'

'Even if you have to contribute to the finding. So tell me the price tag. I am sure there is one.'

'We would like you to come out of retirement, just once, to do a last job for us.'

Anna burst out laughing. 'You have got to be the most utter hypocrite who has ever walked the earth.'

'That also goes with the job.'

'And you felt it necessary to go through all of that blackmailing-type preamble about my dangers and your ability to help me, but only if I helped you?'

'I was feeling my way. Do you accept?'

'You will have to tell me what this job is.'

'Before I do, I wish you to listen to me, very

carefully. This will be the most secret mission you have ever undertaken, and we are turning to you because after due consideration we feel that you are the one, perhaps the only one, who can bring it off.'

'It's so pleasant to be loved.'

'This job has been sanctioned at the very highest level, as its successful completion is regarded as essential not only for the safety of the nation, but for the safety of the world.'

'Spare me the heroic rhetoric.'

'There is, however,' Baxter went on, 'a caveat.'

'Isn't there always?'

'The British Government, MI6, cannot possibly be involved. We will provide you with all the information at our disposal, and with as much back-up as we can, but if you were to be apprehended, either before or after the completion of your assignment, and chose, or were forced, to admit your guilt, we would utterly dissociate ourselves from you; your confession would be the ravings of a madwoman.'

'Doesn't that also go with the job?'

'The same would apply if you accepted the assignment and then chose not to carry it through, but rather to treat it as, perhaps, a story to peddle. Then we would not only disown you, but make life very difficult for you, and yours, no matter where you fled to.'

'It's nearly breakfast time. Do you think you could get on?'

'However,' he continued, now unflappable, 'should you be unable to return from the assignment, we will guarantee the safety and prosperity of your family, your pets and your island for the rest of their lives. And should you succeed in carrying out the assignment, and getting back home, we will also protect you from arrest by any foreign government, providing you with guaranteed alibis for all the time you were away.'

'Tell me about this foreign government.'

'Have you ever heard of a man called Jan Edel?'

'No.'

'He's an atomic scientist. One of the best.'

'And he's been selling his stuff to Moscow? So why do you want him dead? You've locked Fuchs up, not hanged him.'

'Edel has left England.'

'And you think he's in Moscow? Sorry, Billy, I'm going to have to pass. If I'm going to Moscow, I might as well blow my brains out, here and now.'

'He isn't in Moscow. He's in Argentina.'

Anna frowned in genuine confusion. 'What's important about that? Don't tell me they're thinking of building a bomb? Can they? Don't they need enriched uranium?'

'We don't know whether they are capable of building a bomb or not, although there are reports of uranium being found down in the south.'

'That still sounds like an hysterical overreaction to me,' Anna remarked. 'Haven't they got to build all sorts of factories and laboratories, create test sites, et cetera? Not to mention a delivery system. It would take them years to get something like that off the ground. That is, supposing they wanted to, or could afford it.'

'That's another imponderable,' Billy said. 'We do know that this chap Peron is inclined to fascism, and we're pretty sure his government is sheltering quite a few Nazis. Amongst them, Adolf Eichmann. Did you ever meet him?'

'Yes. I thought he was a nasty piece of work. And that was before I knew that he was responsible for the implementation of the Final Solution.'

'A plan, if I remember rightly, that you got hold of when it was first mooted, in 1941. And no one would believe you.'

'And if *I* remember rightly, one of those who wouldn't believe me was you.'

'I know. It was simply too horrendous a concept for a reasonably civilized brain to take in.'

'But you're not sending me after Eichmann.'

'Hunting fugitive war criminals is not in our remit.' He grinned. 'You don't want to forget that in certain circles you are one of them. I just used Eichmann as an example to prove that the current Argentinian government is not averse to fascist ideas. Edel is the man we want. He's not averse to fascist ideas himself. In fact, to get him on our side before the Nazis nabbed him for themselves, we had to kidnap him from Copenhagen; he thought Hitler was one of the best.'

'And that's a reason for wanting him dead? This sounds to me like a pre-emptive strike, Billy. Not my scene. You probably won't believe this, but I have to live with myself. Show me a crime against humanity.'

'You went to Moscow in 1940, to carry out a pre-emptive strike. On Stalin.'

'There happened to be a war on, and in my circumstances, as I'm sure you can remember, I didn't have any choice. Now I do. You'll have to give me a better reason than this character's politics.'

'How about hate, for all mankind?'

Anna blew a raspberry. 'And he wound up working on the Manhattan Project? You people need your heads examined.'

'Look, as far as we were concerned, time was running out. We had to get the bomb before anyone else did. However reluctantly, Edel played a vital part in that; he is the supreme pragmatist. But as his views became more extreme, he was sidelined. He was then caught trying to sell our atomic secrets to the Nazis. Fortunately, they entirely misunderstood its importance. As the war was still on, Edel was convicted of treason and sentenced to death.'

'But you are saying he's still alive.'

'There were a lot of appeals, and the war ended before he could be hanged. So the sentence was commuted to life imprisonment.'

'Again, you people need your heads examined.'

'I know, we have this terrible weakness for letting bygones be bygones.'

'And now he's escaped, is that it?'

'Yes.'

'So what's upsetting you? The only people he could possibly sell the bomb to are the Russians, and they already have it.'

'What the judiciary forgot, or perhaps never knew, was that Edel had access to some very specialized info, which at that time was not considered practical, but which is now very much on the cards.'

'What info?' At last Anna was genuinely interested.

'How much do you know about the atomic process?'

'Not a lot. If, by bombarding it with neutrons or whatever, you manage to split an atom of uranium – the right sort of uranium – you can release an unbelievable amount of energy.'

'Simplistic, but accurate enough. And then you have the ultimate explosive, right? A nuclear device.'

'Right.'

'Only you don't. I mean, have the ultimate explosive.'

'Say again?'

'It is possible to use a controlled nuclear explosion to split an atom of *hydrogen*. In that case, you have a *thermo*nuclear explosion, which is about a thousand times the magnitude of an atomic bomb.'

Anna stared at him. 'I hope you're joking.'

'The bomb dropped on Hiroshima,' Baxter said, 'as I am sure you know, completely obliterated roughly a square mile in the centre of the city. It has been calculated that one of the upgraded bombs, a hydrogen bomb, would be able completely to obliterate virtually *all* of London.'

'I'm afraid that is a bit much to assimilate

before breakfast. And you say this is practical, and not just somebody's nightmare?'

'President Truman has given the go-ahead for work to commence on manufacturing a hydrogen bomb. That will restore America's lead in weapons of mass destruction. The Russians will get it eventually, of course, but the general feeling is that, barring some quite unforeseen catastrophe in international relations, neither side would ever use it, as a war fought with thermonuclear weapons would certainly extinguish civilization. The nightmare is that a rogue state, or a state controlled by a rogue dictator, might come into possession of such a weapon. There are quite a few countries in the world that are theoretically capable of developing atomic power.'

'And Edel—'

'Is one of the very few men in the world who know both the formula and the method required.'

'And you say he's a fascist? I can see why he hates your guts.'

'I'm afraid he hates everybody's guts, here in the West.'

'As do a lot of people,' Anna mused.

'Yes. And you should know better than anyone that if Hitler had managed to obtain the bomb before we did he'd have used it.'

'And you didn't execute this Edel when you had the chance. Isn't a government's prime duty to protect the lives and property of its citizens, no matter what it takes? You people are really not fit to govern anything.'

'You could have a point. Will you correct that mistake for us?'

Anna considered, briefly. 'You say he's in Buenos Aires?'

'He's in Pont del Mar.'

'Bridge of the Sea? What does that mean?'

'It's a fishing port a few miles farther south than Buenos Aires, but it's being developed as a resort. Apparently it's built on two sides of an inlet of the ocean, and has a rather elaborate bridge connecting them.'

'How do you know that Edel is there?'

'We have him under constant surveillance.'

'But you can't do anything about him yourselves.'

'We have him under surveillance from an independent source. We, Great Britain, can't afford to be involved in this. It could cause an international incident; as far as anyone knows, Edel is a world famous scientist who wishes to turn his back on the whole atomic business. There are a lot of ill-informed do-gooders around who would say, thank God for people like him. And with the Argentine government constantly muttering about the true ownership of the Falklands – they call them the Malvinas – it could be tricky.'

'Because your government doesn't want to go to war with anybody.'

'Because our government simply cannot afford to go to war with anybody. It's just about bankrupt.'

'And of course, the arrest and execution, after suitable torture, of an obviously deranged Irishwoman could not possibly have anything to do with you. I'm not altogether unknown in South America, you know.'

'You're wanted for murder in Brazil. But Brazil and Argentina don't have a lot in common. Not even the language. I assume that you do speak Spanish?'

'I took a crash course in it, yes.' She smiled at him. 'When I retired.'

'Are you prescient?'

'Possibly. But I was told to do it.'

'By your CIA bosses.'

'Of course.'

'Because they employ you chiefly in South America.'

'That is something you will have to ask them.'

'So will you do this job for us? We will provide you with a new identity...'

'Irish, of course.'

'Well, you are Irish, aren't you?'

'So tell me why you can't involve the CIA?'

He grimaced. 'We're not exactly flavour of the month in Washington, right now, as regards secrets. They think we've leaked too many of them to the wrong people. They were pretty fed up when Edel's sentence was commuted, and they have no idea that he has escaped. If they were to find out before we can guarantee that he is no longer around, they'd never trust us with anything again.'

'Including, of course, the necessary information on making one of these hydrogen bombs yourselves.'

'I'm afraid you're probably right. That's why

it has to be kept absolutely secret, even from your current employers. Will you do it?'

'You haven't mentioned the fee.'

'Eh?'

'Money, Billy. How much are you offering?'

'When you worked for us during the war, you worked for nothing.'

'The Nazis were paying my bills. But the war is over, Billy. And I'm a big girl now.'

'Hm. I'm authorized to offer you ten thousand pounds in US dollars. This will be paid in cash, and there will be no documentation. That means you do not have to account for any of it. But it will have to cover all your expenses. Anything left on completion is yours to keep.'

'Your generosity staggers me.'

'So, do we have a contract?'

'No.'

'What?'

'I require something more.'

'I am not authorized—'

'Yes, you are. You are authorized to offer me the protection of the British Government, once I complete this assignment.'

'Well, yes. That is what I said.'

'I want the complete protection of the British Government no matter what.'

'I'm not sure what you mean,' he said, uneasily.

'Simply that if any trigger-happy maniac turns up on my island, I am entitled to defend myself, and no questions asked.'

'Is that likely to happen?'

'You never know.'

‘But ... such a guarantee would give you licence to commit murder.’

‘It gives me the licence to defend myself. Now, really, Billy...’ She got up and bent over him; her still wet hair drooped on to his head and her nipple brushed his arm as she kissed him. ‘Do I look like a murderess to you? Think about it, and we’ll talk later.’

CRITICAL MATTERS

Anna went up to her bedroom, where Clive was just surfacing. ‘That was a night I shall never forget. But ... don’t tell me you’ve been swimming already?’

‘I always go swimming first thing in the morning, and it happens to be a quarter to eight. I am going to have a shower to wash my hair properly. Then we’ll breakfast.’ She paused in the bathroom doorway. ‘You’re welcome to join me.’

‘I never wished you many happy returns.’

‘Why, thank you.’

‘Don’t you want to know what I’m giving you as a present?’

‘You’ve already given me my present; your company for a week.’

‘How would you like it permanently?’

She gazed at him in consternation.

‘Don’t you like the idea?’

'It's my favourite idea.'

'Embedded in that statement, there's a but.'

'Well ... you mean you'd be prepared to come and live here, with me?'

'That is what I would rather do than anything else in the world.'

'When did you make the decision?'

'Its been growing on me for a long time.'

'Like ten years.'

'Anna...'

She sat beside him, kissed him. 'I'm not being bitchy. I know what a big decision you're taking. You'll be giving up your life, for me. And I can't give up mine, for you. At least, not right now. Right now, least of all. But if you're prepared to take me on, on that basis, I'll be the happiest woman in the world.'

He frowned at her choice of words, got out of bed, paused by the window to look down. 'He been there long?'

'About half an hour.'

'With you...?'

'It took him a few minutes to get used to the idea. But what he really wanted was that chat.'

'That chat. About Mexico City?'

'There were a few other things.' She stepped beneath the shower, soaked her hair, felt him against her. His arms went round her to hold her close. 'What other things?' he said into her ear.

'You *were* planning to shave?' she countered as his cheek rubbed against hers.

'Yes. What other things?'

She turned in his arms, water bouncing off her head and running down between their bodies.

'You'll have to ask Billy. He's sworn me to secrecy.'

She stepped away from him and used the shampoo.

'I ought to wring his neck,' Clive growled.

She kissed him. 'Perhaps afterwards.'

'After what?'

She gave a wicked smile. 'You'll have to ask him that too. But Clive, the answer to your question is yes. Yes, yes, yes.'

She stepped from the stall, dried herself, and gathered her hair to wrap in a bandanna before putting on her shirt and shorts and going downstairs. She felt absurdly exhilarated. It was not merely the fact that after all this time Clive had formally made up his mind to share her life, warts and all. That needed digesting, savouring, relishing over the next few days.

There was also the London bus syndrome, that after having been called upon only twice in the past three years she was now being required twice in as many months ... and by the British, too. There was no reason why that should exhilarate her; she did not have a drop of English blood in her veins, and after using her to their maximum advantage for six years they had thrown her aside like a worn-out glove. Yet, mainly because of Clive, she supposed, she still regarded them as the principal source of good in the world.

But the exhilaration arose from a more important source, to her. If Billy was to be trusted, and she believed he could be, then once she completed this job she was inviolate, at least, here on Fair Cay, or perhaps anywhere in the Bahamas. That guarantee was worth its weight in gold.

And the assignment? Apprehension, even concern, were irrelevant until she had received all possible information, and had seen the ground for herself. She had gone to Mexico City with no idea of how her mission was going to be accomplished, but a week's reconnaissance had been sufficient both to suggest a way in and a way out, and that had been all she had needed. Of course, Argentina was a little farther away; it would not be simply a matter of getting across the border, unless that had been arranged in advance. That would have to be done, but she remembered that she had escaped from Brazil in 1946, just one step ahead of the police.

There were delicious aromas of frying bacon coming from the dining room, but she went to the radio room first; there were noises.

'Fair Cay, Fair Cay. Come in, Fair Cay. Do you read?'

Anna sat down and thumbed the switch. 'Good morning, Joe.'

'I've been calling you for the past half-hour.'

'I was washing my hair.'

He digested this, no doubt using his imagination ... and his memory. If they had only ever spent one afternoon in bed together, it had been a very long afternoon, and one even she, at that so crowded period of her life, could remember as if it were yesterday. 'You said you had an urgent problem. Anything to do with Mexico?'

'I don't know, which is part of the problem. I don't think we should discuss it on the air. I need to see you, ASAP.'

'Um. I'm kind of tied up ... I'll send Jerry.'

'Who?'

'You remember Jerry Smitten? He certainly remembers you.'

'Shit!'

'You do know that it's illegal to swear on the radio? You must remember Jerry Smitten? You saved his life.'

'I saved his life, Joe, because you sent him to me as a back-up, and when we had our first real problem, and he was facing two armed men, he froze.'

'I know. He's loved you ever since.'

'He loved me before then,' Anna said, absently, remembering the first, and so far only, time *they* had been in bed together.

'Eh?'

'Nothing important. Joe, this time I need a back-up who is capable of doing the job. Even if I'm not around.'

'That Brazil business was three years ago. We reckoned he was pretty good then, even if we knew he wasn't in your class. Who is? But I guess he was overawed by your presence.'

Anna blew a raspberry.

Which Andrews ignored. 'He's come a long way since then. Now he's really good. But when you say you need a back-up even if you're not around ... you talking about the cay?'

'That's right.'

There was a brief pause. 'Anna, you do realize

that our people cannot get involved in any overt activities in the Bahamas. We have no jurisdiction there, and the Brits are pretty jealous of their prerogatives.'

'Joe, you have my word that if Jerry gets involved in anything here on the cay, the Bahamian police will not interfere.'

'You have that kind of clout?'

'I'm about to accumulate it.'

Another brief pause. 'Would you like to tell me what the fuck is going on?'

'Uh-uh! Obscenity on the air! You could be prosecuted. I would love to tell you what is going on, Joe. But I can't do it on the air, and you don't want to come to me.'

'Anna...'

'So I will have to tell Jerry when I see him. Now, it is possible that he may be able to put my mind at rest, but if he can't, I will require his presence on the cay for a few days. The exact dates have not been fixed yet, and before we reach them, he will be able to return to you and put you in the picture. OK?'

'And you may not be there. On the cay.'

'I may have to go away for a few days, yes.'

'And you feel that something, or someone, may be threatening the cay? You're not supposed to have secrets from us, you know.'

'As I have been trying to tell you, this is a secret I am very anxious to share. When will Jerry get here?'

'Don't tell me the Mexican police have traced you? It's that goddamned stupid telephone call you made, isn't it?'

'Just tell me when Jerry will be here.'

'I can have him on a flight this morning. Will you meet him in Miami?'

'That will mean a two-day absence from the cay, and I can't risk that. I'll meet him in Nassau tomorrow. Tell him to check in to the Royal Victoria Hotel.'

'For how many nights?'

'That's up to him. I intend to be back here by tomorrow evening.'

'You know, you'd drive any sane man crazy.'

'So who wants to be sane? I love you, Joe. Fair Cay out.'

The other four were sitting down to the usual sumptuous breakfast, as Anna now did. Everyone was clearly curious, with various degrees of anxiety, as to why and with whom she had spent so long in the radio room, but equally no one wished to ask any questions in front of the others.

Anna ate her bacon and eggs and smiled at them brightly. 'I don't know if Clive has told you,' she said, 'but we're engaged to be married.'

There was a moment's silence, then Jane cried, 'Oh, you darlings! Clive!' She was seated next to him, and threw both arms round him for a hug and a kiss.

'Welcome aboard,' Johann said.

'Well,' Billy said, 'Congratulations.'

'Thank you.'

'Why, Billy, you almost smiled,' Anna commented.

'I wonder if we could have a word.'

'I thought we'd already done that. Billy almost came swimming with me, this morning,' she announced at large.

'Well...' he said, blushing.

'Tell you what,' Anna said, 'after breakfast, and before it gets too hot, I'll show you the island.'

'I say, I'd like that.'

'And Clive can come too.'

'Ah...'

'He is my fiance, Billy.'

'Well...'

'Now, Mama. I shall be going into Nassau tomorrow morning.'

'But ... you were in Nassau yesterday. And tomorrow is Sunday.'

'I know. This is just a little matter that I have to attend to. I'll be back tomorrow afternoon.'

Everyone stared at her, and Clive asked, 'Shall I come with you?'

'I wouldn't bother. It's just to do with the cay.' Which, she reflected, was absolutely true. She finished her coffee. 'Well, gentlemen, whenever you're ready.'

'Some place,' Billy commented. 'Did you create it all yourself?'

'Would you say,' Anna asked. 'That creation is one of my fortes? The creation was by the previous owner. I have merely added to it, and I like to think, embellished it.'

They had walked the length of the island, and stood by the reservoir. As Anna had been pointing things out throughout the stroll, introducing them to Elias and the gardeners, neither Clive nor Billy had been able to ask any of the questions that had obviously been bubbling in their brains, even of each other.

Billy was still appreciating his surroundings, as he looked out over the beach at the sea. 'And there's nothing out there?'

'Of course there is. Abaco is only just over forty miles away. Only you can't see it.'

'And there's a big ship.' Clive pointed to the north-east.

'She's bound for Fort Lauderdale,' Anna said. 'This is the north-west Bahama Passage; it's wide and deep and much used by ocean-going traffic.'

'There's something in the water,' Billy said, also pointing.

Anna squinted. 'That's a shark's fin.'

'What? You mean there's a shark under that?'

'There usually is.'

'But ... it's inside the reef.'

'There's a passage.' She pointed. 'You can see the break in the surf. Big fish sometimes come through, but it's nearly always inadvertent, and they're usually in a hurry to get back out.' She squinted. 'Anyway, that's a ground shark. It's not very big.'

'Is it dangerous?'

'Not as dangerous as some. But there is no shark that you want to swim up to and pat on the head.'

'My word. Even paradise has its dangers, eh? What about hurricanes?'

‘They do have them. But not very often. And we’re sheltered here. The worst of the weather comes from the north-east, and the most dangerous aspect of a hurricane is the storm surge. But on our east side, as you can see, there are several miles of relatively shallow water, and then that arc of islands.’

‘But have you actually experienced one?’

‘Not yet.’ Anna decided that the time had come to talk business. ‘So tell me, Billy,’ she asked. ‘Do you agree to my terms?’

‘I don’t actually have that authority,’ he reminded her. ‘I will have to take advice.’

‘Then I will look forward to hearing from you.’

‘Supposing the answer is affirmative, and I believe it will be, in the present circumstances...’

‘You mean now that I have accumulated one of your own people as a minder? Just to make sure I don’t start shooting people on sight?’

‘Well...’

‘Now look here,’ Clive said.

Anna squeezed his hand. ‘Let’s finish this part of the business first.’

‘That will be an important consideration, yes,’ Billy said. ‘Supposing that I can obtain clearance, how soon can you undertake the mission?’

‘I am not undertaking any mission while Clive is here. We see each other too seldom as it is.’

‘Ah. I was wondering if he was about to resign, and become a permanent resident.’

Anna looked at Clive, who flushed. ‘Well, obviously I can’t just do that. You do understand that, Anna. I have things to tie up, certain obligations...'

'I do understand that, my darling. Having waited ten years for this moment to arrive, I am quite prepared to wait a while longer, until we can get it quite right. Certainly until this present situation is cleared up. So Billy, I will be ready any time after Clive goes back, providing I receive the guarantee, my fee, and all the necessary information as regards locale and contacts.'

'That sounds satisfactory. I have most of what you want right here.'

'You mean there *is* something important in that attaché case?'

'I think I am entitled to know what this "present situation" is,' Clive remarked.

'I think so too. Surely you can trust Clive, Billy?'

'I'm sure of it. But—'

'Tell him first. We can worry about the buts after.'

Billy sighed, and outlined what he had proposed to Anna that morning.

Clive listened in growing consternation. Then he said, 'That is absolutely out of the question.'

'You see?' Billy asked Anna. 'There is the but.'

'It's a job, Clive,' Anna said. 'My very last job, right, Billy?'

'For us, yes. I can't speak for anyone else.'

'It is an act of complete lunacy,' Clive declared. 'And the cheek of it. After Anna has spent six years risking her life for us, we kicked her out without even a thank you much less a pension...'

'Do you need a pension, Anna?' Billy asked.

'That's not the point,' Clive insisted. 'Everyone who retires should have a pension. That is Socialist philosophy. But we not only dropped her as if she was a rotten egg, we told her to get out of England, and stay out. But when we realize that we can't do without her, suddenly all is forgiven. That is the lowest form of hypocrisy of which I have ever heard.'

'All right, you've made your point, and I agree with just about everything you've said. That doesn't alter the fact that we *do* need her, and that she has agreed to help us.'

'I haven't finished,' Clive said coldly. 'You're sending her to Argentina. Under this dictatorship they've accumulated that is just about the most unpleasant country in the Americas, right now. Have you any idea what their secret police would do to her if they had cause to arrest her?'

Billy looked at Anna.

'I think I have rubbed shoulders with some policemen who have got to be the most unpleasant creatures ever to have walked the face of this earth. But I'm still here, and they are not.'

'My God! Talk about hubris! Don't you realize that when you worked for Himmler, you had the entire resources of the SD behind you? When you worked for us, you had MI6 behind you. And when you work for the Yanks I assume you have the CIA behind you.'

'Not when I am on the job,' Anna said quietly. 'Once I'm out, they protect me, so long as they don't have to get politically involved, which is exactly the terms Billy is offering now. And I am only going to undertake this job, if he can guarantee that whatever I may have to do to protect myself, here on the cay MI6 will stand between me and any prosecution. Right, Billy?'

He nodded.

'That doesn't alter the fact that one day you are going to make a mistake.'

'When I do,' Anna said, 'If I have the Brigade of Guards standing by it won't make a damned bit of difference.'

'But why?' he almost wailed. 'Why take a risk you don't have to?'

'Clive, darling, don't you see how important such a guarantee is to me, to us? You and Billy have both suggested that I need to remember that if I break any British laws, even when defending myself or my cay, I could be for the high jump. Now, call it hubris if you like, but I am confident that I can get in, and then out, of just about every situation, and get back here, too. But what I can't prevent is the probability that one day some enterprising villain is going to be able to trace me here. I have to have the right to defend myself and my island and everyone on it. You must understand that because hopefully, one day soon you'll be one of the residents. Don't you want to be able to defend yourself, and me, without being arrested by the local police?'

Clive looked at Billy, who shrugged. 'Sometimes her pragmatism frightens me too. It always did. So, Anna, if you're now working for us at such a high cost, don't you think we're entitled to know what else is going on, that might affect you, and therefore us? That long radio call this morning, this sudden, apparently unusual, extra trip to Nassau tomorrow...'

'Sorry, Billy. It has nothing to do with you.'

'But I'm coming with you tomorrow,' Clive said.

'I'd prefer it if you wouldn't. As I told Mama, I'll only be gone a few hours.' She smiled at them, brightly. 'It's getting hot. Time for a rum punch.'

What a way to start an engagement, Anna thought, as she steered *Fair Girl* through the reef. She had always held the opinion that lovers, when they reached the point of melding, should have no secrets from each other. But then, as a girl, and even as a young woman already launched on her terrifying career, she had held so many opinions that had proved untenable in the cold light of experience.

For Clive and Billy to realize just how vulnerable the cay had suddenly become would add another weight to the burden she was already carrying, and although Billy had, at least in principle, given her the go-ahead to handle a crisis as she thought fit – and in the only way she knew – she had no idea how he might react to the knowledge that the first crisis might already be upon them, before he had obtained the necessary clearance from London.

While for Clive even to encounter Jerry Smitten, would not be a good idea; they had been very close, even if briefly, during her mission to Brazil three years ago. If Clive knew that she had slept with several men, as it had been required by her various assignments, he had only ever known of one colleague, apart from himself. And although he and Joe Andrews had been friends for years, and he had accepted that she had been paying a debt – the saving of her life – she knew it still rankled. While his reaction to her acting the prostitute and what that might have involved had been a shade too orthodox. So it was far better to play it this way and rely on time and an ending of the crisis to keep things peaceful.

Which was not to say that the atmosphere throughout yesterday afternoon and evening, even when softened by pre-lunch and pre-dinner drinks, had not been somewhat frosty. On the other hand, Clive had been as hungry as ever in bed last night, and as she had also been hungry, she felt that she had left him in a contented state.

She had deliberately left early, and they were in Nassau by eleven. 'I'm not sure when I'll be ready to go back,' she told Tommy. 'But it won't be after three.'

'I'll be here Miss Anna,' he promised.

'Miss Fitzjohn!' Charles was delighted to see her again so soon, and looking as attractive as ever, in a pale green frock with matching shoes and handbag, a straw hat with a green ribbon, kid gloves and glowing with jewellery.

'Just for lunch. I'm meeting a Mr Smitten. Has he checked in?'

'Oh, yes, ma'am. He came in last night.'

'Well, will you page him for me? We'll be lunching together.'

'I will see to that, ma'am. But he ain't here, right now. He went for a walk after breakfast, and he ain't come back yet.'

Some people never change, Anna thought; Jerry had always been inclined to think that the world waited on him rather than accept the true state of affairs. 'Well, when he does come in, tell him I'm waiting for him, in the bar.' She turned away, and checked. 'I don't suppose you've seen that woman again? The one who was asking for me a couple of days ago?'

'Now that is a funny thing, ma'am.'

'What?' Anna was totally surprised. 'You mean she's been back here?'

'No, no, ma'am. But James saw her this very morning. James,' he called, 'come over here.'

James hurried round the reception desk. 'Morning, ma'am.'

'Good morning, James. You have something to tell me?'

'Ma'am?'

Anna looked at Charles.

'That woman who was here a few days back, asking for Miss Fitzjohn. You said you seen her again.'

'Today,' Anna reminded him.

'Oh, that woman,' James said. 'Yes, ma'am. I did see she this very morning.'

'Where, and when?' Anna asked, patiently.

'At the fisherman dock, ma'am.'

'She was buying fish?' Charles asked, unhelpfully.

'No, no, Mr Charles. She was hiring a boat.'

'This woman was chartering a fishing boat?'

'You know, that is just what that boy Clarence did say. I was there. He said, "Ma'am, if you want a boat for the day you should go to the Prince George Dock. They got cabin cruiser and thing there. And skippers who knowing the waters. These boats, you can smell them from here, ma'am. They ain't got nothing but fish, and they engines old, and they ain't got no ... well ... "' He paused, embarrassed.

'Toilet facilities,' Anna suggested.

'That is the very thing, ma'am. But the woman said, "I will pay you two hundred American dollars for the use of your boat for today." Well, ma'am, Clarence ain't going pass up two hundred dollars. So he said, "If that's what you wanting."'

'So he hired her his boat. How big a crew did it have?'

'She didn't want no crew, ma'am. She took it, like they say, bareboat.'

Anna looked at Charles for an explanation.

'A bareboat charter is without a crew, ma'am.'

'You mean this woman has taken this boat out by herself?'

'Well, no, ma'am,' James said. 'She had a man with her. Big guy.'

'I see. And what time was this?'

'Not too long. Maybe an hour ago.'

Anna frowned. She and Tommy should have noticed the boat leaving the harbour. 'So she left at ten o'clock.'

'I don't know if she left right then, ma'am, or if she had gear to load.'

'Thank you, James. You've been a great help.'

Anna gave him a ten-pound note, and he retired behind his desk.

'That must be one strange woman,' Charles commented.

'Yes,' Anna agreed. 'Charles, would you have any idea how fast one of those fishing boats can go?'

'Oh, not very fast, ma'am. Them engines does be all beat up. Six, maybe eight knots.'

'Thank you, Charles.' She considered the situation. Obviously she would be able to overtake the fishing boat, even if it had an hour's start, before it could reach the cay, supposing that was where it was heading, and she didn't doubt that. But only if she left herself, immediately. But she didn't want to involve Tommy in the professional side of her life; she had no idea what his reaction might be. So where the hell was Jerry?

And there he was, coming up the steps from the garden., removing his panama hat as he did so. 'Anna!' he cried. 'I can't tell you what a treat it is to see you again.'

She allowed him a hug. 'Right this minute, Jerry, I feel the same about you.'

He held her shoulders to look into her eyes. 'I'm not quite sure how I should take that.'

Jerry Smitten was a large young man, taller than her, which she always appreciated – her erstwhile Nazi masters had all been *little* men – with footballer's shoulders, and narrow hips, displayed by his sports shirt and casual pants, a mop of curly yellow hair, and pleasant features. Although he had a splendid body, as she well remembered, he looked completely harmless, and she had had her doubts when he had appeared in Brazil to act as her back-up in the quest for Martin Bormann. But Joe Andrews had said he was one of the CIA's best, and she had been prepared to accept that, until they had been cornered by the four MGB agents sent by Beria to arrest her and take her back to Moscow for trial.

As they had been travelling in separate cars, two of the Russians had come after her, and two had gone for Jerry. She had disposed of her two antagonists easily enough, but Jerry had apparently been unable to believe that they meant to kill him, as they would have done had she not been able to return to his rescue soon enough.

But again Joe had assured her that he was now an experienced agent. So she said, 'Believe it or not, I need your help, now. Charles, I'm afraid I'm going to have to renege on lunch. Mr Smitten and I have somewhere to go.'

'Oh!' Charles was disappointed. 'Of course, ma'am.'

'But I'll see you soon, and thanks for your help.' She tipped him, and grasped Jerry's arm to take him aside.

'Say,' he protested. 'What's going on? Joe said—'

'That you'd give me a hand. Do you still have that howitzer you used to carry?'

'My Colt forty-five? Well, I have a new one. I believe you threw my old one away.'

'It seemed like a good idea at the time. Is it on you?' But as she looked at his distinctly tropical dress she realized it couldn't be.

'It's in my room. I didn't reckon on needing it, in a place like Nassau.'

'Well, you do now. Nip up and fetch it. But keep it concealed.'

'You figure on shooting someone?'

'I may need you to make a hole in a boat. And I only have my two-two.'

He went off, clearly in a fog, and she returned to the desk. 'James, there is one more thing I forgot to ask you; this boat we were talking about just now, did it have a name? Or a number?'

'Oh, it had a number, ma'am. *216*.'

'*216*. Thank you, James. You've been a great help.'

She summoned one of the taxis, had it waiting when Jerry returned, carrying his hat in his hand; it obviously concealed the revolver. 'You gonna tell me what this is all about?' he asked, as he sat beside her, his hat on his lap.

'When we're on board.'

'On board what?'

'My boat.'

'You have a boat?'

'Well, of course I have a boat. Didn't Joe put you in the picture?'

'He said you'd do that when I got here.'

'Hm. But you do know boats?'

'Well ... I'm from Kansas.'

'Ah. About as far away from the sea as it's possible to be. But wait a minute. You told me that you'd been in the Navy during the war. That you had commanded a submarine.'

'That's right. Subs go under the water.'
'But you must have had some kind of initial training, on a boat?'
'Not really. I volunteered for subs, and things being kind of fraught after Pearl Harbor, it was a rush job. I can tie a bowline,' he added brightly. 'Well, I could once.'
'Shit!'
'Something wrong?'
'I guess we'll manage.' They reached the dock and she paid the driver.
Jerry, still holding his hat in front of him like a shield, was surveying *Fair Girl*. 'Say, that's swell. But there's nobody on board.'
'Well, of course there's nobody on board, Jerry. We're here.'
'I meant, there's no crew.'
Anna went down the steps. 'You're the crew.'
'Eh? I...'
'You'll remember it all as we go along. And –' she looked down at his soft shoes – 'you're perfectly dressed for the part. Mind how you go.'
She took off her shoes, stepped on board, and went below to change her clothes and check that the Walther was fully loaded, less the one bullet she had used on Capillano, but she also had her spare magazine, although if it came to a sea battle Jerry's forty-five would be the superior weapon – provided he got around to using it.
The boat trembled as his weight boarded, and a moment later he appeared in the cabin doorway. 'Some lay-out. Say –' she had taken off her dress – 'you're even more beautiful than I remember.'

'You say the sweetest things.' She buttoned her shirt, pulled up her pants, pocketed the little pistol and the magazine.

'Couldn't we leave this going to sea bit for a while?'

'You know the drill, Jerry. Business before pleasure.'

She attempted to step past him, and he put his arms round her waist. 'I never did thank you for saving my life.'

'That also seemed a good idea. At the time.'

'And that was the last time I saw you. Staring at me along the barrel of a gun.'

'And fortunately for you, there were two Russians in between us. You need to remember that they aren't there today.'

He released her, followed her on deck. 'The people at the hospital told me you packed my wound with mud.'

'If I hadn't, you'd have bled to death long before you reached that hospital. One has to make these instant decisions from time to time, even if one realizes they might have been the wrong decisions, afterwards.' She climbed up to the bridge, watched Tommy pounding along the dock above her.

'Miss Anna?!'

'Tommy! Listen, this gentleman and I are going out for a short spin. I'll be back for you. Hopefully in about three hours.'

He came down the steps, gazed at her reproachfully as she turned the keys to start the engines.

'Only three hours. But you can cast us off.'

He did so, reluctantly, and the boat glided away from the dock.

'You know that guy?' Jerry asked from the after deck.

'My crew?'

'You don't think we might need him?'

'I don't want him to be involved. Besides, I have a crew.'

He didn't seem to have a reply to that, but she didn't feel he could be risked on the narrow side deck, and as the harbour was somnolent in the noonday heat of a Sunday afternoon, once she was clear of the various docks she put the engines in neutral and let the boat come to a stop and drift while she took in the fenders and coiled the warps.

'Anything I can do to help?' Jerry asked.

'Yes, there is. See that dock over there? The one crowded with fishing boats?'

'I got it.'

'Right. In the cabin you'll find a pair of binoculars. Fetch them and have a good look at the boats. They all have numbers painted on the bows. I want you to find *216*.'

'Aye aye, skipper. That's what they used to say in the Navy.'

'There too,' Anna agreed.

She finished her chores and returned to the after deck.

'No joy,' Jerry said. 'Nothing like *216*.'

'That means she must have left. Come up to the bridge and sit down. Bring the glasses and your hat or you'll get sunstroke.'

'What about the gun?'

'Leave that in the cabin for the time being.'

She waited for him to join her, somewhat precariously, and when he was settled beside her, pushed the throttles forward.

'You sure you know how to handle this thing?' he asked as they gathered way.

'What do you think I'm doing?'

He digested this, while they approached the eastern exit, then asked, 'What's that white stuff over there? Looks like surf.'

'It is surf. That's water breaking on a reef.'

'Holy shit! It looks kind of close.'

'It is. You can close your eyes, if you like.'

As she was concentrating on the passage, she didn't know if he did or not. But when they were through to the open water, he asked, 'You gonna tell me what this is all about?'

'You know about Mexico City?'

'Oh, yeah. Joe said you were tremendous, as always.'

'It's nice to be noticed. By the right people.'

'And you got clean away, didn't you? As usual.'

'I thought I'd got clean away. But a couple of days ago this woman tuned up, in Nassau, asking questions.'

'About you? Don't you use a different name in Nassau?'

'Yes. But she had a photograph.'

'Shit! But...'

'That is exactly it. How the fuck did she get hold of a photo?'

'Search me.'

'That is one of the things I want you to do. Get

Joe to search his department and make sure there hasn't been a leak. Now, I've just discovered that this woman, having identified me, and obviously having discovered where I live, has chartered a boat.'

'You mean she's what we're after? But ... out there?'

Apart from the islands to their right, the noonday sea looked entirely empty.

'She'll be making for the cay, but we should catch her up before she gets there. What I want you to do is use the glasses and sweep the horizon.'

'Um. Say, this motion...'

'It's normal.' The sea was calm with a light westerly breeze and a low swell; the Chris-Craft rose and fell rhythmically.

'Shit!' He levelled the glasses. 'You reckon she's alone?'

'No. She has a man with her.'

'And what are you aiming to do?'

'That depends on what she's aiming to do. If she's just checking out the cay, we'll frighten her off. But if she's meaning to finish the job here and now, well...'

'Finish the job? You mean you think she could be on a hit? And you have no idea who she's working for?'

'Not right now. Although I would very much like to find out.'

'Snap! I have a boat out there.'

Anna switched on the autopilot, took the glasses; the boat was further to the west than she would have expected. But...'It's a fishing boat all right. She's giving the islands a wide berth. I suppose she's afraid of the reefs. We'll close her.' She handed him the glasses and resumed the helm to alter course.

'Anna...' he suddenly panted.

Anna glanced at his stricken expression. 'Oh, shit! Give me those.' She took back the binoculars. 'Now hang your head over the rail.'

He did, and vomited violently. Anna put the new course on auto, and studied the distant boat, which was becoming larger by the moment. She reckoned it wasn't more than five miles off, and they should catch it up in an hour. Just in time, as she could make out Fair Cay on the starboard horizon, just a cloud still about thirty miles off. She did not want the people on the cay to have any idea what was happening out here. As for the other cays in the immediate vicinity, as far as she knew they were all uninhabited, although she couldn't be sure. But they were all now a good ten miles off.

Jerry got his head back from over the rail. 'Anna,' he groaned. 'I've puked all over the deck down there.'

'It'll wash off. How do you feel?'

'A little better. I ... oh, Jesus Christ!' His head was back over the rail.

She realized that he was one of those people for whom seasickness was no joke, but a potentially serious medical condition. She reduced speed and engaged the autopilot. 'You have to lie down. Come along, and I'll help you down the ladder.'

'Anna! I'm so sorry.'

'Forget it. It's not your fault.'
'I feel such a no-no.'
'I said, it's not your fault. It's probably something to do with your inner ear, your sense of balance, which gets thrown off by the motion. But how come they let you into the Navy? In fact, how come you survived?'
'I was always sick as a dog the first couple of days. But so was that English guy, Nelson. And he won a couple of battles, didn't he?'
'That's one way of putting it. Now, we're going down together. All I want you to do is grit your teeth and hang on to the rail. Come along.'
She went first, facing the rungs and also gripping the rail on both sides, waited for him to start, his back against her front. She supposed they would look like a pair of vaudeville comedians to any casual onlooker. But a few moments later they were on the deck, by when she felt quite exhausted.
She supported him through the doorway into the saloon and stretched him on one of the settee berths. 'Just lie here.'
'Anna...'
'I know.' She went into the galley, found a bowl and a packet of salt biscuits. These she placed in his arms. 'Try nibbling; it may help.' She went below and fetched a blanket. It was a warm afternoon, but she knew that severe seasickness could act like a shock and lower the body temperature dramatically. Carefully she spread the blanket over him.
'Anna! What are you going to do?'
'What needs to be done.'

INCIDENT AT SEA

Anna checked his revolver to make sure it was loaded; there was a cartridge in each of the six chambers. She tucked it into her waistband, then picked up her Walther and the spare magazine and carried them all up to the bridge, laying them on the facia beside the instruments. The fishing boat had now gained a couple of miles, but she seated herself, switched off the autopilot, made sure her bandanna was firmly on her head, and opened up to her maximum fifteen knots, sending the boat creaming through the low swell, the white wake spreading behind her.

Soon she could make out the fishing boat clearly with the naked eye, although at this distance there was no telling what was happening on board her, whether, in fact, they had even noticed they were being followed. Her advantage was that they could not possibly know who it was behind them. Her disadvantage was that without Jerry, and with no knowledge as to their intentions, she was going to have to play this entirely by ear. But she had had to do that often enough in the past.

Four miles, she estimated. She switched on the autopilot and went down the ladder. Jerry's eyes were closed, and he was breathing stertorously, the bowl clutched in his arms; he had been sick again, at least once. She reckoned he might not recover until they regained the dock.

She picked up the loud hailer, and returned to the bridge. Three miles, she reckoned. And they had noticed her! Through the glasses she could make out someone standing in the stern; from the amount of black hair flowing in the wind she guessed it was the woman. But the fishing boat was continuing towards the cay, now less than twenty miles off. That was still far enough to make it impossible for anyone over there to work out what was happening out here, and now, realizing that she had to be overtaken, the fishing boat was slowing.

Anna closed up to within fifty yards. 'Do you need assistance?' she asked through the trumpet.

'Why should we need assistance?' the woman called back.

It was time to stir the pot. Anna untied her bandanna, and let it drop to the bridge deck; her hair tumbled down her back and immediately streamed in the wind. 'Good afternoon,' she said, 'I am Anna Fehrbach, Countess von Widerstand. Were you looking for me?'

The woman stared at her, then shouted, 'Paolo! It's her! It's the bitch! And she's alone! We can do it now!'

The fishing boat's engine slipped into neutral, and the man emerged from the wheelhouse, carrying a shotgun. The woman had also produced a pistol, but Anna had already levelled the revolver. She had never fired anything quite this heavy before, so she held it in both hands, but even so her first shot missed, a very unusual experience for her.

Her second shot found its target, and the woman uttered a shriek and fell. The man had fired, but *Fair Girl* was still moving forward, and only a couple of the buckshot hit the hull. Anna emptied the remaining chambers and he went down in a welter of blood.

Fair Girl was now in front of the stopped fisherman, moving slowly through the water. Anna put her into neutral, thrust the Walther into her pants pocket and slid down the ladder. Jerry was on his feet, hanging on to the cabin doorway. 'Anna!'

'Go back to bed,' she recommended. 'You look terrible.'

'But...'

She ignored him, selected a coil of rope and carried it forward to make fast to her anchor winch, then surveyed the fishing boat. There was no movement, but with both her engines and that of the fisherman muted she could hear a cry. 'Paolo! For God's sake help me. I'm hit! I'm dying!'

'Just coming,' Anna called, moving up and down the side deck to drape fenders over the rail. Jerry was still watching her, unable to move, it appeared.

'Those people,' he panted.

'I don't think they were friendly.' Satisfied, she climbed back up to the bridge, engaged gear, and turned the boat, carefully manoeuvring it alongside the fisherman. Whcn the two vessels were bumping together, she returned to neutral, slid down the ladder, ran forward to pick up the end of the warp, and scrambled across the two rails, drawing her pistol as she did so, the rope held in her left hand.

But there was no opposition. The woman lay against the engine cowling, still breathing, but bleeding profusely from the wound in her chest; her male companion was lying dead in the wheelhouse doorway, both he and the woodwork shattered by the point four-five bullets fired at such close range. Anna pocketed the pistol, made the warp fast so that the two boats could not drift apart, then stooped beside the woman, nose wrinkling at the stench of fish that pervaded everywhere.

The woman opened her eyes and blinked at her; blood bubbled from her mouth.

'Who sent you?' Anna asked.

Her lip curled.

'I could make dying easier,' Anna suggested.

'Fuck off,' she said, and the bubbling ceased.

Anna regarded her for several seconds, then sighed and stood up. She did not think there would be any point in searching the body, as she was still wearing stretch pants and a loose shirt there was not a lot of room to conceal anything. She stepped over the dead man into the wheelhouse; there was no cabin. But she quickly saw what she wanted, a carryall lying against the bulkhead. This she opened. There was a purse, with a couple of hundred dollars in it, an open return ticket to Miami, and a latch key.

In the bottom of the bag there was a passport. Anna opened it. The name was Lorna Strezzi, and it had been issued in Chicago. Which could be interesting, she thought. But it could also be meaningless; *she* possessed four passports, a German one in the name of Anna Fehrbach, Countess von Widerstand, which actually was out of date, a valid British one in the name of Anna Fitzjohn, a valid Irish one in the name of Anna O'Brien, and a valid American one in the name of Anna O'Donovan!

But beneath the passport, there was a photograph. It depicted a beautiful twenty-year-old girl with long blonde hair fluttering out from beneath her fur hat and down the back of her fur coat. Oh, to be twenty again, she thought. But ... apart from the fact that she was wearing fur, she was standing in front of St Basil's Cathedral in Red Square. The day she and Birgit and Marlene Gehrig had been taken to visit Lenin's tomb! Suddenly her memory came flooding back. The man had said, 'Excuse me, comrade,' and she had turned without thinking, to gaze into the lens of the camera. At the time she had thought nothing of it; she knew the effect her striking looks could have on men, and if one happened to have a camera...

But for it to turn up here, in a bag belonging to an apparently American assassin ... and it had obviously been around; the edges were dog-eared and even torn in a couple of places. But at least she could form some idea as to where this woman had been coming from. What she needed to find out, urgently, was how Moscow had located her. She replaced it and the passport in the carryall and took it outside.

'Anna!' Jerry was seated on one of the deck lockers. He still looked awful, but he would have to do *something*.

'Listen,' she said, 'get up on to the bridge, use the binoculars, and sweep the horizon. I need to know if there is any other boat out there.'

'Right.' Slowly, uncertainly, he climbed the ladder, while she wondered if he was going to fall back to the deck and lay himself out completely. But he made it, sat on the steering bench, and levelled the glasses. 'Take your time,' she told him.

She had already determined that there were only two ways to handle this, in view of the fact that both the bodies had bullet holes. The preferred way was to have them, and their boat, disappear without trace, which would set their employers back a few days while they tried to find out what had happened. But if there was any other boat in the vicinity, there would have to be a fire, which she would have sighted and gone to see if she could help, unavailingly. But if there were to be any witnesses, even at a distance – she had to allow for the possibility that a fire might be spotted by someone on one of the cays – she would have to report it, and while she knew they were in several hundred fathoms of water out here and thus it was very unlikely that the wreckage would ever be located, there would inevitably be interviews, and publicity, and even her picture in the *Guardian*, all of which she did not want to happen.

'There's nothing in sight,' Jerry said. 'Save for those islands over there.'

'They're ten miles off,' Anna said. 'I doubt that anyone over there can even see two small boats out here, unless their attention is drawn to them. Thank you, Jerry.'

'What are you going to do about those stiffs?'

'Bury them.'

Leaving Jerry gaping at her, Anna returned to the wheelhouse and switched off the engine. Then she moved Lorna Strezzi's body, and lifted the lid of the engine box. It was extremely mucky in there, and she grimaced; she had intended to use the heavy Colt cartridges to blow a hole in the bottom of the boat, but having emptied the revolver that was no longer an option. But she could not afford to have anything suspicious about her clothes. 'Come to the rail, Jerry,' she commanded. 'And take these.'

'Eh?' He arrived on the afterdeck in time to receive her shirt and slacks, then her shoes, and lastly her knickers, staring at her in a mixture of admiration and apprehension, as he clearly had no idea what she intended to do next. She also handed him the carryall.

'Put that in a safe place. Now pass me the bandanna,' she commanded, 'and if you will look in the starboard seat locker, you will find a hatchet. I need that as well.'

He found the little axe and handed it across the rails. She laid it down and tied up her hair, returned to the wheelhouse, and dragged the man's body inside. Then she dragged the woman away from the engine box before laying her beside her companion and closing and locking the door. She could not chance a couple of bullet-ridden bodies floating about and being found before the sharks got to them.

Jerry watched her open-mouthed. The sight of a naked Anna at work seemed to have entirely cured his seasickness; she wondered if there was something in that for medical science to use.

Satisfied with the situation on deck, she carefully climbed into the box. Several parts of the engine were still hot, and there were sharp edges which also had to be avoided, although the principal hazard, as she had seen, was the amount of oil and grease and sheer filth that coated every surface.

She felt her way beneath the engine mounting, into the bilge, which was even more noisome than the rest of the space, and was covered with a film of evil-smelling water. She knew there had to be a seacock somewhere, but finding it might take time, and she wanted to get rid of the evidence of what had happened as rapidly as possible.

There was no room to swing the hatchet properly, so she knelt in the water and delivered a series of short blows on the hull, aiming always at the same place, scattering oily water to either side and over herself. As she had expected from the general appearance of the boat, the wood was fairly soft, but it still took her twelve blows to open a seam. Once she was through, however, two more blows had water gushing in. In seconds she was up to her thighs.

She climbed back on to the already sloping deck, handed Jerry the axe while he regarded her as if she were a sea monster. 'I know,' she said, 'I'm a filthy mess.'

She hurried forward, untied the warp, pulled the two boats together, and scrambled over the rail, plucking the forward boathook from its rack. 'There's another hook aft,' she called. 'Push us away.'

He obeyed, and they opened a gap of several feet from the slowly sinking fishing boat. Anna had never seen a boat sink before – when she had been torpedoed in the Baltic in 1944, it had been too dark to see properly what was happening – and she watched in fascinated horror as its decks slowly became awash, and then suddenly it went down with a whoosh, leaving behind only a seethe of disturbed water in which the Chris-Craft bobbed violently. As affected as ever by the many other traumatic events of her life, she replaced the boathook and went aft. Jerry had again sunk on to one of the seat lockers. Anna stowed the axe. 'How do you feel?'

'A little better. But Anna ... those two guys—'

'Had come to kill me. And you, even if they didn't yet know you were on board.'

'The way you do things, so unemotionally, so methodically...'

Unemotionally, she thought; if you only knew. 'I've had a lot of practice.'

'At killing people, and sinking boats?'

'At staying alive.'

She used a rag to wipe the oil and grease from her hands and feet, then went below and stood in her shower. The bandanna hadn't been very efficient at protecting her hair, so she washed that as well. Getting herself clean took half an hour; when she finally emerged, he was sitting on the bunk watching her. 'What do we do now?'

Anna looked at her watch. 'Ten past one. Feel like lunch? There's food in the fridge.'

'For Christ's sake, Anna. I couldn't eat a thing.'

'Hm.' But she wasn't all that hungry herself. She opened the fridge, took out a cold beer, and went on deck. The fishing boat had entirely disappeared. There were a few scraps of flotsam which could probably be identified, but would only add to the mystery of what had happened to her. 'Well, then, we'd better go back to Nassau.'

He had followed her on deck. 'But what do we tell people?'

'We don't tell people anything. You wanted to see what my boat was like, so I took you for a spin. You felt seasick, so we packed it in. We did not see any other boats. Remember that.'

'But that black chap you spoke to as we left...'

'He works for me.'

'And he'll believe what you tell him?'

Anna returned to the cabin and got dressed. 'He will believe that I took you off to some secluded bay for a quiet fuck.'

She climbed on to the bridge and sat at the controls. Jerry joined her. 'You staying in Nassau?'

'No. I'm returning to the cay immediately.'

'Hell, I was looking forward to, well, spending some time together. We didn't have much time in Brazil.'

'No, we didn't,' she agreed. 'But maybe things will work out later on. What I want you to do right now is get back to Joe as quickly as possible. You'll take the passport and the photo; I want this woman identified, I need to know who she works for, and I need to know how she or they got hold of the photo. Right?'

'Right,' he agreed, somewhat gloomily.

'Then, in four days' time, I want someone to come and live on the cay.' Clive had been here three days, and he had come for a week; once he left, she wanted to get the Argentina job over as rapidly as possible.

'With you? Right.' Enthusiasm flooded back. 'It'll be me.'

'I think I'll need more than just you.'

'Hey, wait a minute. Just because I got seasick?'

'No, Jerry. Because I think what I need is round-the-clock protection.'

'*You* need round-the-clock protection? There's a laugh. You reckon this woman's employers may come looking for her? Will they know where to look?'

'Yes. They must have sent her to the Bahamas in the first place.'

'Yeah, but will they know where to look in the Bahamas?'

'Jerry, I would say that she's a professional. She started asking questions two days ago, and decided to act on her info today. I would say that also was on instructions from the top. That almost certainly means that she contacted her boss, probably yesterday, and received instructions from him to check the cay out. That means he now knows the name of the cay.'

'And thought she could take you and the cay with just one back-up? He's gotta be a nut.'

'She wasn't there to take me out. All she was supposed to do was reconnoitre the cay. But when they saw me, close up and apparently alone on my boat, they decided the opportunity was too good to miss. They said so.'

'Well, I guess everybody makes mistakes. So how's her boss gonna find out what happened to her?'

'He isn't. Because there's no way he can. But he's not going to be very happy when she disappears without trace, and now he knows where he can find *me*.'

'So you think he'll send a mob the next time. You don't think I should stay now? We can contact Joe by radio.'

'I won't need you for another four days. And there are things I need that only you can provide.'

He was frowning. 'You're losing me. You don't need back-up now, but you will need it in four days' time.'

'That is correct.'

'Sorry. I can't figure that out.'

'It is simply that in about four days' time I will have to go away for a few days.'

'Go away, where?'

'It's a private business trip.'

'Joe know about it?'

'I said, it's a private business trip.'

'So I'm not to tell him. He'll be curious about

these arrangements you want to make.'

'Of course you can tell him. But it remains none of his business. However, as I'm damned sure this woman Strezzi's turning up here is connected with the Russians, I need to find out who they're employing in the States, and I think I'm entitled to ask for your help in protecting the cay while I'm away. Everyone else living on the cay is absolutely innocent of any involvement in my affairs, and that means, in this instance, in your affairs. I want to keep it that way.'

He brooded some more, while Hog Island came over the horizon. 'And you don't think your people will wonder why I've come to stay with you when you ain't there?'

'I can sort that out. Now listen. I reckon you'll need a team of three, and they all have to be people who can take care of themselves.'

'Three? You sure have a low opinion of CIA operatives.'

'I said, they'll need round-the-clock surveillance.'

'And you don't.'

'No, Jerry. I don't.'

He relapsed into another silence.

'Now listen carefully,' she said again. 'These are what I require. Immediately, which means as soon as you get back to Washington and can see Joe, I need this woman's identity and background and employers. Then I need a date for your return with your squad. And I need you to tell Donald I require two hundred five-shot magazines for my Walther.'

'What?'

'I'm running low.'

'How the hell am I supposed to get a box of a thousand cartridges through Nassau customs?'

'You won't have to. I'll be in Miami in a couple of days and I'll pick them up. When you have your squad assembled, give me your dates, my crew will come across to Miami and pick you up as well.'

'To ... that's two hundred miles.'

'No problem, man.'

'Two hundred miles ... in this?'

'It's two hundred and fifty, actually. Find yourself some good anti-seasick tablets,' she suggested.

Having dropped Jerry off, and picked up a totally mystified Tommy, who had apparently spent the entire three hours they had been away sitting on the dockside waiting for her to come back, she put to sea again immediately, cooking the pair of them a late lunch. 'I'm sorry about this afternoon, Tommy,' she said, the cruiser being on autopilot while they ate.

'No problem, ma'am. You's the boss.'

'Thank you, Tommy. However, I would not like anyone on the cay to know about the gentleman I was seeing. It is a completely confidential business matter.'

'You got it, ma'am.'

She had no doubt that he would keep her secret; not only did he have one of the best-paid jobs going in the Bahamas, with free housing and his keep thrown in, but, even if he had no idea of either her background or of what she was capable, he was totally in awe of her. But he would have to be told more to cover the situation of the boat. 'Because something happened,' she said.

'Ma'am?' He was instantly concerned.

'I thought we could just cruise round while we talked, but the gentleman got seasick.'

'I did see he wasn't looking too good, and that is a fact.'

'So I decided to put into a little cove we saw, drop anchor and give him time to recover. There was another boat anchored there, but I thought nothing of it, only when we approached, a man came on deck with a shotgun and fired at us.'

'Ow, me lord, ma'am! He hit you?'

'Only a couple of pellets. But they marked the topsides. Can you iron them out and paint them over?'

'I can do that, sure, ma'am. But what you did when this guy fired at you?'

'I got the hell out of there. I was scared stiff. I've never been shot at before.'

'Well, ma'am, we got to report this. We can't have people going around shooting at people.'

'I don't want to report it, Tommy. The gentleman I was with can't afford any publicity. He wasn't supposed to be in the Bahamas at all.'

'Well, ma'am, if you saying so. But...'

'Just let's keep it as our secret.'

'Yes, ma'am,' he agreed enthusiastically.

She felt that she had had a successful day in purely pragmatic terms. The fact that her blood-stained tally was now a hundred and four was not something to be proud of, but as with so many of her other victims, Lorna and her friend had been meaning to kill her; she refused to accept guilt for defending herself. And she had done all she could to keep things running smoothly until her return. She didn't at all like the idea of absenting herself from the cay at this time, but she had to believe that after her arrangements it would still be there and functioning when she got back.

Now it was time to concentrate entirely on the task ahead of her, and, of course, to survive the coming evening. It was past seven before they approached the reef, and she felt her way through, at dead slow, using her searchlight and with Tommy in the bow equipped with a powerful flashlight. But they both knew the waters very well, although it was a quarter to eight before they eased alongside the dock, where it seemed everyone on the cay was waiting for them.

Anna had called ahead to warn them she would be late, but they all still seemed to be agitated.

'How the hell did you find your way in through the dark?' Billy inquired.

'We had our light.' Anna hugged and kissed the dogs.

'And you had no problems with your business?' Jane asked.

'None that I couldn't solve. Now, Mama, I had a very light lunch, so I hope there's something good for dinner. And I feel like a stiff drink.'

'I don't suppose,' Clive said, as he got into bed

beside her, 'that you'd care to put me in the picture.'

He had said very little during dinner, or after it, but had been watching her. Having known her now for eleven years, which in real terms made him closer to her moods and idiosyncracies than even her parents, he could tell that she had not spent the day sitting around a desk.

'Off you go, darling.' Anna gave a purring Isis a last kiss and moved the cat from her chest. She had already decided that he would have to know at least something of what was going on; apart from the fact that he could well be involved, she really didn't want to keep secrets from him. 'I was seeing a man,' she said. 'You may remember the name: Jerry Smitten.'

Clive frowned. 'Smitten. Not that character whose life you saved in Brazil, in 1946?'

'That's right.'

'He had got himself shot, hadn't he?'

'That's right, too. That's why I had to save his life; he got himself shot trying to protect me.'

'And now he's come back to show his gratitude.'

'Not quite. He was sent by Joe, because we worked together before, and I have a potentially serious problem on my hands.' She told him about Lorna Strezzi turning up in Nassau and asking questions.

'Shit!' Clive commented 'It's to do with that Mexico job, isn't it? That absolutely crazy telephone call.'

'I had to do that,' she said, quietly.

'I know, my darling girl. I explained that to

Billy. And was this Smitten able to help?'

'Not immediately. I put him in the picture and sent him back to Joe. I need to know who this woman is and who she works for. You see, I have a gut feeling that she's nothing to do with the Mexican police; the photograph she had was taken in Moscow, in 1940.'

'You mean ... my God! The MGB?'

'I thought I was free of them. But are they employing an American squad? I'm hoping that Joe will be able to tell me that, and maybe deal with it at his end.'

'And meanwhile this woman is still hunting around trying to find you.'

'She found me, easily enough. I, and the cay, are well known in Nassau.'

'Jesus! And she'll have reported that to her employers.'

'That's what's bothering me.'

'Do you think she's still around, in Nassau?'

'No. She's no longer in Nassau.'

'How can you be sure of that?'

Anna gazed at the ceiling. 'I believe that her instructions were not only to find out if I lived in the Bahamas, and if so, where, but having done that, to reconnoitre my home and check out its defences, if there were any. So this morning she hired a boat and came out for a look at the cay.'

He frowned. 'How do you know all this?'

'I have friends. Besides, I followed her.'

'So that's why you were so late. And you saw her cruising around the cay. What time was this? Billy and I were on the beach this afternoon, and we didn't see you. Or any other boat.'

'This was around lunch time. And she never actually got within ten miles of the cay.'

Clive raised himself on his elbow. 'You mean you caught her up? What on earth did you say to her?'

'I went alongside, and introduced myself, and asked if I could be of assistance.'

He stared at her. 'Just like that? What did she say?'

'Not a lot. She drew a pistol and tried to shoot me.'

'Holy Jesus Christ!'

'There were actually two of them,' Anna explained. 'She had a male back-up.'

'Oh, my God, my God, my God! You mean you killed them both. You mean you carry a gun on that boat?'

'Well, of course I have a gun on the boat. And what else was I to do? If I hadn't shot them, they'd have shot me, and I wouldn't be here now.'

He got out of bed, and went to the bathroom, to pour himself a drink of water. 'But don't you realize ... who was with you? That black chap, Tommy?'

'No. I left him in Nassau. I didn't want him involved.'

'That makes sense.' He came back to the bed, sat beside her. 'You mean you handled this alone?'

'I had Jerry with me. Not that he was a lot of help. Apparently he gets seasick.'

He gazed at her for several seconds. 'So what are you, we, going to do now? Billy hasn't got you the carte blanche you want yet. There's no guarantee that he'll get it at all. Certainly after this.'

'After what?'

'Anna, my darling, you have just killed two people.'

'I know. The tally is now a hundred and four. That includes that MGB squad in Germany in '46. I know you and Joe and your friends accounted for a couple of them, but the responsibility was mine. It's a bit of a weight to carry around. But these people never leave me any choice.'

'Anna, the war is over. Killing people ad lib is no longer acceptable.'

'I don't think that is a point of view to which everyone subscribes. And until everyone does, I can't afford to do so either.'

'You do realize that they hang people for murder. OK, so it was, as always, self-defence. But the burden will be on you to prove it. Did this fellow Smitten actually see what happened?'

'No. I told you, he was prostrate at the time.'

'And you haven't reported what happened. That's a count against you for a start. What you should have done is either summon help, or towed their boat into Nassau and explain what had happened.'

'I couldn't do that.'

'It would have been tough, yes. And you would probably now be in a cell. But immediately reporting it would have been a big count in your favour. Now...'

‘I couldn’t tow the boat into Nassau, Clive. I sank it.’

‘You did *what?*’

‘I cut a hole in its bottom, and it sank.’

‘But ... they’re bound to find the wreck.’

‘I don’t think they will. It’s in about two thousand feet of water.’

‘And the bodies? They always come ashore. Even if a shark has had a go at them, the bullet wounds will be evident.’

‘I put the bodies in the wheelhouse and locked the door. They’re not going to come out until the wood rots, and they won’t come up then, either, because skeletons don’t float.’

He scratched his head. ‘You did all that?’

‘I’m a professional.’

‘With no help from Smitten.’

‘I work better on my own.’ She squeezed his hand. ‘Have you changed your mind about marrying me?’

‘My darling, I wouldn’t dare. Change my mind, I mean.’

‘Then come to bed. I’ve had a busy day.’

He lay beside her. ‘We have to tell Billy.’

‘You reckon?’

‘Very definitely.’

They sat in the radio room after breakfast, as she was expecting a call, and she put Billy in the picture. She had exercised and had her swim and felt on top of the world. But she was just a little apprehensive; she needed his continued support every bit as much as she needed Joe’s. And Clive’s. He listened without comment until she was finished, then remarked, 'I wonder if the millions of ordinary, innocent men and women going about their daily business realize how fortunate they are. I mean, that there is only one of you on this planet. I don't think they could survive two.'

'You say the sweetest things. Does that mean you're jumping ship?'

'You must be joking. As you reminded me the other morning, I'm on your island. But I need to know how this affects the situation. I mean, these people, whoever they are, are not going to take too kindly to having two of their people rubbed out.'

'I think they are going to take a little time to discover that. Whoever is employing this woman sent her here to find out if I was living here. As far as I could gather from the people at the Royal Vic, she didn't even have a name for me, only the photograph.'

'Which I presume you removed.'

'Yes, I did. Along with her passport.'

'May I have a look at them?'

'I sent them up to Joe Andrews.'

'What? Why?'

'At this moment, Billy, and for the past three years, he has been my principal employer. In fact, until you turned up this time, he has been my only employer.'

'She has a point,' Clive put in.

Billy gave him a dirty look.

'So I regard him as being primarily responsible for my continued existence,' Anna said. 'Besides, it was an American passport. He'll be able to use it to track her down far quicker than you could. The point I am making is that she turned up the day before you two, armed only with the photo. I don't know how lucky she was, but I imagine her plan was to flash the photograph in every hotel, every major shop, and every bank, and see what turned up, but it seems unlikely that she had had any success before reaching the Royal Vic, otherwise she need not have bothered with them at all. But as I'm a regular guest there, she got what she wanted: a name. She must have spent the next day getting an address and as much info on me as possible, which would have been just about nothing, save that I appear to be wealthy and that I've lived here for more than two years. Now, I reckon, that she also got in touch with her bosses, and they told her to make a recce of the island; if they're after me at all, they must have some idea of who and what I am, and would therefore suppose that the cay will be defended. They'll want to know how.'

'Is it defended?' Billy asked.

'It has me on it,' Anna pointed out.

He gulped.

'So,' Anna went on, 'acting on instructions, Strezzi hires a boat yesterday and comes looking. It was her bad luck that was the day I went to Nassau to meet Smitten, and found out about it. Now she and her companion, and the hired boat, have disappeared without trace. Her principals will wait for a couple of days to hear from her.'

'Won't what happened be front page news?'

'Tell me what happened, Billy?'

'Well...'

'A couple of Yanks come over here and hire a fishing boat for the day. Obviously, they're going fishing. They don't come back, and there's no trace of the boat. That might make the front page of the *Nassau Guardian*. But that sort of thing happens fairly regularly in these waters. Either they struck a rock and sank, and they couldn't swim, or they caught a bigger fish than they bargained for. They'll be looked for, of course. But they won't be found. Clarence, the fisherman who hired them the boat, will be counting the insurance money. And after a couple of days it will be forgotten.'

'They'll put it down to the Bermuda Triangle,' Clive suggested with a grin.

'But,' Baxter pointed out, 'if this woman was working undercover for the Mexican police, as seems probable, and had reported back to them before coming out to the cay, they now have both your name and your address.'

'She wasn't working for the Mexican police.'

'How can you be sure of that?'

'Because they want me either to stand trial for murder, or to tell them who was responsible, as I was obviously there. To do either of those things, I have to be alive. That woman was sent to find me, yes, but she was also told, or at least given permission, to finish the job if she had the opportunity. When I turned up alongside her, on a very empty piece of water, apparently alone and with my face hanging out, she thought Christmas had come early. She shouted at her companion, "It's her, and she's alone. We can finish it now." And they started shooting.'

Baxter reached for his pipe, but it wasn't there.

'Hold it,' Anna said. The radio was crackling.

'Fair Cay. Fair Cay. Uncle Joe.'

'Come in, Uncle Joe. May I assume that Jerry got home?'

'Half an hour ago, panting. You sure put that kid through some harrowing experiences.'

'Excuse me?'

'OK, OK. You were at the sharp end. But you say you want him back again.'

'Not just him. I need some capable people on the cay while I'm away.'

'Away where? And for how long?'

'Maybe a fortnight.' Anna gave Clive one of her wicked smiles. 'I'll be honeymooning.'

'What?! You're getting married?'

'Well, that generally precedes a honeymoon.'

'You can't get married.'

'Why not? As I believe you people say, I'm free, white, and over twenty-one.'

'But ... you work for us.'

'Of course I work for you, Joe. But I'm entitled to a private life.'

'Your husband will want to know what you do.'

'My husband already knows what I do. His name is Clive Bartley. You remember Clive Bartley?'

'Holy shit!'

'You *do*. And you're being obscene on the air again. Well, then...'

'You intend to marry that...'

Anna winked at the two men. 'Careful, now. He might hear you.'

'You are saying that Bartley knows you work for us?'

'And for the past three years, yes.'

'And he's had nothing to say about that?'

'He says quite a lot, from time to time. But unlike you, he understands that he has no right to interfere in my business life, any more than you have any right to interfere in my private life. Apart from the two weeks I require, I'm available whenever you want me, that is, of course, providing you keep me and mine alive until then. Which is what this call is about, right?'

There was a brief silence. Then he said, 'It's not on.'

Anna raised her eyebrows, although this was half expected, and what she had feared. 'Are you firing me?'

'Of course I am not firing you, Anna. I am prepared to accept that you have a private life and that you are capable of keeping that private life from interfering with your work for us. I'll even concede that if you are going to marry, Bartley is probably the most acceptable choice, even if he is old enough to be your father.'

Anna smiled at Clive. 'He'd have had to start a little young. So what are you saying?'

'I've referred the matter upstairs, and the decision is that I can't send my people to protect you in the Bahamas.'

'Tell me why not.' Even if she knew the answer.

'Don't you understand that the fact that you

work for us is, and must remain, top secret. We are prepared to give you all the help we can, but it has to be within that parameter.'

'So? Your people will be my guests on the cay. No one will know whether I am here or not.'

'Yes, but if what Jerry has told me is true, whoever is looking for you is liable to be armed and mob-handed. That means my people might have to take them out.'

Anna looked at Baxter. 'I told Jerry to tell you that if they get engaged in a shoot-out they will be immune from prosecution.'

'I'd like to believe that you have that much clout, but even if I do, can you guarantee that they will be immune from publicity?'

Anna glared at the set. But she said, 'So what do you recommend that I do?'

'Well, I assume that if you can guarantee my people from prosecution if they have to shoot somebody, you have that guarantee for yourself. I suggest you postpone this absurd marriage and honeymoon until this business is sorted out. Then if you have to defend the cay, well, it's a Bahamian resident ... correction, beautiful Bahamian resident, gallantly defending her home against pirates. You'll be a nine-day heroine.'

'You say the sweetest things. So how long do you reckon this will take to sort out? You going to help me with *that*?'

'Of course we are. You're still our girl. My people are checking out the passport now, and should have something in forty-eight hours. Then we'll see what we can do at this end.'

'That is very reassuring,' Anna said. 'I look

forward to hearing from you.'

'Anna ... there is no point in going off in a huff. There are certain rules we have to follow.'

'I understand that, Joe. Just as I now understand that I'm your girl when you want me to be, and as long as I'm not a nuisance. However, are you still prepared to arm me?'

'You mean those cartridges you need? They'll be waiting for you.'

'Thank you. In these new circumstances I wish you to add something to that.'

'What?'

'Two tommy guns with adequate spare magazines.'

'Two?'

'There's more than one of us.'

He sighed. 'OK. Two tommy guns. With four spare drums.'

'That sounds great. You're a sweetie, Joe. And a bazooka.'

'A *what*?'

'A bazooka. Surely you know what a bazooka is, Joe. It's an anti-tank missile launcher.'

'I know what a bazooka is, Anna. But what the hell do you want one for?'

'I reckon, if it'll stop a tank, it'll stop a boat if it gets too close. My safest course of action is to stop any mob landing at all.'

There was a brief silence. Then a heavy sigh. 'All right. You'll have a bazooka.'

'You're all heart, Joe. With spare rockets.'

Another sigh. 'With spare rockets.'

'I love you. Fair Cay out.'

She switched off the set, and gazed at the

two men.

'Have you ever fired a bazooka?' Billy asked.

'No. But I've read up about it. Guns, firearms, are my business.'

'So he'll arm you, but he won't actually help you. As I've always said...'

'Then do me a favour and don't say it again. This job of yours ... can it wait?'

'No.'

'Give me a reason why not.'

'Right now we know where Edel is. We don't know for how long he's going to stay there. But we do know that he has been paying regular visits to Buenos Aires for meetings.'

'You mean with the Argentine government?'

'Not so far as we can tell, although they could be intermediaries. As I told you, our man there has to keep a very low profile; at this moment British agents are about as popular in Argentina as Soviet agents are in North America. All surveillance has to be carried out from a distance, and be absolutely discreet. If Edel were to be alerted that we had tracked him and went to the police our man would almost certainly be deported.'

'Poor fellow. But what makes you feel that Edel may move on, all of a sudden?'

'Simply that the impression our man has formed is that he is trying to sell these people something, and he has only one thing to sell: his knowledge and his memory. Whether they are representing international business, or another country, or, as I suggested could be possible, the Argentinian government, or worst of all scenarios, an international crime syndicate, once he concludes a deal he is lost to us. They'll either get him out of the country or put him under such wraps not even you will be able to reach him.'

'And to think that once you had the right to hang him, and passed it up. Don't tell me, you've turned your back on that sort of thing, until it becomes absolutely necessary. I hope you bear that in mind when London is blown up.'

'I'm sure someone will,' Billy agreed

'So solve my problem. I can't leave the cay undefended.'

'I'll defend the cay,' Clive said.

UNWELCOME COMPANY

They both stared at him, open-mouthed.

'You?' Anna asked. 'But—'

'You?' Billy asked. 'What—'

'In answer to your question, Anna, I am still perfectly capable of handling what is essentially a field operation. It so happens that I have actually fired a bazooka. And in reply to yours, Billy, if you want Edel badly enough, you'll just have to give me another fortnight's leave.'

'Well...'

'So, in the circumstances,' Clive went on, 'the sooner we get it done the better. You agree, Anna?'

'Absolutely. If it's possible.' She looked at Billy.

'Oh,' Clive said, 'I'm quite sure he has all the necessary in that attaché case of his.'

'I have all the information we possess on Edel and his habits and whereabouts, yes.'

'And the fee?'

'I have in my bag forty thousand dollars in cash. We presumed that would be the most acceptable to you, Anna.'

'You presumed correctly. Now, this information.'

'You will make your way to Pont del Mar, and there contact a Mr Philip Lustrum. He is a British citizen, working in the construction industry there, and is retained by us for certain tasks. Here is his telephone number.' He pushed a slip of paper across the desk. 'He has been keeping Edel under surveillance, and will be able to tell you everything you wish to know.'

'What does he know about me?'

'Nothing, save that we will inform him that you have been sent from London to replace him in keeping an eye on Edel.'

'Identification?'

He delved into his attaché case and produced a passport. 'He will be informed of your name: Anna O'Rourke.'

'Oh, for God's sake. When are you going to run out of Os?' She opened the little book. 'That photo is getting out of date.' But it had the necessary visas, US, Argentine ... and Chilean and Uruguayan.

She looked up.

Billy was watching her. 'As I said, we don't want to know what you're doing, but it did occur to us that you might wish to leave the country in a hurry, and those are your nearest neighbours. We did not think you'd want one for Brazil. We also felt that you might require to change identities, as we understand you did to get out of Mexico, but without, of course, reverting to your new name of Fitzjohn. Therefore here is another passport, in the name of Anna O'Reilly.' He held it out.

Anna opened it, refraining from commenting.

'You'll see it also has all the necessary visas.'

'Your efficiency terrifies me.'

'Yes, well, please remember not to mix them up. It's O'Rourke on your way in and inside Argentina, and O'Reilly on your way out and back.'

Anna stuck out her tongue at him.

'And you trust this fellow Lustrum not to blow the whistle?' Clive asked.

'He has no whistle to blow. As far as he knows she is coming purely to assess the situation. There will be nothing to indicate to anyone else that Anna is working for us. She is a tourist who is breaking no laws, so far as he knows.'

'He will, after this fellow Edel is found dead.'

'We are assuming that by the time that happens, Anna will have left the country. At which time, if he were to attempt to relate her visit to Edel's death and then to us, we would disclaim ever having known him.'

'I wonder if he understands that,' Anna remarked.

'Whether he does or not is no concern of yours. I would suggest that once you have obtained whatever you wish from him, you drop him.'

'You do realize,' Anna said, 'that you are using the present tense as regards what he does, and does not know.'

'Well...' Billy flushed.

'I see. Another of your pre-emptive strikes.'

'We felt quite sure that you would accept the commission.'

'You are a bastard.'

'Absolutely.'

'So tell us how she gets there and gets out,' Clive said.

'That,' Baxter said, 'is her business. I said we don't want to know.'

'Just as you won't want to know when she is taken and hanged.'

They both looked at Anna.

'I know the drill,' she said.

'So when do you want to leave?'

'The day after tomorrow.'

'Eh?'

'The sooner it's done, the better. All I need now is to be sure that you know everything about how the island works.'

'I really am most appreciative of your enthusiasm to get the job done,' Billy said. 'But there is one small matter outstanding.'

They both looked at him.

'I do not have with me the carte blanche you require.'

'But the carte blanche only applies to the cay,'

Clive pointed out. 'Anna has no protection at all off the cay, save her own brains and skill. So you see, Billy, if I am left alone here to look after her home and family, and I have to shoot someone in doing so, I am the one who will be prosecuted. Then it seems to me you will be in the position that's bothering Joe Andrews. No one will still know anything about Anna, but it is sure to come out that I am an MI6 agent, and that will blow wide open an entirely different can of worms. I can see it now. Questions in Parliament: what is a senior MI6 operative doing, shooting people on a remote Bahamian island? If all goes according to Anna's plan, blowing them up with a bazooka. Front page news, wouldn't you say?'

'You also are a bastard,' Billy commented.

'Well,' Clive said. 'I work for you.'

'But in the circumstances,' Anna said. 'Much as I have enjoyed your company, I think *you* should be the one to leave tomorrow.'

They walked along the beach, barefoot, hand in hand while the dogs frolicked in the shallows. Billy had gone off to Nassau with Tommy early, and they had completed another, detailed, tour of the island, taking in its every aspect. Anna had reintroduced Clive to every member of her staff, told them he was their 'borse' while she was away.

'Even so... I feel a real shit,' she said, 'giving you all this responsibility. And at such short notice.'

'Don't you think I can handle it?'

'Of course I think you can handle any, well, normal crisis. But ... well...'

'What abnormal crisis are you worrying about? You say it's too early for a hurricane.'

'There's not a lot anyone can do about a hurricane. The boys know how to put up the storm shutters, and Tommy will secure the boat. Then it's just a matter of sitting it out.'

'And you're sure the boat will be all right?'

'If she's properly secured, and if everything I've read and been told is correct, yes. That dock has apparently stood up to a hurricane before; the real menace is the storm surge, but it's as sheltered as any of the "hurricane holes" they have around here. As I told you the other day, apparently the worst weather comes from the north-east, and we're protected not only by that row of islands behind us, but by a couple of miles of quite shallow water. We're more vulnerable from the north-west, and that could cause a lot of damage, but there again, any surge, to get at the boat, has to get over the reef and cross the entire island, and there are a lot of obstacles in the way.' She smiled. 'Including the houses.'

'So what's on your mind?'

'Well ... those people may indeed come back mob-handed.'

'And you don't think I can cope with that. While you could.'

'Let's say I have a little more experience than you, at being outnumbered.'

'I was with you at that shoot-out with the Russians outside Eisenach, remember? And I pulled you out of that mess in Brazil, remember?'

'I do. Joe was there too. And you both did your bit. But—'

'You did most of it. I know. Just as I know your secret. You never hesitate, you always shoot to kill, and you never miss.'

'That's why I'm here.' She kicked sand with her toes.

'If the chips go down, here, I'll try to follow your example.'

'You'll have to do more than *try*, Clive.'

'You changing your mind about marrying me?'

'I'm the one who should be asking you that.'

'You're the unique personality. I'm just a hanger-on.' He paused, to hold up his arms protectively as the dogs came out of the sea and began to shake. 'Like these two. Will they really go for anyone I tell them to?'

'Yes,' Anna said. 'They will. But you can only use them as a last resort. They're more important to me as pets than as guard dogs. Your strength is first of all the bazooka. You said you'd fired one?'

'Yes, I have. Do you really think Joe is going to let you have one?'

'His hands may be tied by his rules of engagement, but he has a vested interest in keeping me alive. And don't forget that you also have that riot gun. It has a seven-shot magazine, and the pump action is so smooth you can empty the lot in ten seconds. I keep it loaded with three scattershot and four solid. If the buckshot doesn't discourage the opposition, hit them with the hard stuff. You have five hundred cartridges in the box in the library, half buck and half solid. But remember, the only way they can get at us is by boat. The bazooka is to sort that out.'

'You know that it only has a range of about three hundred yards?'

'That's far enough. Any boat coming within three hundred yards of my dock, uninvited, should be regarded as hostile.'

'You're serious about this, aren't you?'

'Yes, I am, Clive. And you have to be serious too.'

'I know. Anna ... you *are* coming back?'

'Don't I always?'

'I think the correct word would be haven't. Have you any idea as to how you're going to handle this? A plan of campaign?'

'I can't make a plan of campaign until I get there and have a look around.'

'You reckon this fellow Lustrum Billy mentioned will be of help?'

'I'm hoping so. Although I have to remember that he cannot be involved, and that even our meetings have to be totally secret. My real secret is surprise. I know I turn men on, and quite a few women, too. And I know that no one even considers that someone looking like me could ever be lethal, or want to be. That has even applied to people who should have known better.'

'So you reckon you can get close enough to Edel to do the job. It's afterwards that matters.'

'Afterwards always matters, more than before. There have been so many big crimes that have been meticulously planned and flawlessly carried out ... and collapsed afterwards because of human frailty, human greed, human carelessness or just plain human stupidity.'

'And none of those will be involved where you are concerned.'

She smiled. 'Not if I'm working alone.'

'So you obviously have something in mind.'

'Of course. But like I said, I can't make any sort of concrete plan until I get there. Just let's say, that living on this cay and using *Fair Girl* has given me a whole new perspective on life.'

Anna, Clive and her parents sat around the dining table after dinner. 'I'm leaving tomorrow morning at noon,' she told them. 'Tommy and I will cross direct to Miami. That's an eighteen-hour trip, so we'll get in at dawn. There I will disappear, and Tommy will bring the boat back. He will have on board that extra gear we asked for, Clive. When I return to Miami, I will call you from there.' She looked around their faces, which were all very grim.

'Now,' she went on, 'supposing I don't come back...'

'Oh, Anna,' Jane said. 'Do we have to go through that again?'

'I'm afraid we do, Mama. You and Papa may know the drill. But now Clive is involved, and the whole set-up is slightly different. Mama and Papa are my sole beneficiaries,' she explained. 'But I would like you to be, also.'

'Of course I can't muscle in on their inheritance,' he protested.

'I wish you to, and I am sure they will have no objection. The current income is something more than half a million dollars a year. It varies, because as I can't spend even a fraction of that amount no matter how hard I try, the surplus is constantly being reinvested, so that the capital is constantly growing. In any event, my accountant, Paul Stattler, will be here in a couple of weeks. If by any chance I'm not back, I have left a note on my desk instructing him to give you all the gen and bring you up to date, and also instructing him that you, with Mama and Papa, will take over complete control of my investments and capital. However, I don't recommend that you tamper with any of his arrangements, as long as the income keeps coming in. Now, I don't have the time to see my lawyer in Nassau and make a new will, but I wouldn't want to do that anyway; I would prefer to keep our private arrangements private. So, Mama and Papa, in the event of my death, I wish a fifth of my income to go to Clive.'

'Anna!' Clive protested. 'You're talking about a hundred thousand dollars a year!'

'I hope it will be more than that.'

Jane squeezed Clive's hand. 'We will do as Anna wishes. You have our word.'

He drank some brandy.

'Now for the potential problem,' Anna said, 'As you know, my capital and my income is managed by the CIA. I have no reason not to trust them, and certainly not Joe, as in normal circumstances, if I were to disappear it would almost certainly be as a result of working for him. This is different, and I'm sure you wouldn't want Joe to know about the Edel business any more than I would. Apart from being top secret, it's something in which he may feel he should be involved. So if I disappear, the conclusion must be that I paid a visit to Nassau and these heavies, whoever they are, got to me. That should at least put a load on his conscience. Incidentally, I am expecting him to come back to us with some info on these people, whoever they are. You'll have to field that, Clive. Again, tell him that I've gone to Nassau for the day. Same thing if he calls again before I get back. If he gets the impression that I'm miffed and simply don't want to speak to him, well, he wouldn't be so far wrong.' She smiled brightly at their sombre faces. 'Now, I'm off to bed.' She held out her hand for Clive.

'Come in, Luis,' Don Giovanni invited. 'You didn't meet Mr Botten.'

'My pleasure, Mr Ravanelli.' Botten was a tall, cadaverous man, with matching features.

'Mr Botten.' Luis did not take the extended hand, sat in the chair before the desk.

'Mr Botten,' Don Giovanni said, 'is looking for an update on the Fehrbach dame. This countess. I've been telling him how we worked out that she was responsible for that mass killing in Mexico City, and that gave us a lead. Now—'

'We have her,' Luis said.

'Say, that's great,' Botten said. 'You mean you've carried out the hit? You have the proof we want?'

'We haven't done it yet.'

Botten raised his eyebrows.

'Softly softly catchee monkey,' Luis explained. 'I have one of our best women on it.'

'You sent a woman, after Fehrbach?'

'I said, she's one of our best. And she found her, quickly enough. She's living in the Bahamas.'

'In the Bahamas,' Botten said thoughtfully. 'You mean Nassau.'

'If I'd meant Nassau, I'd have said, Nassau,' Luis pointed out. 'She has a home in one of the Out Islands.'

'Of which I believe there are seven hundred.'

'Sure. She owns one of them.'

'Which one?'

Luis gave a cold smile. 'This is our job, Mr Botten.'

'So it is,' Botten said, equably. 'So when do you reckon it'll be done?'

'Should be any day now. You understand that we have to move carefully. The Bahamas are a British colony. We don't have any clout there, any pull with either the local police or the local politicians. So the job has to be slick. In and out. That means, a careful examination of the ground where we'll operate.'

'So?'

'Our woman made a positive ID on this Fehrbach six days ago. She telephoned me the next day to give me the gen. I told her to hire a boat and go out and look at this cay and report back on what she found and what she might need to complete the job. We don't take risks, Mr

Botten. We're professionals.'

'So what did she have to say?'

'We haven't heard from her yet.'

'Let me get this straight, Mr Ravenelli. You told this woman to go and take a look at this cay five days ago, right?'

'That's what I said.'

'How long was this recce supposed to take?'

'Only a few hours. The cay is quite close to Nassau.'

'So she would have been there and back in a day.'

'That's what she said.'

'So we're talking about four days ago, right? And she hasn't reported back. That doesn't strike you as odd?'

'Well, yeah. She should've come back to me by now.'

'And you haven't chased her up.'

'We've been kind of tied up the last few days,' Don Giovanni explained. 'Family business.'

'But you know where she's staying, in Nassau.'

'Yes.'

'Well, you could call her now,' Botten suggested.

'What's bugging you? I said, she's one of the best.'

'I'd take it as a favour. I need some kind of a progress report, for my principal.'

Luis looked at his father, and received a shrug of the massive shoulders. He picked up the phone on the desk and put the call through. The three men waited, regarding each other with varying degrees of disfavour.

'Hi there,' Luis said. 'You have a Miss Strezzi staying with you. I'd like to speak with her.' He listened, a frown slowly gathering between his eyes. 'Slow down, slow down. What d'you mean, disappeared? ... Holy shit! Wasn't there a search? ... Look, pal, a boat can't just disappear. What are the police doing about it? ... The Bermuda Triangle? Don't give me any of that shit ... OK, OK ... What? Why should I? She ain't no relative of mine ... No, I won't give you my name and address. Piss off!'

He slammed the phone down and glared at his father and then at Botten. 'What a fuck-up.'

'Do I gather,' Botten said mildly, 'that your young lady has gone astray?'

'Like if she never existed, save that some of her gear is still in her hotel room, and the bill hasn't been paid.'

'So what exactly happened?' his father asked.

'Nobody knows. Seems she hired this fishing boat for the day last Sunday, went off in it, and never came back. The police went out to see if they could spot her, but they didn't even know in which direction she'd gone. You ever heard of the Bermuda Triangle?'

'It's a legend,' Botten said.

'Yeah. Well, seems boats and planes do disappear around there from time to time. So...' He looked at his father. 'What the shit do we do now? Today is Thursday. Where the hell can she have got to? All she had to do was take a look at this island and report back. So where has she gone? What's she doing?'

'I can tell you where she has gone, Mr Ravanelli,' Botten said. 'In fact, I can tell you where she now is, give or take a few miles.'

'How the shit can you know that?'

'Let's say that I can make an educated guess. Your young lady is at the bottom of the sea, together with her boat, somewhere between Nassau and this cay she was supposed to be investigating.'

'You have got to be joking. She was taking Paolo with her.'

'Paolo being one of your best men, I assume.'

'Yeah, he is. And he used to be a professional seaman.'

'Just as, no doubt, he used to be alive.'

Luis looked about to explode. 'Just what the shit are you trying to say?'

'I wonder if you'd bear with me while I tell you a little story.' He looked from face to face. 'It concerns Anna Fehrbach. As you know, she used to belong to the SS. Actually, this was a branch of it, called the SD, the Sicherheitsdienst, the most secret of all the German secret services. Her profession was assassin, and she was the best they had.'

Both Ravanellis were looking sceptical, but he continued urbanely. 'You can forget what I told you about her collecting Jews for the gas chambers. Her work was more specialized than that. Just before the German invasion of Russia in 1941, she was in Moscow, her brief to assassinate Stalin. The NKVD caught her before she could bring that off, and locked her up in the Lubianka to await trial. She escaped, the only person ever to do so, and left behind her two very senior officials, dead. Later that year, the NKVD tracked her to Washington, and sent a squad of six to arrest her and take her back to Moscow for execution. Again she disappeared, and the six agents were all found, dead. They caught up with her again in Warsaw in 1944. This time they had a squad of twelve. She shot six of them, dead, before the rest got away, without her. When the Soviets were about to take Berlin, they caught her trying to escape. But they couldn't hold her, and three more went the way of all flesh. After the war ended, she disappeared again, but they found her again, in Scotland. Four agents, four more dead bodies. Again she disappeared, but they located her in Brazil. Four more in the morgue. Next, she returned to Germany to collect some money she'd left behind at the end of the war. This time she had some friends with her, so that when the NKVD, who by then had become the MGB, found out what she was doing, they sent twenty-two picked men after her. That meant twenty-two more dead. Like I said, she had support on that occasion, so maybe she didn't do them all herself, but no one has any doubt she did most of them. Then, only a couple of days later, when another four-man squad caught up with her in Geneva, Switzerland, they also went.'

He paused to look at their faces, which were revealing total consternation. Luis was the first to recover; he had majored in Maths at college, and had been keeping count. 'You telling us this dame has been responsible for fifty-one killings?'

'No. I am telling you that this woman has killed fifty-one *Russian* agents, so far. God alone knows how many she's put away besides those, not to mention the five in Mexico City.'

'Shit!' Don Giovanni commented.

'And you sent a woman and an itinerant sailor to do the job,' Botten said, contemptuously.

'They were only supposed to check the place out,' Luis said, defensively.

'Well, they must've overplayed their hand. So we're forced to conclude you guys just aren't up to it. They said you're the best in the business. Well, give me back my money and the photo and I'll go elsewhere.'

'Strezzi had the photo with her,' Luis muttered.

'Oh, for God's sake! That's the only one we had. But you have the name she's using, and the address. Let me have it.'

Luis looked at his father.

'Don't let's be hasty about this, Mr Botten,' Don Giovanni said. 'OK, so we underestimated the opposition and fouled up. But now we know what we're up against, we can handle it.'

'You'll need an army.'

'We can raise an army. But ... it'll cost us, to bring in outside help.'

'How much?'

'Another ten grand should swing it. Can you manage that? If you want this dame badly enough.'

Botten regarded him for several minutes. Then he nodded. 'You'll get your other ten thousand.

But just remember, the whole lot is on loan, until the job is completed.'

'We understand that.'

'So when will it happen?'

'We'll need a couple of days to set things up.'

'A couple of days.' Botten got up. 'The extra ten will be delivered tomorrow morning. And I'll see you in a week's time.'

He left the office. 'What an asshole,' Luis commented. 'Who the hell does he think he is, reading us the riot act? I'm surprised you let him get away with it, Pa.'

'Dummo,' Don Giovanni commented. 'This guy ain't no itinerant with a grudge. He's working for the Russian government.'

'Eh?'

'It's as plain as the nose on your face. How do you think he got all that data on this countess's record? Well, the last thing we need is a bunch of MGB heavies turning up on our doorstep.'

'Well, say, can't we hand the whole thing over to the Feds? They're not going to look too kindly on a bunch of Reds muscling in in this country.'

'Listen,' his father said 'If there is one thing I've learned from my years in this business, it's that you don't buck no governments. We've always got along fine because we get on with the cops. We don't bother them, and they don't bother us, and if the going gets too rough there's always someone willing to take a backhander. If we ever get involved with the Feds, we're done. And if we ever fall out with Stalin's lot, we're even more done.' He pointed. 'You get on to Solly.'

'Solly? For Jesus' sake, Pa. We don't want to involve that asshole. He's crazy. Look, I'll handle the dame myself. I should've done it from the beginning.'

'And you'd have got yourself killed.'

'By a dame?'

'This ain't no dame you or I have ever come across before. What kind of muscle can you raise?'

'A dozen good guys, with no trouble at all.'

'The Reds had twenty-two at that shoot-out in Gemany, and it didn't do them too much good. You get hold of Solly and bring him in for a chat. He has men, he has a boat, and he knows the Bahamas.'

Despite what she had told Clive, Anna had, as always, prepared herself as meticulously as she could until she had actually seen the situation for herself, planning her wardrobe and her appearance down to the last detail. She went below as soon as they were alongside in Miami to change from her seagoing clothes. For travelling through the airport where it was still possible that the police were on the lookout for a good-looking long-haired and perhaps flamboyant blonde, she had decided entirely to reverse the pattern she had followed in leaving Mexico. Thus she wore a plain grey dress, and pinned up her hair beneath one of her slouch hats, no jewellery at all save for her crucifix, which was anyway invisible, and her plain cheap watch. Her shoes were wedges, and she carried an inexpensive cloth coat slung on her arm; May/

June was the depths of the Argentine winter, and although according to her encyclopaedia the temperature in the north never dropped much below fifty that was a lot colder than Miami or the Bahamas in high summer. Equally she wore no make-up and a cheap perfume. Her jewellery was all stowed in her shoulder bag, along with her pistol and two spare magazines as well as her gun belt and Baxter's forty thousand US dollars, not to mention her four passports and her *Fodor's Guide to South America*. She also packed her Italian sunglasses, and instead wore a pair of horn-rimmed spectacles; the glass was of course plain.

She inspected herself in the mirror, slung her shoulder bag, picked up her suitcase, and went up the companion ladder. Tommy blinked at her. 'Ma'am?'

'What do I look like, Tommy?'

'Well, ma'am...' He was embarrassed.

'Say it?'

'You remind me of a schoolmistress I had when I was a boy.'

'Tommy, you are a darling; that is exactly what I wanted you to say. Now, I want you to wait for a couple of hours; I'm expecting some goods to be delivered to the boat. As soon as you receive them, head on back to the cay. Can you manage on your own?' She knew he could, but she liked him to know she cared.

'No problem, ma'am. I'll put in to Bimini for the night, and be home tomorrow.'

'Great. The goods will probably be in three boxes, which you will deliver to Mr Bartley.'

'You got it, ma'am.'

'And I'll call you from here, when I'm ready to go home.'

'No problem, ma'am.'

She stepped ashore, carried her suitcase across to the street, and hailed a cab. 'Petersen's Bookshop, please.'

He made no comment, and she was there in a few minutes. She paid him and went inside. There were two customers, browsing. Anna went straight to the counter, where a man sat reading the *Miami Herald*. He was bald and had a big nose, and looked up without a great deal of interest. 'Yeah?'

'Would you have,' Anna asked, 'a copy of *Leaves of Grass*, signed by Whitman himself?'

He slowly lowered the newspaper, and blinked at her. 'Holy shit!'

'Please,' Anna requested.

'Yeah. Could be one in the back room. You'd better come through.'

'Thank you.' Anna carried her suitcase through a door into an inner office, remembering how, back in 1939, the Nazi spy she had dealt with in London had also operated a book shop. Nothing ever really changed, except that this man was entirely on her side.

He closed the door. 'Who're you trying to be?'

'Miss Absolutely Nobody. You see Jerry a couple of days ago?'

'Yeah. He was all shook up. What do you do to these guys?'

'I didn't know he gets seasick. He give you my

message?'

'He did. The goods are waiting for you. Two hundred five-shot magazines for your little gun. Two tommy guns with spare drums. And a bazooka with five rockets. You aiming to start a war?'

'You never know your luck.'

'So, you taking them now? They're quite a load.'

'My boat's on the dock. Can you deliver?'

'Sure. This afternoon.'

'I won't be there, but my man, Tommy Rawlings, will receive them. I wouldn't like him to know what's in the boxes.'

'You got it. You travelling on company business?'

'Private. I'll see you, Donald.'

She took a taxi to the airport, went to the Pan Am desk, and bought a ticket on the next flight to Buenos Aires.

'You stop in Belem for fuel and a crew change,' the woman said.

'Ah,' Anna said. The last time she had been in Belem, she had been on her way out of Brazil, in a hurry. But, she reflected, she had then been flying in an RAF machine, and it was very unlikely that any Rio policeman would be at Belem airport. In any event, they too would be looking for a good-looking long-haired blonde.

'Only an hour,' the woman said reassuringly. 'You'll be in BA in the morning. Now, the return flight?'

'Make it a week today.' She had no intention

of using it, but having a fixed departure date was always reassuring to local immigration officials.

'Of course, Miss O'Rourke.' She checked Anna's passport to make sure that she had a valid visa; but the three did not include Brazil. 'You understand that without a visa you will not be allowed to leave Belem airport?'

'I wasn't thinking of doing that.'

'And, ah, payment?'

'I'll pay cash.'

The woman raised her eyebrow, but took the several hundred dollar bills and, somewhat laboriously, dealt out the necessary change. 'You'll be called in an hour.'

Anna retired to a quiet corner of the huge departure lounge and hid herself behind a newspaper. She felt, as always when working, totally relaxed. If she still had no idea what she was going to, she had no doubt that she would be able to cope with it, and afterwards. Having so carefully studied both Buenos Aires and Pont del Mar, using both the encyclopaedia and *Fodor's Guide* she was already forming her plans for afterwards.

It was dark when the aircraft touched down at Belem, and she, and the other transit passengers, who were mainly South Americans of varying nationalities, were allowed to stretch their legs in an almost deserted terminal building. They were all very jolly, but to her relief, no one showed any great desire to get close to the somewhat dowdy woman with spectacles even if she was travelling on her own. And the next morning she was in Buenos Aires, where the temperature was distinctly cool. She took a taxi to the railway station, but annoyingly, she had just missed the train to Pont del Mar, which was not, as Baxter had said, a few miles south of the capital, but in fact three hundred, served by only one train a day. Again using her *Fodor's*, she checked into a good hotel and spent a quiet day. The hotel was on the front, overlooking the Parque de Diversiones and the Avenue Costanera, and from her bedroom window she could look out at the huge estuary of the River Plate. Just across there was Uruguay, but here the word 'just' meant some thirty miles, while Montevideo was over a hundred miles towards the mouth of the estuary. That suited her just fine.

Next morning she put on a red woollen dress with a side vent – as she had no idea what she was going to encounter she wore her gun belt – matching high heels, and a panama hat with a matching ribbon. To go with this colourful outfit she added her gold bar earrings and her Junghans, but left her ruby ring in her shoulder bag along with her money and spare magazines. She then stowed her false glasses and put on her winged dark ones. Her hair she left loose save for a red retaining band. An angel going to war, she thought as she smiled at herself in the mirror. She would be remembered going in. But not coming out!

When she paid her bill, in US dollars, she took the opportunity to change a couple of hundred for pesos to use as change. The train left at eight, and for the next ten hours, punctuated by several stops, Anna gazed at flat uninteresting country on her right and the sea on her left. There was no way she was going to be able to leave this country in a hurry, or at all, in safety, except by sea. She thought that her two years of owning *Fair Girl* might turn out to be the most valuable of her life.

The train was full, and now she did attract glances, but mainly because she was so obviously not an Argentinian, and this was not the tourist season. And at last one man sat beside her as she ate her lunch; there was no dining car but a man pushing a trolley with beers, soft drinks and bocadilloes; these huge, hard ham rolls took a good deal of eating, and she was concentrating on the task when she discovered that she had close company, to make room for whom all her immediate fellow travellers had obligingly moved away. She put him down as the middle thirties; he was not very tall, but had a good body and quite handsome, aquiline features to go with his black hair, although his lips were a little thin. And he exuded a good deal of confidence. 'You are going to Pont del Mar, senorita?' She was not wearing gloves, and her fingers were bare.

'Wouldn't that seem to be obvious?'

'Your Spanish is very good.'

'Thank you.'

'But the accent...?'

'I am Irish,' Anna explained.

'Ah,' he commented, as if that covered everything. 'The reason I asked about your destination is that this train does not stop in Pont del Mar.'

'I beg your pardon?'

'Oh, it stops there for tonight. But it goes further south tomorrow. It continues to Mar del Plata. Mar del Plata is a much more, how do I say, go-ahead place. Pont del Mar is just a fishing village being developed for tourism.'

'I understand. Well, senor, I am stopping in Pont del Mar.'

'You have friends there?'

'No. I am a tourist.'

'You know this is not the season?'

'I like visiting places off season. They're more real.'

'I agree with you. But you see, as it is off season, most of the hotels will be closed. But of course you have a booking.'

'I'm afraid not. Surely some will still be open?' She hadn't considered that possibility.

'It may be difficult. May I recommend one?'

'Can you?'

'The Excelsior. It is open all the year round. But it is not cheap. Will that bother you?'

'Not really.'

'I did not think it would.' Even without her ring there could be no doubting her wealth. 'If you will permit me, there is something ... special about you.'

'You say the sweetest things. What do you think is special about me?'

He shrugged. 'It is indefinable. But very present. An aura.'

'You wouldn't be trying to get fresh with me, I hope.'

'No, senorita. I would not dream of getting

fresh with you. But I would like to help you. Go to the Excelsior, and tell them it was recommended to you by Carlos Guimard.'

'Did you say Carlos?'

'It is Spanish for Charles. You do not like this name?'

'No, no. It's just that I knew a man named Carlos.'

'He must have been fortunate.'

'It was a very brief acquaintanceship.'

'You mean you did not like him. Then he was not so fortunate.'

'I never actually had time to form an opinion about him,' Anna confessed. 'We were ships that passed in the night.'

'But you obviously remember him very well. So he made an impression on you. I would like to think that I may have done so, also. Now I must leave you. Have a nice stay in Pont del Mar.' He got up. 'Perhaps I will see you again.'

'I shall look forward to that,' Anna said, not quite sure whether she was lying or not. He seemed a very pleasant and personable man, whose company could well be enjoyable ... in other circumstances. But she did not intend to be in Pont del Mar long enough to make friends.

It was dusk when the train reached Pont del Mar. Anna looked for her new friend as she disembarked, but he was not to be seen on the crowded platform. So she took a taxi to the Excelsior, where a uniformed doorman carried her bag into a sumptuous foyer.

'Good evening, senorita,' said the receptionist,

regarding her somewhat sceptically. 'You have a reservation?'

'I'm afraid not.'

'I see. Unfortunately, the hotel is full.'

'Oh! You were recommended to me by Senor Guimard.'

He stiffened. 'You were recommended by...'

'Senor Carlos Guimard. He said you would know his name.'

'Yes, senorita. Of course. Boy!' He snapped his fingers, and a bellhop hurried over. 'Number 7. If you would be so good as to sign the book, Senorita...?'

'O'Rourke.' Anna signed.

'Senorita O'Rourke. It is a very great pleasure to have you staying with us, senorita. For how long would you like the room?'

'I think about a week. Do I have to be definite?'

'Oh, no, no, no. I will put you down for a week, with an option for longer if you wish.'

'You're very sweet. Do you require payment now?'

'Oh good heavens, no, senorita. You pay when you are ready. Gerardo will take you up. The room is on the front, you understand. Overlooking the sea.'

'That sounds delightful. There is just one more thing. Is there a telephone in the room?'

'Of course.'

'And do I make the call through you, here on the desk?'

'Oh, no, no, senorita. All our room telephones can be connected direct to the exchange. Just press number nine. The call will be charged to your account. If you wish anything in the room, food, drink, laundry, anything, you will call here, that is number zero, and I will arrange it.'

'That sounds incredibly civilized.'

'Would you like me to book you a table for dinner?'

'No. I have been travelling all day and am very tired. I'll just have something in my room.'

'Of course.' He presented her with a menu. 'May I recommend the tuna? It is caught off these very shores by our very own fishermen.'

'You have a fishing fleet, here in Pont del Mar?'

'Oh, yes, senorita. Before the area began to be developed as a tourist centre, fishing was the main industry. It is still important. The fleet goes out three times a week.'

Manna from heaven. 'Then of course I will have the tuna.' She scanned the drinks list 'And a bottle of Pouilly Fuissé.'

'A bottle, senorita?'

'I wish to sleep well.'

'Of course. And when would you like this served? Nine o'clock? Ten o'clock?'

'Senor, I said that I wish to sleep well, and long.' She glanced at her watch; it was six thirty. 'Half past seven.'

'Half past seven,' he remarked, incredulously.

'Thank you.' She gave him a bright smile and followed Gerardo to the lift.

The room was palatial, and although it was now too dark to see anything from the balcony, and too chilly to stay out there for more than a few minutes, it clearly had spectacular views. Anna wondered just how much it was setting her back, but she only intended to spend a couple of days here, nor, as she would be leaving in a hurry, would she be paying the bill.

She made sure the door was locked, then sat at the desk and picked up the phone, dialling the number, which was repeated at the other end a few minutes later. 'Mr Lustrum?' she asked.

'Yes,' was the cautious reply.

'Anna O'Rourke.'

There was a moment's silence. 'I did not expect you until next week.'

'So I'm early. Does it matter? When can we meet?'

'Where are you staying?'

'I'm at the Excelsior.'

'The Excelsior? That's a very exclusive hotel.'

'So I gather. It was recommended to me by someone I met on the train. A Senor Guimard. Would you know the name? Everyone else seems to.'

Another brief silence. 'Did you say Guimard?'

'That's what I said, yes. *Do* you know the name? He seems to carry an awful amount of clout.'

'Is his first name Carlos?'

'That's right. Carlos.'

'Captain Carlos Guimard is Pont del Mar's chief of police.'

It was Anna's turn to be silent.

'Miss O'Rourke?' Lustrum asked. 'Are you all right?'

Anna's brain was racing, but she said, 'Yes, I'm all right. My meeting him had to be sheer coincidence. He was absolutely charming.'

'He is always charming,' Lustrum said. 'Even when he is pulling out your toenails.'

Anna swallowed. 'It was a coincidence,' she insisted. 'You haven't said where we can meet.'

'You mean you are going to remain here? Despite...'

'A coincidence? Really, Mr Lustrum, I have not come all this way just to turn round and go home again.'

'I cannot be involved in this.'

'Mr Lustrum, all I need from you is five minutes of your time, to put me in the picture. I was told you would provide this. If you are not prepared to do so at this late stage, I cannot answer for the attitude of my, and your, superiors in London, to whom I shall have to make a full report.'

Another silence. 'If you will walk along the waterfront tomorrow morning, just beyond the fishing dock you will come across a bar coffee shop named The Matador; we will meet there, by accident, at ten o'clock.'

'Excellent.' She had intended to walk along the front tomorrow in any event.

'How will I know you?'

'Why, Mr Lustrum, I shall be the most attractive woman there.'

She hung up, and a few minutes later her supper arrived. She ate, and drank, slowly and thoughtfully. But meeting Guimard *had* to have been purely coincidental. She had realized from the start that he was a very confident man, without deducing any real reason for the confidence. Now she had the reason, which made it entirely reasonable for him to chat up an attractive woman. But there was no possible reason for a local police chief to suspect anything sinister about an itinerant tourist.

At the same time, the pulling out of toenails bit was no help to her digestion. If she was no stranger to difficult situations, she could not forget that the only time she had had to take on a local police force on their own ground and without a back-up had been when she had been confronted by the NKVD in Moscow in 1941, and then she had wound up in the Lubianka having jets of ice cold water hurled at her naked body. She, or her corpse, would be still hanging in that never to be forgotten torture chamber but for the amazing intervention of Joe Andrews.

But such negative thinking, or allowing her brooding concern as to how a photograph of her taken by a Russian in Red Square nine years ago had got into the hands of an American female killer to occupy any of her thoughts right now, would be highly dangerous. Depending on what Lustrum had to tell her, and what the harbour could produce, she could be out of Argentina in forty-eight hours, job done.

She slept soundly, and was awake early, to the sound of church bells. Just a week ago she had encountered Lorna Strezzi! She bathed, breakfasted in her room, put on slacks and a shirt, and went for a walk, her bag slung on her shoulder;

today she was not wearing her pistol, but it was within easy reach. From her bedroom window she did indeed overlook the beach and the sea; the beach was long and luxuriant, and reminded her of Copacabana, although not on the same scale. But the first thing that struck her as she left the hotel was that the entire town appeared to be a vast building site. Cranes rose in every direction, towering over half completed edifices which were undoubtedly going to be blocks of flats, hotels and restaurants, but on a Sunday the only sound was the pealing of the bells.

In contrast the docks, reached by crossing the very elaborate foot bridge that apparently gave the place its name – the railway line and highway were about half a mile inland, where the sea inlet dwindled to nothing – seemed a relic of a bygone age, although to her surprise they were busy. The fishing boats had apparently only just returned, and were unloading their catches on to a quay crowded with eager recipients, from both food stores and restaurants, anxious for the fish to be taken to the depot for auction.

Anna watched them for some time, studying the boats and their hard-working crews. The boats were reassuringly large, far bigger than any of the Nassau smacks, with sizeable cabins, suggesting that they were intended to keep to the sea for more than a few hours. On the debit side, each had a crew of three, but she did not regard that as an insuperable obstacle.

This morning she had left her hair loose; it floated about her in the brisk on-shore wind. Thus, as she had anticipated, she attracted attention, and it was not long before one of the buyers stood beside her. 'Good morning, senorita. You are well?'

'Very well, thank you. And you?'

'Oh, very well. You like the fish, eh?'

'I like the boats.'

'Ah. You know boats?'

'No, I don't. But they fascinate me. Do you think I could meet one of the skippers? That one.' She pointed. After a couple of days at sea all the crews were unshaven, unwashed, and untidy, but the one she had selected at least looked reasonably young and good-humoured; she felt that, properly groomed, he could even be handsome.

'Ah,' her new friend said. 'Salvador. Hey, Salvador, the lady wishes to speak with you.'

Salvador looked surprised, but he said something to his two crew and then walked towards them, regarding Anna with increasing interest as he approached, before making the standard Spanish greeting. 'Buenos dias, senorita. Bien?'

To which Anna made the standard reply, as she had to the first man. 'Muy bien. Usted?'

'Si, muy bien.'

'The lady is interested in your boat,' the first man explained.

Salvador raised his eyebrows.

'It is a big boat,' Anna explained. 'Do you have to go far to catch your fish?'

'There are fish everywhere, senorita. But the further out, the better the catch, yes.'

'You have a big engine?'

'Oh, yes. It is a Gardner diesel. You know of this?'

'I have read that Gardners are the best,' Anna said fervently. 'What sort of speed does that give you?'

'Eight knots.'

'That's very good. And what about the range?'

'Oh, we have two thousand kilometres. Not that we have to go so far to find the fish, you understand.'

'Of course. But it is always good to have something in reserve.' And two thousand kilometres would be more than sufficient for her purpose. 'Would you show it to me? The engine?'

He looked her up and down, paying particular attention to her feet, but she was wearing her wedges, which had reasonably soft heels. And the breeze was flattening her shirt against her breasts, a picture as attractive as her fluttering hair; he could tell she was not wearing a brassiere. 'You understand that the boat is not clean, senorita,' said the other man. 'The fish, you know. When it is all landed, they will hose it down.'

'Well,' Anna said, 'perhaps I should come back when it has been washed. May I do that, Captain?'

'Of course, senorita.'

'And you will show me over your boat?'

'I will show you anything you wish to see, senorita.'

'That sounds very exciting. Is that a promise?'

'Of course,' he said, looking her up and down

again.

'Then shall we say ... oh! When will you sail again?'

'This morning, when the fish is landed, we clean up and then we go to church. This evening we get drunk. Tomorrow we sleep, and tomorrow evening we put to sea again. It is the season when the fish are running.'

'What an exciting life you lead. I will come to see you tomorrow. When you are awake.'

'I will be awake, senorita, whenever you come.'

'But what time do you sail?'

'We sail at dusk.'

'Well, then, I must come before dusk. You have not told me the name of your boat.'

'The name is *Bruja del Mar*. You understand this?'

'Oh, yes. In English, that is Sea Witch.'

He clearly did not understand *her*. So she added, 'Hasta la vista, senors. 'Dios.'

She left the two men muttering at each other; she had a pretty good idea what they were saying. If the captain obviously could not believe his luck, his friend was equally warning him to be careful about going too far with an – judging by her clothes and jewellery and general appearance – obviously rich tourist, even if out of season, and who, equally obviously, was so innocent as to be slightly fey. But she had an idea the skipper's lust would prove a more powerful factor than caution.

She strolled along the dock and soon spotted the

sign, El Matador. The interior was gloomy, and did not smell a great deal better than the dock. There were three male customers seated at a table, and a solitary bartender. All their heads turned as she appeared. 'Good morning,' she said brightly. 'Is it possible to have a cup of coffee?'

'You want a cup of coffee?' the bartender asked.

'I think that's what I said,' Anna pointed out.

'Then you sit, eh? I will bring it.'

'That is terribly kind of you.' Anna chose a table on the far side of the room from the three men, sat down and crossed her legs, the shoulder bag now resting in her lap. The machine gurgled and a few minutes later the bartender brought her a large cup of black coffee. 'You want sugar?'

'Thank you.'

He was obviously not offering any milk, but returned a moment later with a bowl of coagulated brown sugar in which a spoon was stuck. Anna estimated that it had been there for several days, except when temporarily withdrawn to stir other cups of coffee. On the other hand, her cup was still boiling hot, so she supposed whatever was on the spoon would not do her too much damage.

'You want brandy?'

As she knew that this was a Spanish habit even at half past nine in the morning, she said, 'Why not? You have cognac?'

'Cognac?'

'Ah. Well...'

'This is made here,' he said proudly.

Then it obviously was unlikely to be made from grapes, she reflected. 'You mean you make your own, here in this bar? Or upstairs in the bathtub? You do have a bathtub?'

He regarded her for some seconds, then suddenly grinned. 'Senorita makes the joke.'

'I know, it's a bad habit I have. Bring on your Argentinian brandy.'

He returned a moment later with a small glass. 'This is made from the plum. You drink this...'

'And I'll get hair on my chest. That's what bothers me. Salut!' She tasted, and suppressed a shudder. But actually, it wasn't all that bad.

The bartender gathered that he had been dismissed, and wandered off. She sipped the brandy and the coffee alternately, watching the doorway. At five to ten a man appeared, and the morning, which had been going quite well, took a sudden turn for the worse. The man entering the bar, wearing a crushed suit and a greasy fedora, with a tie that had clearly not been removed during his last meal, was small and narrow-shouldered, with matching features. Anna was quite prepared to accept that men came in all shapes and sizes, but this one reminded her irresistibly of the Gestapo agent, Feutlanger, who had once tried to torture her. She could feel her hackles rising.

Having looked around the room, the little man advanced to stand above her and blink at her. 'Miss O'Rourke?' His tone was incredulous.

'That's what it says on my passport,' Anna

acknowledged. 'And you, I assume, are Lustrum.'

He sat down, and snapped his fingers. 'You unhappy with that?' He switched to English.

'Not really.' Anna also switched languages. 'It's just that you remind me of someone.'

The bartender had arrived, and Lustrum ordered coffee and brandy. 'You make that sound as if you didn't like this guy,'

'Actually, I loathed him.'

'Oh. Still, I guess you can't choose who you have to work with.'

'That is very true.'

'And you aim to take over watching Edel? For how long? He'll spot you a mile away. And you're not resident. And if Guimard has his teeth into you, you're liable to wind up being deported. After a session in one of his cells. He'll enjoy messing about with you.'

Anna gazed at him, and he flushed. Then she gave one of her bright smiles. 'That is no longer your concern. After this morning, you will never see me again, and thus, happily, I will not see you. What I require from you is the information that our mutual employers tell me you possess. You have the address where Edel is living.'

'I've written it down for you.' He felt in his pocket and gave her a folded piece of paper that was every bit as stained as his tie.

Anna opened it; at least the handwriting was reasonable legible. 'Seven Calle Victoriana.' She refolded it, and put it in her shoulder bag. 'What is it?'

'I told you. It is where he lives.'

'I understand that. But is it a flat, or a house, or what?'

'It is a flat.'

'In what sort of building?'

'It is a new block. Quite up-market. He seems to be well-off.'

'There's a relief. What floor?'

'The fifth.'

'And is there a lift?'

'Yes. But it doesn't always work. What, you aiming to get that close?'

'I know: he'll spot me a mile away. Now, I assume he has some kind of help in the place.' The way her plan was working out, the job would have to be carried out in the middle of the day.

'There is a woman who goes in every morning.'

That was a relief.

'But she is only to clean,' Lustrum said.

'You mean he cooks his own meals. Or does he eat out?' A possible complication.

'No, no. His wife does the cooking.'

'His *wife*?'

'You did not know that he has a wife?'

'No,' Anna said. That bastard Baxter had not mentioned that small detail. Although perhaps he had not known. 'This wife is Argentinian, right?'

'No, no. I believe she is Danish.'

'Are you saying that he met and married a Danish woman, here in Argentina? My information is that he only left England a couple of months ago.'

'That is correct. But his wife was already here, waiting for him. Frankly, it's my opinion that she knew he was going to escape. As far as I have been able to discover, she has lived here for several months, waiting for him to arrive.'

Therefore Baxter *must* have known about it. She had a strong temptation just to catch the next plane out of here. But the mere fact that Edel had a wife did not mean that he was any the less a threat to mankind. In fact, if she had been waiting for him to escape, and had a home waiting for him here, she was almost certainly part of whatever he was up to.

'But she's not too difficult to avoid,' Lustrum went on. 'She takes the kid to school every morning, spends most of the rest of the day out, and then picks him up again every afternoon.'

INCIDENT IN ARGENTINA

Anna felt as if she had been kicked in the stomach. 'Did you say, kid?' she asked in a low voice.

'I guess you didn't know about that either,' Lustrum observed, with some satisfaction.

'What sort of kid?'

'A boy.'

'Age?'

'Well, I don't know that, for sure. Somewhere about six, I'd say.'

'Six. And you say she picks him up from school every afternoon. What school?'

'The Convent of the Sacred Heart. It's only a ten-minute walk from the apartment block. You going to tell me what the real score is?' He grinned. 'With the wife and kid?'

Anna stood up. 'You can pay for the drinks. And have a nice day.'

She left the bar and returned to the hotel, picking up a street plan at the desk before going straight up to her room, throwing her hat and bag on a chair, kicking off her shoes, and lying full length across the bed, head buried in her hands.

It had all been so simple. That was the trouble. It had been too simple. Simply knock on the door, do the job, and leave again. But the timing had to be perfect, so that she arrived on the dock just fifteen minutes before the fishing boat was due to leave. That meant ... she sat up and unfolded the plan. The Calle Victoriana was about half a mile from the dock, therefore if she left the building at half past five she should make it comfortably. So simple. But the kid, and his mother, would surely be home at half past five. Billy Baxter, she thought, I am going to wring your goddamned neck. Supposing she ever had the opportunity.

She did not feel like seeing people, so she rang down for a room service lunch, sticking to the fish as it was more digestible and her stomach was feeling distinctly tender. But a couple of glasses of wine helped, then she pushed the trolley into the corridor, locked her door, and went to bed.

She was up soon after three, dressed in her most casual gear and wore her hair in a bandanna, and went for a walk. At four o'clock on a Sunday afternoon the town seemed totally somnolent; she strolled along the Calle Victoriana, pausing every so often to admire the architecture, such as it was, and paused for a few moments in front of number seven, which appeared, as Lustrum had suggested, to be both new and fairly upmarket. She was about to cross for a closer look when a woman and child came along the street, both very smartly dressed, and clearly having just left church. Anna immediately deduced that this had to be Edel's wife, because she was blonde, not unattractive, with high cheekbones, and an expression of utterly sad resignation. She did not look the sort of person she would ever wish to kill. And the little boy was a charmer, skipping along the pavement, constantly chattering, although Anna could not hear what he was saying. Nor did his mother pay too much attention to him.

They reached the apartment, and disappeared inside, the mother using her latchkey. Anna gave them a few moments, then wandered across the street and checked the list of names. Edel was on the fifth floor, as Lustrum had promised. And there was a bell beside each name. That seemed simple enough.

She surveyed the street. At four thirty it remained empty. But this was a Spanish-oriented social system; people would just be waking up from their siestas. And sure enough, as she continued her walk, the town gradually came to life, bars opening and being filled with custom. Whether or not this would prove to be a help or a hindrance remained to be seen.

She returned to the hotel, had a room service supper, and considered the situation. She had no doubt that the job had to be done. But it had to be done without endangering either mother or child. Or herself, more than was inevitable. But ideas were already filling her brain.

As usual, she slept soundly, had a late breakfast, pushed the trolley into the corridor, hung out a Do Not Disturb sign and locked the door, then had a leisurely bath – there was no saying when she would be able to have another – and was just drying herself when there was a tap on the door. She pulled on a dressing gown, feeling distinctly irritated, unlocked the door, pulled it open. 'Can't you read the—?' She stepped back in consternation.

'Oh!' Carlos Guimard looked her up and down; he could tell that she was wearing nothing under the dressing gown. 'I am intruding.'

He was wearing uniform, which included a pistol holster on his belt, and several medal ribbons on his left breast. Anna got her brain into gear. 'I was having a bath.'

'I am most terribly sorry. This is unforgivable of me. But ... ah ... may I come in?'

'One should never argue with the chief of police.' She stepped back, and he entered the room, closing the door behind him; the latch clicked into place. 'Is this an official visit?'

'I just happened to be passing, and thought I

should stop by and see that you were comfortable.'

'Oh,' Anna said. 'And here was I thinking you came to pull out my toenails.'

'Eh?'

'Just a joke. Do sit down.' She did so herself, allowing the dressing gown to fall away so that her legs were exposed from her thighs to her feet. This was another ploy that had been advantageous in the past when enduring a possibly hostile interview.

Guimard took the other chair in the room, arranging it so that he exactly faced her without the table in the way. 'People have been telling tales about me.'

'Only that you are the chief of police. And that's what policemen do, isn't it?'

'Is that what your police in Ireland do?'

'Absolutely. The number of people in Ireland without toenails is astronomical.'

He studied her for several seconds. 'The senorita is very fond of her little jokes.'

'Well, I'm Irish, you see.'

'I think you are enchanting.'

Anna suppressed a grimace, as she remembered Roberto Capillano. And Adolf Hitler.

'You do not like to be told that?' Guimard continued to study her.

'A woman always likes to be complimented.'

'That is true. I would like you to have lunch with me.'

'Today?'

'You have another appointment?'

'Ah ... no, no. Of course not. But I will have to

get dressed.'

'Of course. And I have my duties to attend to. My car will call for you at two.'

'Two?' Anna could not prevent her voice going up an octave.

'You would prefer it to be later? Just name the time that would suit you.'

'I would prefer it to be one.'

'One o'clock? You wish to eat at one o'clock?'

'Well, you see, my stomach hasn't yet got used to your habits. If I don't eat until two I will be biting holes in the carpet.'

'What an entrancing vision that conjures up. But I would not wish to upset your stomach. My car will call for you at a quarter to one, and I will take the afternoon off, so that we can spend the rest of the day together, eh?'

Shit, Anna thought. Shit, shit, shit. She said, 'That sounds absolutely delightful. But are you sure your wife will not object?'

'I do not have a wife, senorita.'

'Oh.'

'Do you have a husband?'

'Well, actually, not right this minute. I am divorced.' Which was perfectly true: Ballantine Bordman had divorced her, in absentia, back in 1940, when he had discovered who and what she was.

'Well, then –' he got up and bent over her hand – 'I will be counting the minutes.'

Anna closed and locked the door, then leaned against it while she considered the situation. Clearly the captain was thinking of taking her somewhere after lunch, with sex in mind. And Spanish, and therefore she estimated, Argentinian lunches, were usually lengthy affairs in any event. But supposing the meal lasted until four, there would still be time to visit Edel and reach the dock by a quarter to six. To accomplish that she would have to decline his invitation to move on from the meal, which would undoubtedly disappoint him, and he did not strike her as the sort of man who would readily accept disappointment. On the other hand, there was a simple solution, one that she had used often enough in the past, and it could be sweetened by a promise that the moment her period was over she would happily get together with him. As he would certainly know that she was booked into the hotel for at least a week, there was no reason for him to disbelieve her.

She wore her red dress, but as she still could not conceive that Guimard had any plans other than to get his hand into her knickers, left her pistol in her shoulder bag, along with her gun belt. Equally, however, as she was about to leave the hotel for the last time, she packed her pants and shirt and wedges and bandanna also in her shoulder bag, along with her spare magazines, her money and her passports, but wore all of her jewellery. As usual, the rest of her clothes would have to be abandoned. There was just one thing left to do. She sat at the table, used a sheet of the hotel stationery, and wrote rapidly, using a large and very clear hand, then folded the paper and placed it also in her shoulder bag.

Satisfied, she brushed her hair but left it loose,

not bothering with a hat. Then she sat down and waited, as usual keeping her mind deliberately blank; from here on she had to take every moment as it came.

At five to one her phone rang. 'Senorita O'Rourke, there is a car here for you.'

'Thank you. I'll be right down.' She got up, put on her coat, pulled on her gloves, and surveyed herself in the mirror. She looked good enough to eat; she could only hope that was not what the captain had in mind.

A uniformed policeman was waiting for her, and the hotel staff were clearly intrigued. He saluted and escorted her to a police car. She sat in the back, and watched the blocks and the building sites rolling by; gradually thinning in number; with every second she was being taken farther away from both the docks and Edel's apartment.

She leaned forward. 'May I ask, senor, where you're taking me?'

'To the captain's villa, senorita.'

Oh, good lord, she thought. If this was some kind of luncheon party... 'And the villa is in the country?'

'No, no, senorita. It is just outside of town. We will soon be there.'

Soon being a relative word. Anna reckoned they were at least five miles from the front when the car pulled into a concrete drive, the gate of which was roofed. 'We are here.'

She was not surprised to see that it was a luxurious house, and very obviously newly built, fronted by a veranda on the lower floor and a balcony above it, this outside, she guessed, the master bedroom; as the building was situated on a slight rise, she also guessed that the upper floor had a view of the sea beyond the town.

The gate was opened for them by another uniformed policeman, and the car drew up on the paved patio outside the front steps. Guimard was waiting – he had changed into casual civilian dress – and came down the steps to take her hands as she got out of the car. 'Senorita, you have the amazing facility of being able to appear a completely different woman every time I see you.'

'You say the sweetest things. But is that not what every woman seeks to achieve?'

'Do you know, I have never considered the matter from that point of view.' He gestured at the steps. 'My home is eager to welcome you.'

'Thank you. Does this car wait for me?'

'No, no. He cannot wait there indefinitely. I will call for a car when you are ready to leave.'

'Ah.' She allowed herself to be escorted up the steps and into a large lounge, with open windows to allow the drapes to rustle as the wind drifted through. Anna took off her gloves and her coat and Guimard laid them on a chair, then went to an elaborate sideboard. 'You'll take a glass of champagne?'

'Thank you.' Anna sat on a settee, crossing her knees and placing her shoulder bag beside her. 'What a lovely house.'

He gave her a glass and sat beside her. 'I will show you the rest of it later.'

'That would be very nice. But you say you

have no wife, and you must be a very busy man. Who looks after it for you?'

'I have a housekeeper, and various servants. But I have given them the afternoon off. I was afraid that their presence might embarrass you. But do you know, I am beginning to doubt that anything would embarrass you.'

'I try not to be. But do you mean that we are entirely alone?'

'I wished to enjoy you all to myself. Does this alarm you?'

'I don't see how I can be alarmed in the presence of the chief of police.'

'Touché. You said you like to eat at one, and it is half past. Would you like to eat now? The meal is all ready.'

'If it will not inconvenience you.'

'Not at all. Suddenly I am also impatient to eat.' He escorted her through an arched doorway into the dining room, where a large table was set with two places, the cutlery being silver, as she saw at a glance. The sideboard was a mass of hot plates, all of which emitted delicious smells. 'What would you like?'

'I think you will have to serve me,' Anna suggested. 'I have no idea what any of them are.'

'It will be a pleasure, and I will explain them to you.' Which he did as he ladled helpings on to her plate. But Anna wasn't really listening. Her instincts, born of long experience, were warning her that all was not as it seemed. She had not doubted for a moment that he intended to make a pass at her, and that it was going to be a serious pass had been revealed by the way he had carefully emptied his house of servants. She had been quite prepared to cope with this as she had planned; her sole objective was to be away from here by four o'clock, although this far out of town that would be cutting it very fine. But now she had become aware of something more. She had put him down from the moment of their first meeting as a very confident man; that had been explained by learning he was the chief of police. But she had been courted by many confident men, from Hitler and Stalin down, and they had all, certainly in their initial encounters, been as much in awe of her beauty as she of their power. This man, while saying all the right things, regarded her as already his.

The food was certainly delicious, and the wine, a red she did not recognize, very drinkable. He made small talk throughout the meal, inquiring where she intended to go after she left Pont del Mar. She suggested that she might travel further south, and have a look at Mar del Plata, but he did not seem to be terribly interested, and as soon as they had finished their dessert, some kind of unusual fruit, announced, 'Now I would like to show off the rest of my house.'

'Oh,' she said. 'I was hoping that we might have a cup of your delicious coffee.'

'I think the coffee can wait. It is always better after one has digested for a while.' He pushed back his chair and got up.

Anna obediently also rose, slinging her shoulder bag.

'Do you carry that bag everywhere?' he asked.

'It has become a habit, I suppose.'

'Or is it that you carry around all your wealth with you?'

'Not *all* of it,' Anna admitted modestly.

He indicated the stairs in the hall outside the dining room and she went up. 'On the left,' he suggested.

She entered a large bedroom. As she had supposed, it was the one with the balcony, and there was a view of the sea. She went through the open french doors. As she had suspected might be the case, Guimard might have dismissed his servants, but the armed policeman remained, seated in the shade of the roof over the gate. 'What a superb view.'

'It is good, isn't it? Let's close these.'

'Must we? The breeze is delicious.'

'It will soon turn chilly. And you see –' he closed the doors – 'they are double glazed. So that no noise can get in. And equally, no noise can get out.'

'You believe in being cosy.'

'A bedroom should always be cosy. Will you put down that absurd bag?'

Anna laid the bag on the table.

'Thank you.' He sat in an armchair, leaned back. 'Now, will you take off your dress? In fact, take off everything.'

'I beg your pardon?'

'I wish you to undress.'

This was definitely not merely a pass; it was a command. She abandoned her original feminine plan; she needed to find out what had inspired his change of attitude. 'I think you have the wrong idea, Captain. I am not a whore.'

'I never thought you were, Miss O'Rourke. But you see, I would like to ask you some questions, and I have learned, over the years, that people under interrogation are more likely to tell the truth when they are naked. Being nude robs people of complacency, and indeed, confidence.'

'You have clearly studied the matter. But shouldn't all this be happening in your office, or torture chamber, or wherever?'

'If your answers to my questions are not satisfactory, I will certainly take you to my office.' He smiled. 'To my torture chamber. But I thought, as you are clearly a refined young lady, that you would prefer to have a preliminary chat here in private. In my torture chamber, there will be other people present, you see, and you might find that embarrassing. Whereas, if you answer my questions sufficiently honestly to convince me of your innocence, you will suffer no inconvenience or embarrassment at all, save that of revealing your undoubted charms to me.'

'Innocence? Am I accused of some crime?'

'Whether you are accused or not depends on your answers to this preliminary examination.'

'But you do admit to having, and using, a torture chamber? Where you pull out people's toenails.'

Another smile. 'I do not *admit* to anything. I do not have to. I am charged with keeping the peace and eliminating crime. My methods are my own business, as long as I get the right results. As for pulling out people's toenails, that is terribly medieval, and of course, it leaves the evidence of what has been done to them. We are much more sophisticated. We use electricity. That produces instant results, and leaves no trace whatsoever. On the flesh.'

She understood that he was serious, and that he did indeed have a reason for suspecting her of ... what? Thus he simply had to be challenged, in order to find out what he had learned of her, and from whom. And if that involved ... a chief of police! But she was rapidly developing an intense dislike for him. She smiled at him. 'You mean you attach electrodes to various parts of your victim's body, preferably somewhere sensitive and attractive to you, and switch on the current.'

'I see you have read about it. That is about right. And I'm sure you understand that the idea of pushing an electrode up your ass is extremely attractive.'

'I do understand that, captain,' Anna said. 'I have experienced it.'

The humour left Guimard's face, and he sat straight. 'You have been tortured?'

Almost Anna thought he had bitten off the word, already. 'It was applied by a man called Reinhard Heydrich, you may have heard of him. And you are quite right in claiming that it leaves no marks.'

He stared at her. 'You were a prisoner of the Gestapo? You?'

'Well, no. Actually, I was employed by them. Or more accurately, the SS.'

He relaxed, slightly. 'You are lying. The SS did not employ women.'

'I see you have studied that matter as well. And again you are quite correct. But the SD did. Employ women, I mean.'

'You were SD? In what capacity?'

'I killed people,' Anna explained, and picked up her bag, at the same time opening it to draw her Walther. 'I still do. Although not for the SD, of course.'

He stared at the gun, then at her face. 'You admit this? To me? I am the chief of police.'

'Except for a few very close friends,' Anna pointed out, 'the people I admit this to never hang around long enough to give evidence against me. Now tell me how you got interested in me in the first place.'

'You think I am afraid of you? I am Captain Carlos Guimard. Mention my name to anyone in this country and they start to shake.'

'Is that why they have stuck you in a backwater like this? Come along, captain, I haven't got all afternoon.'

He snorted. 'You can't frighten me. Working for the SD! Ha! Do you actually know how to fire that thing?'

'Captain.' Anna levelled the pistol. 'Hold up your right hand.'

'What?' But he obeyed her.

'Now extend the forefinger.'

Again he obeyed, mystified.

Anna fired. Guimard uttered a scream and fell out of the chair, turning on to his hands and knees; the bullet embedded itself in the wall.

Anna moved to the window, and looked down; the sentry continued to sit, reading his newspaper. 'You are absolutely correct,' she said, 'This double glazing does keep the sound in.'

Guimard was hugging his hand, which was dripping blood. 'You shot away my finger. I am bleeding to death.'

Anna stood above him. 'I have a strong feeling that you are not going to do that. *Bleed* to death, I mean. Tell me why you wish to investigate me.'

'You must help me,' he moaned. 'I am in pain. I am bleeding.'

'I will help you, I give you my word. When you have answered my question.'

'Lustrum,' he muttered.

'What? You have arrested him?' Then she was in deeper trouble than she had feared.

'Not yet,' he groaned. 'But you telephoned him, the night you arrived.'

'And the hotel phone was tapped?'

'No, no,' he groaned. 'It is Lustrum's phone that is bugged.'

'Why? Is he a crook?'

'He is a very shady character. We have been keeping an eye on him for some time. He has links to organized crime, but he also has links to the British Embassy in Buenos Aires. Senorita, you must help me. I am bleeding. Senorita...'

'In a moment. What are these links to the British Embassy?'

'We do not know. But he goes there from time to time. There is no reason for him to do this if he is not receiving instruction or giving information.'

'But you have never actually arrested him.'

'Well no, he is a British citizen, and we have no proof of any actual wrongdoing. Senorita...'

'I am an Irish citizen. And I have broken no laws here in Argentina. Yet you arrested me.'

'Well—'

'Can that be because, unlike Lustrum, I am an attractive woman, and as you said, you felt it might be interesting to shove an electrode up my ass?'

'Senorita ... you said you will help me.'

'To stop bleeding,' Anna agreed. 'I will do that, permanently.' She shot him through the head.

What a mess, she thought. But if the police were intent on interrogating her, and probably Lustrum, she did not see that she had had any alternative. And Lustrum, as the man she had contacted immediately on getting there, was up to his ears in any event. But he would have to sink or swim on his own, and if he revealed that he was working for MI6, and so was she, that was between him and his employers – who should have vetted him more carefully in the first place; she could not possibly be held responsible for their catastrophic choice of a local agent. Her business was to complete her assignment and get out. It was half past two, and she did not reckon she had any time to waste. If Guimard had given instructions that he was not to be disturbed until he called for a car, she was safe until then, and he had suggested that he had looked forward to spending the whole evening with her, so no one would be alarmed if he did not call for several hours. But she was still five miles outside of the town, without transport, and she had to be on the dock by a quarter to six at the latest, after visiting Edel!

She took off her dress and high-heeled shoes as well as her jewellery, packed them away in her shoulder bag, and put on her slacks and shirt and soft shoes, tying her hair in the bandanna. Then she surveyed Guimard. She felt he was definitely not armed. But his uniform hung on a hanger behind the door, his belts suspended beside it. And there was a holster!

She unclipped it, and gazed at a Luger! A weapon that had seen her through countless lethal situations; it had twice the range and stopping power of the Walther. She drew it and checked the magazine; it was fully loaded with a dozen nine-millimetre cartridges. She put it in her bag, moved back to the window.

The sentry was still there. She did not suppose he would stop her leaving, but once she did that, there would be no reason for him not, as time went by, to look in to see if his boss needed his assistance; she did not know how much time he would allow to elapse before wondering why there was no sound or movement from within the house. Nor could she just shoot him, as he was almost certainly going to be relieved at some time this afternoon, and she did not know when that was due to happen.

She surveyed the area. Thc nearest house was about a quarter of a mile away, and was also a prosperous-looking villa, as were all the other houses she could see beyond. This was clearly an upmarket neighbourhood. It was also siesta time, and there was no immediate sign of any activity, but as she watched a car went by ... and then a bus, heading for town.

She went into the hall, and to the other bedroom, this at the rear of the house, overlooking a rather scrubby lawn enclosed by a high wall. She studied it, reckoned it was about six feet tall, which was not insurmountable, providing ... she continued to gaze at it for some moments, but could see no sign of any broken glass along the top. And why indeed should a much-feared chief of police need to protect his property with broken glass?

Beyond there was an open area in which she could see no sign of life at this moment, although there was a house in the process of construction a few hundred yards to the right. As there was no activity there either she assumed the workmen were also en siesta. Anyway, it was her only exit.

She returned to the bedroom, slung her bag, as always looked around herself to make sure there was no evidence of her presence – not that it mattered on this occasion as the sentry knew she had been here – then went down the stairs and into the lounge, watching the front door as she retrieved her gloves and coat. But the sentry was definitely somnolent.

She folded the accessories also into her bag, which was now stuffed to full capacity, then went through the kitchen. The back door was bolted, but it gave access to the garden, and a few moments later she stood beneath the wall. Taking a deep breath she jumped, got her arms on the top, and heaved herself up to sit astride, the bag bumping on her back.

To turn left would mean that once she reached the road, to get back to the town she would have to walk past the front of the house, and the sentry. So it had to be the building site. She turned right, picking her way over the uneven ground, and a few minutes later was in the midst of concrete mixers and wheelbarrows, piles of timber and bricks, and several men, sprawled in the shade, and not all asleep. 'Hey!' one said. 'You want something, senorita?'

'As a matter of fact, yes. How often does the bus run?'

'It is every half an hour. You want this bus?'

Anna looked at her watch. It was just three. And a bus had just passed. So the next one would be at half past, if it was on time. 'And how long does it take to get back to town?'

He shrugged. 'An hour, maybe.'

So she would get back at half past four, which should give her just sufficient time. 'And where is the bus stop?'

'Just out there on the road. But senorita, why you want to catch this bus? Why you no stay here with us? We work from four until six, then our own bus comes for us. You could wait and ride into town with us. We would make you very happy. We have wine.'

'That sounds entrancing,' Anna said. 'But my husband is waiting for me. Thank you, senor.'

She continued on her way, and the man shouted, 'But, senora, where you come from?'

'Back there,' Anna assured him.

She half expected him to follow her, but fortunately he did not think it worth his while, and a few minutes later she was at the halt. Guimard's villa was about four hundred yards to her right, but there was no sign of the sentry, who was clearly still seated in the shade. There was no seat or shelter at the halt, so she walked slowly up and down, keeping her mind empty of any possible agitating thoughts. But the bus was only five minutes late.

There were only three other passengers, and she sat at the back, visited by a rather sad looking dog, who apparently belonged to one of them. 'I would love to stroke you,' Anna said. 'But I have a terrible suspicion that you have fleas. So bugger off.'

He accepted the menace in her voice and retreated.

It was twenty to five when the bus finally reached its depot, but this was only a ten-minute walk from Edel's apartment building. She rang the bell, and again, but there was no reply. Shit, she thought. If he was out, for any reason, she was up the creek without a paddle. But the wife and child were surely at home. She tried again without success, and was turning away in disgust, when a voice behind her asked, 'May I help you?'

Anna turned, and faced Mrs Edel, who had her son at her side; school must have ended late today. ‘Perhaps you can,’ she said. ‘I am trying to find a Senor Jan Edel. I see his name here, but he does not answer the bell.’

‘He never answers the bell,’ Mrs Edel explained.

‘Do you know him?’

‘I’m his wife.’

‘Oh! I didn’t know. I am sorry. And this is...?’

‘Little Jan. Our son.’

‘How sweet. Do you think I could see Senor Edel?’

‘What do you wish to see him about? He is a very private person.’

‘I’m from *Time* magazine. I’d like to do a story on him.’

Mrs Edel gazed at her for several seconds, and Anna knew exactly what she was thinking: how in the name of God did anyone from *Time* find us? But she also knew that she had created a situation that simply had to be addressed. ‘Then you had better come up,’ she said.

The elevator was apparently working. Anna smiled at Little Jan as they rode up, and a few minutes later she was in a small but comfortably furnished lounge. ‘Off you go to your room, Jan,’ his mother said. The boy hurried down a hallway. ‘My husband is in his study,’ she explained. ‘I’ll just tell him you’re here.’

‘Thank you.’

Mrs Edel also went down the hall, but only as far as the first door on the right, which she opened and then closed behind her. Anna wandered around the room, looking at the books on the shelves, but these were all in Danish, a language she did not have, thus she could not understand the sudden explosion of sound from beyond the wall, also in Danish, although she had a fairly good idea what was being said, especially as it was accompanied by the sound of a slap and a thud.

She faced the hall entrance. As always when she was working, her brain was ice cold, completely divorced from her normal persona; she had turned herself into a machine, a killing machine.

The door opened, and Mrs Edel emerged. There was a bruise on her cheek, darker than the flush that suffused the rest of her face, and her clothes were slightly dishevelled. 'My husband will see you now,' she said. The words were indistinct; Anna deduced that her mouth was filled with blood.

'I am most terribly sorry,' she said. 'I had no idea...'

Mrs Edel's mouth twisted. 'That my husband is a violent man? So I must warn you to be careful. He thought ... well...'

'That he was safe here?'

Mrs Edel's head came up.

'From prying journalists,' Anna explained. 'Again, I am sorry to have inflicted this upon you. But I have my job to do.'

'I understand that. And frankly, I am glad it is over.'

Anna had moved towards the door. Now she checked, and turned back. 'What is over?'

'This running. This hiding. This living a false life.'

'I can see that would be tiresome,' Anna agreed, with feeling. 'May I ask you a very personal question?'

Mrs Edel shrugged.

'Do you love your husband?'

Her mouth twisted again, and she looked over Anna's shoulder.

'Well?' Edel snapped. 'What is that bitch telling you about me?' He was quite a big man, grey-haired but still possessing powerful shoulders, which he carried slightly hunched. His features were regular enough, but distorted by ill-humour and impatience; his eyes were concealed behind horn-rimmed glasses which were slightly tinged, as if he did not like exposure to light.

'She was telling me how much she loves you. Senor Edel?'

'Of course I am Senor Edel.'

Anna held out her hand. 'Anna O'Rourke. *Time* magazine. May I have a word?'

He ignored the offered fingers. 'I wish a word with *you*,' he said. 'Come in here.'

Anna glanced at Mrs Edel, who mouthed something, but she couldn't be sure what it was. She followed him into the office.

'Now close the door.'

Anna obeyed and turned to face him, right hand resting on the catch for her shoulder bag. The room was book-lined with but a single window, closed; the only furniture was a large desk, covered in papers which were themselves covered with scrawling handwriting. Edel sat behind the desk, leaving Anna standing in front of it.

'Who are you working for?' he demanded.
'I told you...'
'Bullshit! How could they find me?'
'We have correspondents all over the place. In every nook and cranny.'
He glared at her, and she smiled at him. 'And they sent you, a chit of a girl, to interview me?'
'I really am very experienced,' Anna assured him, as always seeking to stick to the truth.
'Bullshit! What is it you want to know?'
Anna opened her bag and took out a pad and pencil, fingers brushing against both of the guns. 'First of all, I'd like to be sure I am interviewing the right man.'
'What?'
'You are Jan Edel?'
'Well, of course I am, you silly bitch.'
'And you are a Dane by nationality?'
'Is that important?'
'I am sure it is to you. You are an atomic scientist, who was persuaded to leave Denmark in 1940 to go to America and work on the Manhattan Project?'
'If you know my name, that is a rhetorical question.'
'And while working on that project, you became aware that splitting the atom, creating a nuclear bomb, was only a stage on the way to the ultimate explosive device, a thermonuclear bomb.'
Now he was frowning. 'How in the name of God do you know about that?'
'I find it difficult to believe that God knows, or wants to know, anything about this business.

Unless, of course, He has allowed us to discover this knowledge so that we could destroy ourselves and save Him having to do so. As to how we found out about you and the H-Bomb, we have, as I said, sources everywhere. However, to continue with my résumé, you were always a fascist, indeed, a Nazi, at heart, and when your employers detected this, they removed you from the project and returned you to England, under strict surveillance. This surveillance you managed to escape sufficiently to open negotiations with a Nazi agent with a view to selling your expertise and knowledge to them.'

She paused, because his frown had faded and he was staring at her with undisguised venom. 'I would really appreciate it if you would correct me if anything I am saying is inaccurate. However, you were found out, of course, and charged with treason. You were convicted and sentenced to death, but the sentence was reviewed, I assume because you had a wife and small child, and commuted to life imprisonment. However, a few months ago you managed to escape, and fled, here to Argentina, where your wife and child already were. Now, the really important question, and the one to which we require an answer, is to whom are you now trying to sell this enormous, and horrific, expertise you possess. And, of course, whether you are at all concerned about its eventual use.'

'We being *Time* magazine.'

'We have a reputation for our in-depth coverage and analysis of stories of great importance.'

'You are a lying bitch. However, if you're interested, I have no concern whatsoever as to what the bomb is used for. I am a scientist, not a moralist or an apologist.'

'You do not care that thousands, perhaps millions, of people may die if the bomb falls into the wrong hands?'

'What makes you think that the Americans, or the British, are the right hands? The moment the Americans got hold of the atom bomb they used it. Twice.'

'I think you will find that their argument was that they were actually trying to save lives.'

'Don't make me laugh.'

'Well, you see, their point of view seems to have been supported by the evidence they have obtained from Japanese archives since the war ended. That Japan was within six months of achieving a bomb of their own. That the Japanese military leaders had determined to fight to the last man, even if that involved the total destruction of their country. That they had already concentrated over two million regular troops, backed by four million state employees, backed by twenty-eight million civilian "volunteers", all of whom were dedicated to dying for their emperor. You may recall that Hitler had the same idea, but the German people had no six-thousand-year religious belief in an immortal emperor.'

'You should be a lawyer, not a journalist. I am not interested in western rhetoric. And you've stuck your neck out just too far this time, young lady. What you do not seem to be aware of is that

I am a guest of the Argentine government, and therefore any idea you may have of applying for my extradition is a waste of time. Something else you should know is that here in Pont del Mar I, and my safety, is the personal responsibility of the chief of police.'

'Ah,' Anna said. 'Would that be Captain Guimard?'

'I see you have heard of him.'

'He has quite a reputation.'

'He does indeed,' Edel agreed. 'And I have no doubt that he would enjoy widening that reputation on your body. So I think I will telephone him now and have you picked up.' He reached for his telephone.

'I wouldn't waste your time with that,' Anna said.

His head turned back to her, and he was again frowning.

'I had lunch with him today,' Anna explained.

'You, had lunch with Captain Guimard?'

'At his villa.'

Edel abandoned the telephone to stare at her. 'Then he knows that you are not what you pretend?'

'Well, he sort of worked it out. I think he had a gut feeling.'

'And he has just turned you loose?'

'Well, no. I don't think he intended to do that. But I persuaded him.'

'Persuaded him?'

'Well, actually, I shot him.'

Edel's gaze was taking on the aspect of hypnosis. 'What...' He licked his lips as Anna's hand emerged from her bag holding the Walther.

'I was sent here by the British Government,' she explained. 'They have concluded that commuting your death sentence was a grave mistake. I will confess that I came here with an open mind, well, relatively open mind. But our little chat has convinced me that they are absolutely correct in their judgement. So...' She levelled the pistol and shot him between the eyes.

GONE FISHING

Anna opened the office door. Mrs Edel stood in the centre of the lounge, hands clasped together. 'Are you all right?' she asked. 'That noise...?'

'I'm afraid that I have just shot your husband.'

'You –' Mrs Edel ran to the door, and Anna stepped aside – 'my God! Is he dead?'

'Well, when I shoot people, they generally do die,' Anna explained.

'But ... why?'

As Anna had suspected, and hoped, would be the case, there was no evidence of grief.

'He was too dangerous, to all humanity, to be allowed to live.'

'You knew him? I have never seen you before today.'

'I never saw him before today either. You never had the time to answer my question. Did you love him?'

'I –' Mrs Edel licked her lips – 'he was the father of my child.'

'Nothing more than that?'

A faint shrug. 'I went for a genius. Some people can't resist that. And when I became pregnant, he said he would marry me. So...'

'Do you have any family?'

One of those now familiar twists of the lips. 'In Denmark.'

'Can you not go back to them, with the boy?'

'If I can raise the fare, perhaps.'

'Didn't Edel have any money?'

'Not really. He is, was, being paid a pension by the Argentine government. But that has just been enough to live on. The apartment is theirs.'

'Hm.' Anna opened her shoulder bag, replaced the pistol, and took out her money. As she had not paid her hotel bill, and had no intention of doing so, she had spent less than a thousand of the original forty. But she was going to need a few thousand to get home. She peeled off thirty thousand, watched in fascination by the woman. 'Will this be sufficient to get you home?'

'Thirty thousand dollars? My God! But—'

'I have caused you a considerable inconvenience, and am going to have to cause you more. Where will you go, in Denmark?'

'I will go to my parents, in Copenhagen, until I can find a job and some place of my own.'

Anna indicated the table. 'Write down their address and give it to me.'

Frowning, Mrs Edel obeyed, while Anna looked at her watch. Time was ticking by, but this was something she had to do. Mrs Edel held out the piece of paper, and Anna stowed it in her bag 'Now, do you have any clothesline?'

'In the kitchen.'

'Show me.'

There was a long length of strong line. 'I do not believe that you will betray me,' Anna said, 'but in my business I cannot afford to take any risks, and besides, you have to be absolutely innocent of any involvement in what has happened. So I am going to tie you up and gag you. Will you please lie down on that sofa.'

Mrs Edel looked at her, then at the bag, then at the money, decided that any attempt at resistance would not be worth the risk, and obeyed. 'Thank you.' Anna rolled her on her side and tied her wrists together behind her back. 'I know it is not very comfortable,' she said apologetically. 'But I will send someone to release you in a little while. Meanwhile, I shall place the money under this cushion, so that only you will know where it is. I will then give you a month to get back to Denmark, at which time I will wire you a hundred thousand US dollars. I think that should enable you to find a place to live and get settled into a new life.'

Mrs Edel's eyes were enormous. 'Why are you doing this?'

Anna considered. 'I think, when you take something, you should give something back.'

'But ... when I am released, what do I do? I should call the police.'

'I have an idea that it will be the police who release you. At which time you should tell them the exact truth: a woman you have never seen before called here this afternoon, and asked to see your husband. You allowed her in, she went into your husband's office, and shot him. She then threatened you with her pistol, tied you up, and left.'

'They will want a description.'

'Then give them one. Remember to tell the truth.'

'But ... if they catch you ... Do you know what they will do to you?'

'If that was going to keep me awake at night, I wouldn't have come here in the first place. Now, I'm afraid that I am going to have to gag you, and lock the door of Little Jan's room.' She did so, returned to the lounge, looked around her, and closed the office door. 'Adios,' she said, and closed the apartment door behind her.

It was twenty-five minutes to six when Anna reached the fishing dock, which was a hive of activity as the fleet prepared to sail. She threaded her way through the throng to reach the *Bruja del Mar*. The two crew were still furling their nets, while Salvador stood on the dockside with his hands on his hips. 'Salvador!' she called. 'Sorry I'm so late.'

'Senorita! I did not think you were coming.'

'Well, here I am.'

'But there is no time to show you anything. We are to leave.'

'No problem. I will come with you.'

'You wish to come with us? To sea?'

'Why not?'

'But ... we go for two days.'

'I don't mind. I don't have anywhere to go.'
'There are only two bunks.'
'I am sure we can work something out.'
He rolled his eyes. 'I do not understand why you wish to do this.'
'Let us go on board, and I will tell you.' She climbed over the rail, watched in amazement by the crew; Salvador followed. 'I am a writer,' Anna explained. 'I wish to write a story about fishing boats at sea, and to do this I must have first-hand experience. You understand? Listen, how much do you expect to make from this trip? In US dollars.'
'In dollars ... sometimes we make three, four hundred. Maybe five.'
'I will pay you one thousand dollars, cash, if you let me come with you.'
He scratched his head. 'You have one thousand dollars?'
Anna opened her shoulder bag, thrust her hand inside, knuckles brushing the two pistols, and drew out a wad of ten hundreds. Salvador's eyes gleamed.
'Who is this woman?'
Anna turned, to look at a handsome if slightly overweight woman with curling dark hair, standing on the quayside with her hands on her hips. 'Who is *this* woman?' she inquired.
'This is my wife, Luciana,' Salvador said, uneasily.
'Ah.' Anna could understand his discomfort; Luciana was not looking the least contented. 'I am pleased to meet you, senora. Anna O'-Rourke.'

'What are you doing on my husband's boat?'
'He is taking me to sea with him.'
'What? You? With him?'
'You must not worry,' Anna explained. 'I am a lesbiana.'
'What?'
'What?' Salvador shouted.
Luciana burst out laughing. 'When you come back, you come and see me, eh?'
'Of course,' Anna agreed. 'As soon as I come back.'
'Ha ha,' Luciana commented, and strode off.
Salvador stared after her with his mouth open.
'Well, you see, senor,' Anna pointed out. 'You learn something new every day, even about your wife. Now listen, I need to make a telephone call. I will not be five minutes.' She had spotted the call box on the far side of the dock. 'Don't leave without me.' She patted her bag. 'One thousand dollars, eh?'
She went ashore and hurried to the box, dialled the police number. 'Good afternoon, senor,' she said to the voice answering. 'Listen carefully.'
'Who is this speaking, please?'
'Just listen. If you will go, or send someone, to Number Seven, Calle Victoriana, and go up to Apartment Five, you will find a woman who needs your help very urgently. The door is open.'
'Senorita? What is your name. Where are you calling from?'
'Just do it,' Anna recommended. 'Apartment Five, Number Seven, Calle Victoriana.' She hung up and hurried back across the dock.

* * *

The engine was already rumbling, and the crew were standing by to cast off the warps. Most of the other boats were already on their way out of the harbour. Anna joined Salvador in the wheelhouse. 'I am so excited,' she confessed. 'I have never been on a boat before.'

He considered. 'You will get seasick.'

'Then I must suffer for my art. But you must show me what everything is. What is this round thing, with the needle?'

'That is the compass.' He watched the crew coiling the warps. 'Senorita, my crew, they wish to know why you come with us. Why I take you. I tell them you have paid me. Paid us.'

'Well, that's true, isn't it?'

He glanced at her. 'I tell them you have paid two hundred American dollars.'

'Ah.'

'You understand this?'

'Of course. You're the skipper. I would have done the same. What are their names?'

'The tall one is named Pedro. The short one is named Carlos.'

Shit, Anna thought. She had only met two men named Carlos in her life, and both were now dead. She hoped that wasn't an omen; she really had no desire to harm any of these rather gormless young men.

'You do not like these names?'

'I think they are lovely names. So easy to remember.'

'You feel all right?'

The boat had now passed the pier heads and

was rising and falling to a long but quite large swell; Anna guessed that there might be weather about.

'I feel fine. You were telling me about these instruments. What is this one?'

'That is the revolution counter for my engine.'

Anna peered at the needle. 'And you are going at six hundred kilometres an hour?' She looked out of the window. 'It does not look like that to me.'

Salvador chuckled. 'No, no, senorita. That is how fast the engine is turning. From that I can tell how fast we are going.'

'You must have to know an awful lot to be skipper of a boat,' Anna said, admiringly. 'And what is this thing? It is making a funny noise.'

'That is my radio.'

'Gosh! You mean you are in touch with the shore?'

'Oh, yes, senorita. This is necessary, to find out about the weather and so we can report if there is an emergency. Send a Mayday, eh?'

'Do you have to do that often?'

'I have never had to do that,' Salvador said, proudly. 'This is a good boat, and I am good sailor. Experienced, eh?'

'That is very reassuring. And you say this radio is on all the time?'

'Every minute.'

'What sort of range does it have?'

'Six, eight hundred kilometres.'

'Gosh!'

'It is MF,' Salvador said, proudly. 'You know what this is?'

'Should I?'

'It is medium frequency.'

'How many frequencies are there?'

'In terms of range, there is medium frequency, high frequency, that is very long, thousands of kilometres, and very high frequency.'

'I get it. Very high frequency is longer yet.'

Salvador smiled at her ignorance. 'No, no. Very high frequency is short range. Maybe seventy kilometres.'

'It is very confusing.'

'Now, you see,' Salvador was warming to his theme, 'We deal in megacycles. There are hundreds of these, for different purposes. You see this radio, it is set on 2182.'

Anna peered at the dial, 'So it is. Is that yours?'

'That is the Shipping Band. All ships at sea listen on that band. If the call is for you, personally, you will hear it on that band, and then, when you have replied, you will be told to go to another band to talk.'

'It is very complicated.' Anna smiled at the two crew as they came into the wheelhouse. They both looked embarrassed as they went down the companionway, 'Are they going to bed already?'

It was in fact quite dark, but they were surrounded by the lights of the other boats, all apparently heading the same way.

'No, no, they go to cook our dinner. You are hungry, eh?'

'As a matter of fact I am.' Lunch seemed a very long way away. 'When do we start fishing?'

'Oh, not until tomorrow. When we reach the best ground.'

'And you all fish together?' That was a complication for which she hadn't allowed.

'No, no, we split up.' He tapped the side of his nose. 'Each skipper thinks he knows where is best, eh?'

'I'm sure of it. Now tell me about your sleeping arrangements. You said you have only two bunks.'

'Well, when we are at sea, you see, one of us must always be on the helm. So we only need two bunks. But one of them will be yours, for this trip,' he said, gallantly. 'The other one of us will sleep on the deck. Unless –' he glanced at her and took a deep breath – 'what you said to my wife. Was it true?'

'What did I say to your wife?'

'Well ... that you do not go for men.'

'I might go for the right man,' Anna said, fluttering her eyelashes.

As she had feared would be the case, the cabin turned out to be not very clean and distinctly odorous. At the after end there was a toilet compartment, which also had a washbasin, but this was even less salubrious, while the bedclothes turned out to be a well-worn sleeping bag that was the least salubrious of all. The things I have to do for England, she thought.

But the meal, if swimming in grease, was surprisingly tasty, even if, although fish, it had to be washcd down by a couple of tumblers of a very rough but drinkable red wine; there was apparently nothing else available save for water, and that wasn't very salubrious either. But the meal was finished with some very palatable cheese, which suited her purpose, as it enabled her to drink some more wine, and as she was clearly unused to alcohol, she allowed herself to become equally clearly intoxicated, and could hardly stagger to her bunk before passing out.

She lay with her shoulder bag clutched against her stomach, listening to their muttered conversation, which, had she not been Anna Fehrbach, might have terrified her, as it varied from a speculative analysis of various bits of her anatomy, annoyingly concealed by her shirt and pants, through a derogatory discussion of 'lesbiana', by way of wondering whether a 'lesbiana' might not be more enjoyable than an orthodox woman, to arrive at where she might be keeping the two hundred dollars she had promised them, and what else might be in her bag.

But any immediate intent was quashed by Salvador, who made it perfectly plain that she was his, and that any investigation of either her or her bag was his prerogative. In fact, when she gave a gentle snore, he stood above her for several minutes, staring at her. But she allowed herself a few more snores, and he went away again, to sleep in the other bunk.

The cabin light was turned down, and Anna slept herself, her hand inside her bag. In view of his obvious ambitions, and the fact that if he came on too hard she might reveal to the crew that he was planning to cheat them of eight hundred dollars she did not fear an interruption, not that, with her hand resting on her two pistols, she *feared* an interruption, anyway.

She awoke refreshed, to considerable motion; overnight the wind had freshened and the sea had become distinctly lumpy. But she was pleased to discover, on going up to the wheel-house, that there was no other boat in sight, although she guessed that they might not be very far off, hidden by the now large ocean swell.

Salvador was on the helm. 'Good morning, senorita. You sleep well, eh?'

'Yes, I did. Where are the other boats?'

He waved his hand. 'They are fishing.'

'When do we start fishing?'

'As soon as we have had breakfast. You wish breakfast?'

'Yes, indeed.'

'You no have the head?'

'What is a head between friends?' She tapped the chart, which lay on the console beside the helm. 'Do you know where we are?'

'Of course, senorita.'

'Show me.'

'Well, you see, we left Pont del Mar at six o'clock yesterday evening, and it is now eight o'clock this morning. That is fourteen hours,' he announced triumphantly.

'You are a brilliant man,' Anna acknowledged.

'So, you see, we have made a steady eight knots, thus we have covered a hundred and twelve nautical miles.'

'You mean you worked that out in your head?'

'It is my business,' he said proudly. 'I am a

navigator.'

'Of course. And in which direction have we been travelling?' She watched the sun, which was still rising just off the starboard bow.

'North-east. Now, there is a little bit of current, but I estimate that we are –' he used a pair of dividers – 'here.' He made a little pencil mark on the chart.

'Amazing!' Anna studied the chart. 'But that means that we are only a hundred and twenty nautical miles from Montevideo.'

'That is true.'

'So, we could be there in fifteen hours. If we altered course now, we could be there at three o'clock tomorrow morning.'

'That is also true. But why do we want to go to Uruguay?'

'Oh, I think it would be a lovely idea. I have never been to Montevideo. Have you?'

'Well, no. But why should I want to go there? I am Argentinian.'

'I would like to go there,' Anna said.

'You wish to go to Uruguay?'

'You have such a quick brain.'

'But senorita, as you said, that will take us all night, and another full day back again. We are here to fish.'

'For which you will earn a thousand dollars. But I will pay you another five thousand dollars to take me to Montevideo.' She smiled past him at Carlos and Pedro, who were just emerging from the cabin. 'Do you not think that is a fair offer?'

'I do not understand this,' Carlos said. 'Five

thousand dollars?'

'This woman is mad,' Salvador declared.

Carlos preferred to concentrate on what mattered. 'You have five thousand dollars, senorita?'

'I do.'

'In that bag?'

'Show it to us,' Pedro said.

'If you wish.' Anna opened the bag, took out the five bundles of notes. 'See?'

He reached for them.

'Not so fast,' Anna said, putting the money back into the bag and wrapping her fingers around the Luger. 'You will get the money when we reach Montevideo.'

Carlos and Pedro looked at each other.

'There is something wrong,' Salvador said. 'You are escaping Argentina. You are a criminal.'

'It takes all sorts,' Anna agreed.

'I must take you back to Pont del Mar. I will call them to tell them what you are trying to do.'

'I am not *trying* to do anything,' Anna said. 'Except to be reasonable. And generous. I am offering you a large sum of money, several times what you can hope to earn from this fishing trip, to take me to Montevideo. That is all you have to do. Then you can go back to fishing, or go straight back to Pont del Mar. It is entirely up to you.'

'I must call. You could be a spy.'

'What an exciting thought. But I would prefer you not to call. Now, I wish you to alter course.'

Salvador bristled. 'You cannot give me orders

on board my own boat.'

'But I have just chartered your boat,' Anna explained, patiently. 'For five thousand dollars, for one night. You will never do a better business deal. I doubt you would get five thousand dollars if you put this boat up for sale.' She looked at the crew. 'Do you not agree?'

'Oh, yes, senorita,' Pedro said. 'We agree.'

'I will take you to Montevideo,' Salvador said, with dignity, accepting that he might be outvoted. 'But I must call Pont del Mar first. If I do not, and you are a criminal, I could be locked up, and have my boat confiscated.'

'I don't think you need to worry about that,' Anna assured him. 'Because you are being coerced. So...' She had already determined, from watching their faces, that they had every intention of getting hold of her bag, at the very least, the moment they saw their opportunity. 'I will remove temptation.' She drew the Luger and put a shot into the radio, which obligingly exploded.

'Madre de Dios!' Salvador shrieked, releasing the wheel and jumping back.

'You have that wrong,' Anna said. 'I'm told that I come from the other direction. And you have forced me to form the opinion that you are not to be trusted.' She looked at Pedro and Carlos, who had shrunk against the after bulkhead, almost holding hands. 'Pedro,' she said, 'go below and bring up the rest of the cheese, a fresh bottle of wine, and a bottle of water. You have three minutes to do this.'

Even if she supposed that it was unlikely they

would have any sedative material on board, as usual she did not believe in taking risks.

Pedro was back well within the time limit, placing the food and drink on the table, while Carlos and Salvador stared at her in mesmerized horror.

'Thank you,' she said. 'Now, I made you an offer, which at least your crew were prepared to accept, and I always keep my word. So –' she felt in her bag with her free hand and took out the money – 'here, Carlos.'

Cautiously he came forward and took the bundle of notes.

'Now, you, Salvador.' She felt in her bag again and took out the receipt she had carefully written out in her room at the Excelsior. 'Sign this.'

'What is that? You are committing piracy.'

'Of course I am not committing piracy. I have just chartered your boat for one night for five thousand dollars. I wish you to sign this receipt to make it legal.'

He glared at her, then at the pistol, then laid the receipt on the table and signed it.

'Thank you.' Anna restored it to her bag. 'Now, I would like you to go below into the cabin and stay there. I intend to lock the door, and if there is any banging on it I will come in and shoot you all.'

'You?' Salvador asked, getting some of his nerve back. 'Will shoot us?'

'It is my profession.'

'Your...?'

'Shooting people. But I really do not wish to have to shoot you. So down you go.'

Pedro and Carlos had already disappeared, but Salvador still hesitated. 'But who will sail the boat?'

'Me.'

'You? A woman cannot sail a boat.'

'You are not exactly making me your friend, Salvador.'

'You do not know how. You told me you had never been on a boat before last night. You do not know how to navigate. You will wreck us.'

'I'm sure I'll pick it up as I go along. And I promise you, if I wreck the boat, I will let you out. Down.'

Reluctantly he went down the companionway. Anna followed, pistol in hand, closed and locked the door, then returned to the wheelhouse. Unhelmed, the trawler was yawing all over the place, but a glance over the stern at the wake, informed her that there had been no great deviation from the course.

She put the engine in neutral, found a pair of binoculars, and swept the horizon. There was no other boat in sight. She busied herself with the chart, taking Salvador's estimated position as accurate, and laid a course for Montevideo, then re-engaged the gear. Lacking an autopilot she knew she was in for a long fifteen hours, but she had supreme confidence in her stamina, both physical and mental; she had lasted just as long in her escape from Mexico City.

And as the day went on, it steadily brightened, even if the swell remained big enough to indicate even more that there was weather out there somewhere. She began to enjoy herself, taking an occasional bite of cheese, washed down with a sip of either wine or water. There was no sound from below, although she did not doubt there was a good deal of discussion going on.

Steering with one hand, she took out her *Fodor* and studied Montevideo, noted the long mole jutting into the mouth of the River Plate, and also that the international airport was immediately on the outskirts of the city. The day drifted by and it became dark. She was now very tired, but she forced herself to stay awake, and at about midnight made out a flashing light ahead.

She doused her own navigation lights, put the engine into neutral and let the boat drift, then stripped, went on deck to do what was necessary over the side, returned to the wheelhouse to use the last of the water on her face and armpits, applied perfume, put on her red dress and her coat, both now sadly crushed, laid her gloves on the console with her high-heeled shoes beneath them, packed away her shirt and pants, and wedges, leaving her feet bare, and relaxed for a couple of hours.

Now there was a banging on the door. 'Senorita!' Salvador shouted. 'What has happened? Why are we stopped?'

'Go back to sleep,' Anna recommended.

The noise subsided. Now there was a problem in keeping awake. She went on deck and walked about, listening to the waves slurping against the hull, watching the distant flashing light. At three o'clock she lowered the blue and white Argentine flag. Then she started the engine again, and moved towards the light.

It was just dawn when she sighted the mole, on her starboard hand. To port was a fort, the entrance to the harbour proper was between them, but she did not intend going that far. She had no doubt that the watch on the fort had sighted the visitor, and was now reporting it, but a single itinerant fishing boat was not going to cause an emergency. The city itself, behind a fringe of date palms, was just waking up, lights appearing in house windows, traffic just starting to growl. She used the binoculars to discern several iron ladders let into the stone sides of the mole, nosed alongside one of these, stopped the engine, put on her gloves, slung her shoulder bag, picked up her shoes, and stepped on to the ladder, dropping the cabin key overboard as she did so. At the top she put on her high heels and dark glasses and turned left to walk towards the houses.

'Hey, you! Senorita!'

Anna stopped, and turned to face a policeman. 'Me?'

'Yes, you. You have come off that boat.'

'Yes, I have.'

'That boat cannot stay there. Where has it come from, anyway?'

'I do not know.'

'What? But you were on it.'

'Briefly. It came in ... oh, about an hour ago. I had been unable to sleep, so I had come down here for a walk in the morning air, and these men called me, and asked me to go on board for a drink.'

The policeman peered at her. 'Just like that? And you went? You did not know these men?'

'No. But they seemed very nice. But when I got on board they made a pass at me, so I left.'

Almost she thought he was going to scratch his head. 'You have identification?'

'Of course.' Anna felt in her bag, located the right passport, and gave it to him.

He flipped it open, looked from the photograph to her face. 'Anna O'Reilly. You are Irish?'

'Well, of course I am Irish,' Anna said indignantly.

'Ah,' he commented, as if that explained everything. 'And you have a visa.'

'If I did not have a visa, I would not have been allowed in.'

'You are working here in Uruguay?'

'I am on holiday.'

'Ah,' he said again, even more obviously reflecting that only an Irishwoman would choose to holiday in the middle of winter. He handed her the passport. 'You were very foolish to go on board a strange boat with strange men. But you will come with me and we will deal with them, eh?'

Anna took off her glasses in alarm, and fluttered her eyelashes at him. 'Deal with them?'

'They wished to assault you, did they not? And they have no right to be here. That is not a Montevideo boat, and anyway, it is not allowed to moor on this pier.'

'But they are no longer there,' she pointed out.

'Eh? What?' He swung round to watch the *Bruja del Mar*, which Anna had deliberately not moored, drifting away from the dock. 'They cannot do that. I will call the harbour police. You stay here.'

'But senor, I cannot stay here. I must go for breakfast.'

'What? Where will you go for this breakfast?'

'To my hotel.'

'You are staying in a hotel?'

She remembered that it *was* early in the day, and he had probably been on duty for several hours, 'Of course I am staying in a hotel, senor. The Splendide.'

'The Splendide. That is very expensive.'

'Is it? Senor, I think, if you really wish to speak to those men, you should hurry, or they will drift right out of the harbour.'

He turned again; the trawler was a hundred yards away from the dock. 'Madre de Dios! Are they asleep? But you said...'

'They were drunk,' Anna said, disparagingly. 'Listen, senor. You go and get the harbour authority and sort them out. I will go to my hotel and have breakfast, and then wait for you to come to see me.'

'Yes. Yes, that is what you must do. I must do. And you are Senorita O'Reilly.'

'What a good memory you have. Hasta la vista, senor.' She hurried along the mole.

She found a taxi rank and was taken to the airport. 'I do no think there are any flights at this hour, senorita,' the driver warned.

'Then I will have to wait,' Anna said bravely. She reckoned it was going to take a good hour for the *Bruja del Mar* to be recovered and

Salvador and his crew freed, and then another hour or so of interrogation for them to convince the police that their side of the story was the truth, certainly once the Luger was found as it certainly would be, and perhaps the five thousand dollars as well. If she were lucky, they might still begin the search for her at the Splendide, even if Salvador would claim he had brought her from Pont del Mar.

The airport was indeed just waking up, but the restaurant was open. Anna had breakfast, then went to the PanAm desk where the first ticket clerk was just taking her place. 'Miami?' she remarked. 'Today? Yes, there is a flight at ten o'clock. But economy is fully booked.'

'I wish to travel first,' Anna pointed out.

'First?' The woman looked sceptical as she regarded her; even if clearly expensive, her clothes were crushed and untidy.

'I will pay cash.' She opened her bag and took out her last four wads of hundred dollar bills.

'That was a quick trip,' Donald remarked. 'Five days?'

'Things went better than I expected. I'd like to use your radio to call the cay.'

'Sure. Help yourself.'

'Anna?' Clive almost shouted. 'You're back already?'

'Seems like it. Any problems?'

'Not a thing.'

'That's great. Would you ask Tommy to come across and get me?'

'Of course. But ... ah ... you saw...'

'Not on the radio,' Anna said. 'Yes, I saw him. We'll talk about it when I get home. I'll expect Tommy tomorrow. Over and out.'

Donald had returned to the shop, but there were no customers at the moment. Anna joined him. 'All correct?' he asked.

'Yes, but he can't get here until tomorrow. How'd you like to put me up for tonight?'

'Put you up? Well ... wow! You've never asked me that before.'

'Because I've always stayed in a hotel before. But right this minute Miami is a little hot for me; there are at least two groups of nasties looking for me. And I don't have any clothes.'

'What?' He peered at her. 'Say, you went out with a suitcase.'

'I lost it.'

'Just like that?'

'These things happen.'

'Can't you buy a new outfit?'

'As I said, I feel it would be a good idea to keep a low profile here in Miami for the next few months. So how about it?'

'I'd love to put you up, Anna. But I'm not sure how Jennie would take it.'

'Jennie being?'

'My wife.'

'I didn't know you had a wife.'

'And how. I mean, don't get me wrong. She's a sweet kid, but she's kind of highly strung when it comes to other dames.'

Well, Anna reflected, even secret service agents are entitled to have private, domestic lives ... just as she was trying desperately to do.

'Well, then—'

'But say, you can stay here.'

'Where?'

'There's a put-you-up out the back.'

'With a bathroom? I desperately need a bath.'

'Well, no. There ain't no bath.'

'Shit!'

'There's a toilet, and a washbasin. And hell, it'll only be for eighteen hours.'

'And what do I eat? In the last twenty-four hours I have had a lump of cheese, a light breakfast and two totally cardboard airplane snacks.'

'Tell you what, I'll nip out and get you some hamburgers and a couple of bottles of beer. That'll keep you going until you're on your boat. Won't it?'

'I suppose it'll have to,' Anna said sadly. 'Just remember that I like lots of mustard and ketchup.'

'You have no idea how good this feels,' Anna told Tommy, as they stood together on the bridge of *Fair Girl* and helmed her out of Miami harbour.

'It's been a hard week, ma'am?'

'Uncomfortable. So you take her for a while. I'm going below.'

'You got it, ma'am.'

She dumped her dirty clothes on the cabin floor, then stood beneath her shower for half an hour, soaping again and again and then washing and rinsing her hair time and again. Then she wrapped her head in a towel and collapsed on to her bunk. Nothing had *ever* felt so good. She had to suppose that once upon a time Donald's put-you-up had had springs, but that had clearly been a long time ago, so that it was now some forty-eight hours since she had had any proper sleep, and to be between her own sheets and with her head on her own pillow, as much as knowing that she was on her own boat and in the safest of hands, was luxury personified.

And the racing big seas of the Gulf Stream were soporific. She slept like a log for six hours, then got up, put on clean knickers, clean shirt and clean pants, and cooked a good lunch. They were by now across the Stream, and the Biminis were in sight to the south but as they were now in the open water of the North-West Providence Channel Tommy was able to put the boat on autopilot and join her in the saloon.

She poured them each a glass of cold beer. 'So tell me what's been happening on the cay. You had rain?'

'Yes, ma'am. We had one heavy storm the day before yesterday. All night it was. Must have been six or seven inches.'

She knew he would hardly be exaggerating; summer rain in the Bahamas could be tropical in its intensity. 'Well, that must have topped up the cistern.'

'Yes, ma'am. It's all but overflowing. They do say there's a tropical storm down by Haiti, and it could well freshen up and come this way.'

'What, on June two? That's early.' The hurricane season officially started at the beginning of June. 'But you've had no visitors?'

'No, ma'am.'

'No ships or yachts coming close to the cay?'
'No, ma'am.'
Anna gave a sigh of relief, and finished her beer, 'Well, then, let's get this lot washed up.'
'You putting in to Bimini, ma'am, for the night?'
Anna washed plates and cutlery while Tommy dried. 'No, there's still four hours of daylight left. We'll go on to Great Harbour Cay and drop the hook, I don't feel like company, and it'll shorten the trip tomorrow.'
'You got it, ma'am.' He followed her back up to the bridge where she regained control. 'You know what ... I didn't say, but there was that aeroplane yesterday.'

Anna turned her head, sharply. 'What?'
'Just after you called, ma'am. I got the boat out just as soon as Mr Bartley told me, and I was just passing through the reef when this plane came down.'
'Came down? You mean, in the sea?'
'No, no. It just came low, over the island. Over me and the boat too. Then it went up and turned, and came round again, dipping low. It did that three or four times. You know what I am thinking, ma'am? I am thinking that it was taking photographs.'
Shit, Anna thought. Shit, shit, shit. But her voice was calm. 'Were you able to see how many people were on board?'
'Oh, yes, ma'am. It come that low. There were three men. And one was using what I think was a big camera. You knew they was going to do

this, ma'am?'

'No. I did not know they were going to do this.' But I should have, she thought.

'Well, you know what I am thinking, ma'am: if you didn't give them permission to fly low over your island and take photographs, that is an invasion of privacy. We should report them to the police in Nassau.'

Tommy's law-abiding approach to every problem, she thought. 'Well,' she said. 'I don't suppose they were doing any harm. It's a beautiful and obviously thriving cay; they probably want to put us in a glossy magazine. Take her helm a moment.' She went down the ladder and into the saloon, unrolled the chart. But as she had known would be the case, even Great Harbour Cay was too far from Fair Cay for her VHF, and while the temptation to keep going all night was tremendous, it would be the height of irresponsibility to risk striking an unseen reef in the dark; if they left at dawn tomorrow, they'd be home for lunch.

And as they approached the cay in the glow of the noonday sun, everything looked absolutely peaceful and normal. To her own surprise, Anna had slept well, lulled by the gentle motion of the boat riding to its anchor, and even more by the patter of rain on the deck above her head, just before dawn. Now the cay looked as green and prosperous as always, and as she had called ahead as soon as they were within range, there was the usual enthusiastic reception committee on the dock to greet her.

But after hugs and kisses all round, she was

anxious to get Clive alone in the radio room. 'I am assuming all went well, and successfully,' he said.

'All went successfully, in the end,' Anna said. 'But not well.'

'Oh, no. You all right?'

'I am fine. But Baxter's set-up was full of shit.'

'Tell me.'

'It's what he did not tell me, that mattered. Like that Edel had a wife and a kid.'

'Oh, my God! You didn't—'

'No, I did not. But that was pure luck. She'd fallen out with her husband and was happy to be rid of him, even if perhaps not quite so finally. But as for my so-called contact, Baxter also didn't tell me, or perhaps he didn't know, that Lustrum is a small-time crook who is under surveillance by the police. Although I have a feeling that all of those references should be past tense by now.'

'You mean...?'

'No, I did not kill him. But his phone was being tapped, and as a result I was arrested.'

'*What*? But...'

'As you can see, I'm still here. But the local chief of police isn't.'

'Holy Jesus Christ! What—?'

'Don't worry about it. He was a nasty piece of work. And they're looking for a wild Irish woman named Anna O'Rourke. Unfortunately if, as I suspect will have happened, and as they know I telephoned Lustrum when I got to Pont del Mar, they may have taken him as part of their investigation into Captain Guimard's death, and applied some pressure...'

'You think they'll have tortured him?'

'They were certainly meaning to torture me. And that was before I'd shot their police chief.'

'Then he may reveal that you were working for MI6!'

'The words you want are *will* reveal.'

'Shit! Look, my darling, I had better get back to England just as rapidly as possible.'

'That figures. But you will be coming back? We have a marriage to sort out.'

'I'll be coming back.'

'Bringing my carte blanche as well as my wedding ring.'

'I'll bring the wedding ring, certainly. But Anna ... you do realize that MI6 are going to have to disown any knowledge of Anna O'-Rourke? And Lustrum.'

'I know that.'

'Therefore, well...'

'Clive, there is no possible connection between an Irish assassin Anna O'Rourke and reclusive Bahamian resident Anna Fitzjohn.'

'That seems obvious to you and me, but it may not be obvious in London. They won't sell you out. They can't, without admitting that you did this job for them. But they may not be happy about giving you carte blanche to kill anybody else.'

'In that case you had better tell Billy not to show his face here again, or he'll be top of the list.'

'I'll do that.'

'Now tell me about Joe. Has he called?'

'Yes. And it's not good.'

'Tell me.'

'Well, first of all, he was pretty browned off to discover you weren't here, but I was.'

'Hasn't he got the message that you are liable to be here permanently, from now on?'

'At your side. He's a suspicious cuss.'

'But what did he have to say about friend Strezzi?'

'Ah. Now here's the problem. They've identified her as a member of the Ravanelli Family. Do you know these people?'

'Never heard of them. But would I be right in assuming that the word 'family' in this context means a Mafia connection?'

'You would be. That's what's bothering Joe. The woman of course wasn't actually kin; she worked for them. But they're not people to tangle with.'

'Even for the CIA?'

'There's the rub. The CIA could certainly handle one of these families, but dealing with domestic thugs is not their remit. That's FBI stuff. And involving the FBI in handling the mob to protect you means telling the Feds who and what you are. You're not supposed to be working for the US Government. For God's sake, you're not supposed to be *alive*. And these people have long memories. They haven't forgotten 1941, when they had you cold for killing those six Russians and were told to keep off the grass. That rankled. Apparently it still does. J.

Edgar Hoover never forgets.'

'And the Russian connection? As I have never had anything to do with the Mafia in my life, there has to be a connection.'

'He agrees. That photo of you was certainly taken in Moscow. Would that have been in 1941?'

Anna shook her head. '1940.'

'You remember it?'

'Very vaguely. I had just arrived, officially as a secretary in the German Embassy, and was being shown the sights by this Intourist guide. And suddenly this character pops up and snaps me. I thought nothing of it. I was only a kid and I knew I attracted men. Anyway, as I had never had anything to do with the Reds either, at that time, I couldn't believe they had ever heard of me, much less had any idea who I was and what I was there for.'

'And when they found out, and you slipped through their fingers, they put the whole state mechanism to work, and came up with that photographer. And as since then they have tried to grab you on God knows how many occasions and failed every time, they're employing the Mafia to have a go. And,' he added bitterly, 'your gallant employers, the CIA, seem quite happy to let you sink or swim, on your own, without lifting a finger to help you.'

'Just as my other gallant employers are happy to send me off on a pretty tricky assignment with no relevant information and a totally duff contact.'

He sighed. 'I know. I suppose Billy was worried that if you knew about the wife and kid you'd have said no dice.'

'And he would have been absolutely right.'

'Anna, you simply have to get out.'

'So tell me how I do that. Right now, it'd mean that I'd have the MGB, the Mafia, the CIA, and MI6, all on my back. And it would mean giving up the cay. I'm not going to do that.'

'Are you saying that you have to charge blindly onwards until one of your pursuers finally catches up with you, or your employers give you a job even you can't complete?'

'My plan is to outlast them all, or all who matter.' She gave one of her wicked smiles. 'I look at it this way. I'm forty-one years younger than Stalin, thirty-odd years younger than Beria, more than twenty years younger than either Joe or Billy. If I can keep alive another few years they'll all just fade away. I will, of course, need some help from my friends to do that.'

'Therefore I can't possibly leave you alone here to cope.'

'You have to, for a couple of days, anyway. You have to tell Baxter that the job has been completed, and that he may have a problem with Lustrum. You also have to point out that as I have fulfilled my part of the bargain, I expect him to fulfil his. That needs to be stressed at the very highest level you can reach. You are the only person who can convince them that I have no intention or desire to kill anybody unless I am instructed to or in self-defence. Will you do that?'

'If I can't, I am resigning on the spot and

coming back to join you here.'

'Just remember to bring the wedding ring with you.'

INCIDENT IN THE STORM

'What happens,' Clive asked, as they walked down to the boat the next morning, where Tommy was waiting to ferry him to Nassau – Anna had used her radio to call ahead and book him a seat on the overnight flight to London, 'if our friends decide to pay you a visit before I get back? They've been taking a look at us, you know.'

'I do know. Tommy told me. Taking photographs.'

'Real military reconnaissance stuff. So what do you reckon is their next step? With you virtually alone on the cay?'

Anna pointed at the sky. 'Ever seen those before?'

Clive looked up. 'No, I haven't. Piled on top of one another like that? Does it mean something?'

'Yes. It means there's a hurricane out there.'

'My God! And you never told me! But isn't it a bit early for a hurricane?'

'The season officially starts in June, and today's the fourth. There have been hurricanes on the first day of the season before. It all depends on the sea temperatures. Anyway, it's not confirmed that it's coming this way yet. I'm going to get a weather update from Nassau in a few minutes. But it's close. And it's our best protection for the next few days. No one in their right mind moves around, either at sea or in the sky, while there's a chance of running into one of those.'

'And you expect me to rush off and abandon you to face that as well as a bunch of heavies?'

'Yes. Because you have more important things to do than nursemaid me, and you have to get out while you can. First thing they do if a hurricane gets too close is to ground all aircraft. I told you, I'm perfectly safe. This island has taken a direct hit before, and it's still here, and while the weather is around I'm not likely to receive any visitors, welcome or unwelcome.' She kissed him. 'Now hurry. Tommy,' she called, 'back as quick as you can.'

'You got it, ma'am.'

She waved them through the reef, then returned to the house, found Johann in the radio room. 'Latest update,' he said. 'The eye passed just north of the Turks and Caicos a couple of hours ago. They're taking a pounding; sustained winds are a hundred and twenty miles an hour.'

'Then it's a big one. Speed and track?'

'North-west, sixteen knots.'

'And travelling fast. At least that means it'll be gone by tomorrow.' She looked at the big chart of the Bahamas pinned to the wall, and used a pair of dividers. 'When was that update timed?'

'Six this morning.'

'Shit! That's three hours ago. When you say it

passed the Turks and Caicos a couple of hours ago, is that what the report said?'

'Well, yes. Is that important?'

'It could mean that the eye passed the islands five hours ago! They're about three hundred and fifty miles to the south-east. If it passed them more than five hours ago, travelling at sixteen knots, it could be not much more than two hundred and fifty miles from us right now. If it maintains that speed and track it'll be here by midnight tonight. That's the eye. The hurricane wind will be getting up well before that, perhaps several hours. I think it's time to batten down the hatches, PDQ.'

'Maybe we should have gone into Nassau with Clive.'

'Now, Pa, we're not going to be afraid of a little wind, are we? I'll take care of what we have to do.'

Dogs at her heels, she went to Desiree's house. 'There's a storm coming, Desiree,' she said. 'It could be a big one. Do you want to stay here or go up to Eleuthera?'

'Ow me God, ma'am. You staying here?'

'Yes.'

'Then we should stay with you.' She hesitated.

'There's a but.'

'It's me mother, ma'am. She ain't too well since me daddy died. I don't think she could cope with no big storm.'

'And she's in Eleuthera?'

'Yes, ma'am. She living in Bluff.'

'Then you must go to her. As soon as Tommy

gets back. Meanwhile put your shutters up.'
'But you must have yours up too, ma'am.'
Anna nodded. 'I'm going to get the boys on it now.'
She went to the vegetable garden and brought Elias up to date. 'I know you'll want to get home,' she said. 'And you'll go with Desiree and Tommy as soon as he gets back from Nassau. Meanwhile, drop all this and put the shutters up on the house.'
'You got it, borse. You staying here?'
'Yes.'
He chewed his lip uncertainly.
Anna smiled at him. 'I can manage on my own for a couple of days. And you have your houses and families to think of. Let's hurry.'

The morning was filled with activity, as the storm shutters were carried from the store shed and put in place. The operation was simple in terms of mechanics – each shutter was fitted with bolts which slotted into sockets let into the walls of the house – but as they were great heavy things carting them about required a good deal of strength and effort.
The upstairs windows were far more simple, as there the shutters were built-in, with iron bars across. Anna attended to these herself with the help of her mother. She also wound down the aerial, as that was extremely vulnerable to a strong wind and she had no intention of making, or receiving, any calls.
The job was completed by one, and Anna sent the staff off to have lunch and pack up their gear;

as Tommy had left at half past eight, he would have dropped Clive and be on his way back by now. She, Johann and Jane ate in the shuttered gloom of the dining room. 'What do we do now?' Jane asked as they cleared away the dishes.

'We wait,' Anna said.

She took the dogs for a walk, watched the clouds building to the south-east, while it remained clear overhead. As what might be going to happen was outside her experience, it was impossible to form any plan of action beyond utilizing the knowledge she had gained from books and from what she had been told. But she was trying to think of every eventuality.

She could do nothing about the poultry, who would have to survive as best they could; while she would be sorry to lose any of them, they could be replaced. From a human perspective, a more serious potential problem was the cistern. This was situated about ten feet above the normal water level; a lot would depend on the height of the storm surge, if there was one. But again, she could do nothing about that until after it happened, save ... she returned to the house.

'I think we need to fill all three bath tubs,' she told her mother. 'To the very brim. Then we stick to showers until this is over. That way, if the cistern is contaminated, we'll have enough drinking water to last us a week or more, which should allow time to get a tanker up from Nassau.'

'You really think there could be that big a surge?'

'I hope not. But we have to allow for it.'

'You're always so calm,' Jane observed.

'I had to learn, at an early age, that getting agitated only ever makes things worse.'

Jane squeezed her hand and got to work.

Anna went up to her bedroom veranda and used her high-powered binoculars to survey the sea to the south. Although the clouds were building very fast and coming closer, now more black than white, the wind remained light and the sea calm. And immediately she gave a sigh of relief as she spotted the Chris-Craft, moving towards the cay at speed. There was no other shipping in sight, but from habit she swung the glasses to the west and north, sweeping the deep water channel. And frowned.

There was something out there, at the very limit of the binocular range even when positioned some thirty feet above sea level, perhaps forty miles. It was too far off properly to make out, but it had to be a boat of some sort, and she did not think it was large enough to be a liner hurrying for shelter, and in any event, it was coming this way. Most probably it was a trawler. Although she would have thought any trawler late returning would be heading for Nassau rather than Eleuthera; the only really snug harbours on the big island were on the south-eastern end, which was well over a hundred miles away from the cay, much less out there at sea; the vessel wouldn't make it before the arrival of the hurricane ... at the south-eastern end of the island.

She went down to the dock to greet Tommy.

'Any problems?'
'No, ma'am. Mr Bartley must have been in good time for his plane. You boys help me bed this down,' he told the gardeners, who were waiting along with Desiree.
They fell to, carrying out double warps in every direction, massing the topsides with fenders.
'Any other shipping about?' Anna asked, casually.
'Nobody in his right mind going to sea right now. Saving me.'
Anna decided against telling him about the craft she had just sighted. He could do nothing about it, and he might just be so agitated that he'd refuse to leave the island. As it was, he asked as they boarded the runabout. 'You sure you going be all right, ma'am?'
'That is the very thing bothering me,' Desiree put in.
'I'll be all right,' Anna assured him. 'Just make sure *you're* all right. That's a big stretch of open water between here and North Eleuthera.'
'Ah, is only thirty miles, ma'am. We be there in an hour and a half. And we coming back just as soon as the sea go back down.'
'Just don't take any risks. And make sure the runabout is safe.'
She waved them off, watched them steering over the shallows to the north-east, while she fondled the two dogs. Suddenly she felt intensely lonely, even if she knew that they had to go, both on account of the coming storm and because she couldn't risk having them here if

there was trouble coming out of the west. But with them gone, she could concentrate on the problems nearer to hand. She looked up at the sky, which was now entirely black.

'Come along, chaps.' She led them back up to the house, but before they got there the skies opened in a drenching downpour. She ran the last fifty yards, arrived laughing and panting, while the dogs barked with delicious excitement. 'Now shake,' she commanded, when they gained the veranda. They obeyed and she opened the door. 'You're spending the night in here.'

That seemed to delight them, and they followed her up the stairs to her bedroom, where they were regarded with outraged scepticism by Isis. Anna took her binoculars on to the veranda again. The squall had swept across the island and was now over the passage, obliterating visibility for the moment. Then it cleared, and she could see the mysterious boat again.

It was definitely coming straight for the cay, and now that it was some thirty miles off she could just about estimate that it was something over fifty feet long, and therefore capable of carrying at least twenty people in reasonable comfort.

She continued to study the stranger for some minutes, trying to ascertain its speed. This was certainly not very fast, about eight knots, she thought. That meant it would reach the outer reef in about three hours time, just about dusk. But there was only the one narrow passage, which required local knowledge, and within the reef there was no shelter, just open beach. As they had to know there was a storm on its way, if they were coming here they would need to round the south side of the island and gain the more sheltered shallows, and hope to get into her little harbour.

If they were coming here. But that was an increasingly likely scenario. She went downstairs, accompanied by the dogs, still excited at being allowed the run of this unknown territory, and opened the wooden cases, which had already been unsealed by Clive. Two hundred five-shot point-two-two magazines for her Walther. But she didn't think they would be too much value in a major shoot-out. Two tommy guns, loaded, and with four spare drums each. Perfect! It was three years since last she had fired a tommy gun.

And then, the rocket-launcher. Although a heavy weapon it was both simpler and lighter than she had expected, and fitted neatly into her shoulder; open at both ends there would be no recoil to worry about. There were six rockets, each containing about three and a half pounds of penthalite, an explosive powerful enough, it was claimed, to penetrate five inches of armour; it should certainly get through a couple of inches of wood, once the enemy came within the rather limited range of three hundred yards. The gap through the southern reef was just about that distance from the dock.

'Have you ever fired one of those?' her father asked from the doorway.

'There's a first time for everything.'

'But you think there is going to be a first

time?'

'It could happen. Papa, you understand the drill about handling a hurricane?'

'We've been through it often enough.'

'Tell me. Word for word.'

He frowned, then concentrated. 'When the storm is very close, there will be a catastrophic fall in barometric pressure, which in a confined space can be dangerous. So, as the first force will approach from the north-east, we open a shutter on the south-west side to equalize the pressure inside the house. This is safe until the eye passes over, when the wind will drop right away and the skies may even clear. But within a few minutes the wind will resume from the south-west, perhaps stronger than before. During the eye, therefore, shutter number one must be closed, and a north-east facing window opened.'

'Perfect. Remember all that, and you can't go wrong.'

'But you're going to be here, aren't you?'

'That is my intention. But you never know. I'm going out for a little while. Lock the door behind me, and don't open it again until I call. Promise?'

'Anna ... there is trouble, isn't there?'

'Come with me.' She took him upstairs to her bedroom, showed him the approaching boat, which was now visible to the naked eye.

'You think that could be coming here?'

'It's beginning to look like it.'

Now that it was within about ten miles of the island, the boat was altering course to the south-east, for the passage through the main reef.

'But ... aren't they just seeking shelter?'

'Papa, that boat has come from far away. As everyone knows there is a storm coming, it shouldn't be out there at all. If it hasn't been listening to the forecasts, which is hard to believe, and has suddenly realized it's in danger, it should be making for Nassau. It's only forty miles, and it's out of the direct path of the storm. But it's not doing that. It's trying to get in here, where there is no shelter at all, where there's no room for a thing that size with my boat in place.'

'You think they may be ... what?'

'I think they may be Mafia.'

'What? But you have no connection with the Mafia. Do you?'

'They are in the employ of the MGB.'

He stared at her, ashen-faced. 'How long have you known this might happen?'

'A few days, now.'

'And ... but you've sent everyone away.'

'I work better on my own.'

'My God! What are we going to do?'

'You are going to do as I said, sit tight and keep the doors locked.'

'You mean you're going out to confront these people? But surely you'll be better off here, with all this fire power, and under cover. I'd help you.'

'Have you ever fired a gun in your life?'

'Well ... no.'

'Then now is no time to start. But I'm leaving you a tommy gun just in case. You don't have to aim it, just point it in the general direction of anyone who breaks in and squeeze the trigger. As for my staying here, that would be to give them a free run of the island. God knows how much damage they could cause. And we wouldn't know what they were doing, what explosives they might be planting around us.'

'And you think you can meet them on the beach? You? A—'

'Please, Papa. Don't say it.'

'I was going to say, alone.'

She kissed him. 'Then I forgive you. Just sit tight. You're in command until I come back.' She went down to the radio room, put her Walther and a couple of magazines in her shoulder bag, just in case, and added the spare drums for the tommy gun as well as the rockets. It weighed a ton, but she didn't have far to go. She slung it, added the tommy gun, tucked the bazooka under her arm, and smiled at her father, who was watching her with increasing apprehension.

'Do you mean to kill all the people on that boat?'

'I mean to defend the cay, Papa. And the only adequate defence is offence. And the best offence of all is the pre-emptive strike. So wish me luck.' She slung her binoculars round her neck. 'You guys stay here and guard the house,' she told the dogs.

Her mother was in the hall. 'Anna—'

'This is no time for talk, Mama. Papa knows what to do. But I shouldn't be all that long.' She kissed her, and opened the door.

* * *

It was only five o'clock, but the weather had deteriorated dramatically: the clouds were so low and black it was almost dark, and they hurried by, driven by a strong but not yet storm-force wind, and accompanied by driving rain squalls, rumbles of thunder and vivid flashes of forked lightning, most striking the surface of the sea; she had hardly left the shelter of the veranda when she was soaked to the skin.

She reached the slope leading down to the dock, and saw the large motor boat slowly feeling its way towards the reef. She chose her spot behind a casuarina tree and waited, as the ship came through the passage – she obviously had someone on board who knew the waters – and approached the dock, now rolling violently in the surging waves that swept across the sound to break on the dock and the beach. From the shelter of the swaying casuarinas Anna used the glasses to study the approaching vessel, pushing wet hair from her eyes. Now there could be no doubt that Fair Cay was her destination, and she was showing no lights, while as Anna focused the glasses she could make out several men on her deck ... and that they were carrying tommy guns of their own.

That removed any lingering idea that they were simply coming for shelter. She knelt against the tree, opened her bag, stowed the binoculars. And fitted a rocket into the launcher, then held it to her shoulder to peer through the sight. She waited until the trawler yacht was within a hundred yards of the dock, sighting all the time, aiming at the hull which rose some eight feet out of the water to make a target she could not possibly miss, then drew a deep breath and squeezed the trigger. Even without a recoil the force of the discharge seemed to travel right through her body, throwing her back against the tree, driving the breath from her lungs. But despite her discomfort she was already fitting another rocket to the muzzle before peering down the sight again.

At pandemonium. The trawler had yawed violently, away from the dock, and there was a gaping hole in her hull, just above the waterline. That did not mean that she was about to sink, even if she was obviously taking water with every roll. Anna aimed just below the previous mark, and fired again, then lowered the bazooka to rub her shoulder and use the glasses.

Taken entirely by surprise at the suddenness and violence of the attack the would-be invaders seemed to be panic-stricken. Several were firing their guns, but as they could not see her and had no idea where the rockets had come from, they were simply making a noise. Others had climbed up to the top deck behind the flying bridge and were unlashing a rubber dinghy. Still others were running in and out of the wheelhouse.

Anna reloaded the bazooka, aimed, and fired, this time aiming at the wheelhouse itself. It seemed to explode in a kaleidoscope of shattering instruments. She did not know if she had killed anybody, although it seemed likely, especially as the house burst into flames, but the boat was now completely out of control, drifting helplessly, and now definitely sinking, as she heeled slowly to port. With the wind where it was, Anna estimated that she would be driven back on to the reef before she went down, although in any event with only about twelve feet of water out there, she was not going to go down very far.

Several men had already jumped into the water to make for the beach. Others were still freeing the dinghy and pushing it out to the rail. Anna laid down the bazooka, which had served its purpose, and picked up the shotgun, sending a shot into the middle of the group. Men fell left and right, and the dinghy exploded with an obvious gush of air which she couldn't hear above the rattle of the rain and the howl of the wind.

It was time to turn her attention to the men in the water. Some were in trouble, waving their arms and clearly calling for help, although she couldn't hear them either. But others had reached the shallows, and were wading or staggering ashore, buffeted and occasionally knocked down by the breaking waves. But most of them were still carrying their guns.

Anna laid the shotgun alongside the bazooka, pulling fallen leaves over both guns to conceal them, unslung her tommy gun, and crawled through the trees to a better vantage point, immediately above the beach, and close enough, she felt, for them to hear her even in the wind.

The survivors were just coming ashore. There were six of them, and she counted another six still floundering in the sea. Four more were still on the sinking ship, now virtually on her beam ends, and Anna reckoned that there had been about four in the burning wheelhouse. Twenty men, she thought, sent to kill one woman.

That did not encourage her to feel the least sorry for any of them, but she was reluctant to kill them all, unless she had to. She cupped her hands round her mouth. 'I have you covered,' she shouted. 'Throw down your weapons and put your hands on your heads. If you do not obey me, now, I will fire into you.'

There was a moment's hesitation, then someone shouted, 'It's the bitch, right up there.' As he spoke the man opened fire, as did his companions. Anna lay flat, her hands over her head, and the bullets sliced through the trees and bushes. Then the firing stopped, and she rose to her knees again, but as she did so there was the loudest noise she had ever heard, a screaming howl like an express train entering a tunnel at full speed with its whistle blowing. The hurricane wind had arrived.

Instinctively she dropped on to her face again, digging her fingers into the soil. What the men were doing she had no idea; every sound was obliterated by the howl of the wind, now joined by the booming crashing of the waves. Although she was lying still she found herself gasping for breath, and then realized that she was being moved, or perhaps the whole island was being moved.

Desperately she tried to grasp the trunk of the nearest tree, but that was moving too, the entire roots being torn out of the ground. She released it and threw herself away from it, as it came down with an enormous scything sound, striking the ground with an earth-shaking crash and taking several smaller trees with it. But by then Anna was far away. In escaping the falling casuarinas she had inadvertently risen to her knees, and was now carried along by the wind, crashing through various bushes, bouncing off trees. The tommy gun had long flown from her hands, but the shoulder bag, held by its strong leather strap, was still round her neck and she clutched it against her breasts and stomach to protect herself as best she could.

Then suddenly she found herself in a pool of water. For a moment she supposed she had been driven up the hill and into the pool, but this was fresh. Then, the cistern? But that was very nearly a mile from the dock.

She again rose to her knees, but while the wind continued to howl, it was no longer driving her along, and she realized that she had fallen into a hollow, and that the water had just been dumped here by the rain, which continued to teem down.

There was another tearing, scything sound, and she instinctively ducked into the water, and again felt the earth shake as another tree came down, right over her head, bridging both sides of the dip. Branches flailed her head but she was relatively unhurt, and she realized that she was now as safe as she could possibly be, protected by the dip from the full force of the wind, and by the tree from any more debris. So she lay, totally immersed save for her head, against the side of the hollow, and gasped for breath.

Anna had no idea for how long she lay in her

ditch. She later realized that she must have nodded off from time to time, so that when the thunder dwindled and the wind suddenly dropped, she came to with a start. Looking at her watch, she discovered it was eleven o'clock, and the moon was shining brilliantly from an apparently clear sky. The eye!

As she reckoned it had been about seven when the storm had hit, she had lain here for four hours. Now she had a tremendous sense of urgency to find out what had been happening. Slowly she pushed herself up. She was dripping water, even from her hair, as the bandanna had long blown away, she was shivering with cold, and she felt as if she had been ridden over by a horde of elephants, but as she felt her legs and arms and ribs she realized that she was only bruised.

She climbed out of her hollow, looked around at a scene of utter devastation. The darkness hid the worst of it, but there were fallen trees everywhere. She made her way to the dock, and saw to her immense relief that *Fair Girl* was still riding to her mooring; the water inside the dock was relatively calm, and when she went down to it she saw that although three of the warps had snapped, the others had held, and she reckoned the amount of water both on deck and in puddles on the dock itself had been caused mainly by the rain; as she had estimated was likely, the long area of relatively shallow water had prevented any big storm surge from reaching the cay. Fortune, she thought, favours the brave. Or the ungodly.

On the other hand, the trawler yacht had entirely disappeared, either torn to pieces on the bottom or broken up on the reef. There would be time enough to check that out tomorrow. But the men! They were not to be seen either. Yet they, or their bodies, had to be around somewhere. That was assuming they had all perished.

She retraced her steps to the bushes where she had left the bazooka and the shotgun. Remarkably, while the bazooka was missing, the shotgun was still there. As the rocket-launcher was by far the heavier piece of metal, that had to be a freak of the wind ... Or someone had found it. But as the other rockets were still in her bag, it wouldn't do its new owner much good.

And there was no use looking for any of the invaders in the dark, and with the wind likely to return in the next few minutes. She climbed the rise to the house, increasingly aware of her aches and pains, but so relieved as she got closer to see the chinks of light through the shutters: thanks to her precautions, the electrics had not failed.

She banged on the door, and the dogs barked. 'Anna?' Johann asked.

'It's me.'

The bolts were drawn, and Anna was in his arms. 'I'm afraid I'm very wet,' she warned.

He hugged her tighter.

'Anna!' Jane was awaiting her turn. 'It was so long. We thought ... oh, we thought...'

'I was sheltering in a ditch. But it filled with water.' She turned her attention to the dogs. 'No problems, here?'

'I think one of the trees got struck by lightning,' Johann said. 'There was a terrible crash.'

'We'll have a look in the morning.'

'But the ship?' Jane said. 'Did you see it?'

'Yes, I did.'

'And was it coming here?'

'I really can't be sure. It sank.'

'But ... what about the people on board?'

'I can't be sure about them either. I was trying to stay alive. The wind arrived before I could get back to the house. Have you had dinner?'

'Well ... we ate something.'

'I am ravenous. I am also filthy, as you can see, very wet, and very cold. I would also like a stiff drink, Papa. Meanwhile, I'm going to have a hot shower.'

'But what are we going to do?' Jane asked.

'Mama, there is nothing we can do until tomorrow morning. We'll pick up the pieces then.'

Isis lay on the bed and stretched as she watched her mistress strip off her sodden clothes; Anna wondered if she had even noticed there was a storm on.

She was still in the shower when the wind started again, howling around the house while the thunder boomed and the lightning flashed, but Anna felt that it was not as intense as before, although she recognized that could be because she was now under shelter instead of actually out in it.

She washed her hair, wrapped it in a towel and herself in a dressing gown, and went downstairs to enjoy the hot rum toddy prepared by her father and the meal prepared by her mother. Who continued to be anxious. 'What are we going to do?' she asked again above the roar of the wind and the crashing of the rain.

'I told you, sit it out,' Anna replied, 'until this abates. It should have done that by dawn.'

'What about the storm surge?' Johann asked. They could hear the crashing of the waves even above the wind.

'There is nothing we can do about that either, Papa. If it comes, it comes. As this house has been through a hurricane before, I'm quite sure it'll do so again. But we can't attempt to assess the damage and pick up any pieces until it's daylight and the wind drops.'

'I was thinking of the people on the boat,' Jane said. 'They can't *all* have drowned. Some of them must have come ashore.'

'In which case, we'll find them too, in the morning. Now you both go to bed, and get some sleep.'

'What are you going to do?' Johann asked.

'The same,' she assured him, and stroked the dogs. 'You're on watch.'

Anna slept with Isis in her arms, awoke at six, not quite certain where she was. With the shutters closed the room was still dark, and the heavy wood also shut out all normal sound ... and there was no other.

Isis had moved during the night, so she rolled out of bed, opened the shutters and then the doors to the veranda, went outside to gaze at a very turbulent sea, with tossing whitecaps in every direction, both within and outside the reef. But that was a residue of the storm, because this morning the wind, if fresh, had lost most of its force, and the sky was a clear empty blue, although there was a heavy cloud bank to the north-west to suggest that somebody else was catching it.

But that the storm had passed this way was evident wherever she looked. There were trees down to every side; even those coconut palms that had not been uprooted were bent almost double, and as her father had suspected, one of the casuarinas had come down in the pool, which was in any event overflowing, flooding the coronation and into the garden around it. But that would be mostly rainwater.

She dressed in pants and a shirt, sandals and a sun hat, leaving her still damp hair loose, then emptied the shoulder bag of the rockets and three of the drums, retaining one. As she had no idea what she might be going to encounter, she also left the Walther and the two magazines, then carried Isis downstairs and set her before a saucer of milk.

Both her parents were up. 'Is it over?' Jane asked.

'The storm, yes.'

'You mean...'

'There should be at least a couple of bodies lying around. I'm talking about drowned,' she hastily added as she saw her mother's expression.

'Do you want breakfast?'

'It's very early. I'll have a look outside first.'

'I'll come with you,' Johann volunteered.

'Thank you, Papa.' She went into the radio room, reloaded the shotgun with scatter shot, slung it and the reserve tommy gun, then wound the aerial back up and listened for a few minutes. The airwaves were busy with both contact calls and calls for assistance, but none of them appeared to be directed at Fair Cay.

She joined her father and mother. 'Now, Mama,' she said, 'we're not going to be long, but you must keep the doors shut and locked until we come back One or two of those characters may have survived.'

Jane nodded, face grim with determination. Anna had considered leaving her a weapon, but she knew that, like her father, her mother had never fired a gun in her life and in any event would be quite incapable of shooting a human being. Besides, with the storm shutters still in place and the doors locked the house was just about invulnerable. So she kissed her, and let the dogs out, followed by her father, to stand on the veranda and take long, deep breaths. 'Doesn't that smell good?'

'Where do we begin?' Johann asked.

'North beach first. We need to know how high the surge came last night.'

They stopped by the generator house, picking their way over fallen trees and scattered underbrush. 'The garden is ruined,' Johann commented.

'It'll grow again.' She surveyed the little house. A tree had actually come down very close to it, but no damage had been done, and it growled reassuringly. Anna topped up both the oil and water from the cans that always waited beside the machinery, then led the way over the slight rise to look down at the beach.

'There's a sight,' Johann said.

Beyond the reef the seas were still a mass of tumbling whitecaps, crashing into the rocks, and the beach itself had been scoured so that there were coral head poking up through what was left of the sand.

'Where's it all gone?' Johann wondered.

'It'll come back,' Anna assured him. She was more interested in the evidence of the surge, indicated by where the bushes had been flattened. 'That was about eight feet,' she said. 'Thank God for that.'

'You reckon?'

'It shouldn't have got to the cistern. Let's go find out. But we'll check the east beach first.'

They stood on the rise and looked down on the dock. The sound was still turbulent, but, as she had observed during the night, the dock was undamaged and so was *Fair Girl*.

'Think the staff will get across today?' Johann asked.

'I sincerely hope they don't try. Not only are they likely to be swamped in that open boat, but we need the cay to ourselves for at least today.'

He raised his eyebrows, and she smiled at him. 'They don't know anything about what our visitors might have wanted, and I aim to keep it that way. Just for starters, there is a bazooka and a tommy gun lying around somewhere. But they can wait. There should be some interesting objects on the beach.'

He followed her as she climbed down the rocks. 'But that boat. Where did it go down?'

'It went on to the reef.'

He followed the direction of her pointing finger. 'I don't see anything.'

'She broke up in the storm. I imagine there are bits scattered along the shore. And...' She pointed as they reached the sand.

'Oh, my God! That's a leg.'

'It looks like one. There'll be others.'

'But ... how many?'

'I don't know. I think there were something like twenty people on board. But only six definitely came ashore.'

'And you hope to hush that up?'

'Of course not. There was this boat, apparently trying to make shelter, and she hit a rock or something coming through the reef, and went down. As this was just as the full force of the hurricane hit, there was nothing we could do about it.'

'But if you shot these people...'

'I did not shoot anybody, Papa. I was going to, but the storm hit first, and threw me into the bushes. I couldn't move for four hours, by which time ... Well, the boat had gone and so had all the people I could see. On the other hand, they were carrying guns when they left the boat, and some of those may have come ashore. We'd better have a look.'

Over the next hour they uncovered four more bodies, and two tommy guns. 'Leave those,' Anna said, 'and we'll take them up to the house when we find my gear. After we've checked the reservoir.'

'But ... what are we going to do about these bodies?'

'There is nothing you and I can do about them, Papa. They all drowned. When the boys come back, probably tomorrow, we'll be able to do something. Meanwhile, we'll call Nassau, tell them there's been a tragedy here, and ask for help. You come up from there,' she told the dogs, who were sniffing around the corpses.

'You said you thought that six men came ashore.'

'Yes, I did.'

'But—'

'There are only five bodies. He could have been dragged back out to sea by the undertow, or –' she looked up at the trees – 'if he's ashore, he'll turn up.' She tucked the shotgun under her arm. 'Just let's check that reservoir.'

Johann followed her up to the land, wiping his brow with his handkerchief.

They regained the path. The Rawlings' cottage appeared undamaged, and if the orchard was carpeted with fallen fruit, only two of the trees had come down; the rest had been protected by the grove of casuarinas in the midst of which she had spent the night. The vegetable garden was far more devastated, although Anna reckoned that most of the damage had been done by the rain.

But the hen run ... it was deserted. 'Oh, fuck it!' she muttered.

'All of them!' Johann said. 'Fifty fowls! That is tragic.'

Anna looked out to sea, wondering if they were all floating out there, but even the lagoon was still too disturbed to make out anything. Then she was startled by a sudden squawk behind her. She swung round, instinctively levelling the shotgun, and saw the cock rising from the bushes, whence it had been disturbed by the dogs. And now it was joined by a host of hens and chickens, clucking and squawking. They weren't all there, but she did not think more than a dozen were gone. 'Oh, you darlings,' she cried, feeling close to tears.

'I have an idea,' her father remarked, 'that you value these animals more than most human beings.'

'I think it's that I haven't been all that lucky with most of the human beings I happen to have encountered.'

She hurried on to the reservoir. This was overflowing, but when, having laid down the shotgun, she waded ankle-deep to the actual cistern and stooped to taste the water, it was all fresh. 'Do you know,' she said over her shoulder. 'We have been quite phenomenally lucky.'

For reply there was a startled exclamation from Johann, and a low growl from Jupiter. Anna turned, still stooping in the water, and saw that a man had emerged from the bushes and was standing with his arm round Johann's neck and a Browning automatic pistol pressed to his head. His appearance had surprised even the dogs, who were uncertain whether to attack him as that would have involved attacking Johann as well. Anna couldn't risk that, so she said, 'Stay Jupiter! Stay Juno! Wait.' While she slowly rose to her feet, mentally cursing her own carelessness; her tommy gun was still slung, and the shotgun was on the dry ground eight feet away.

'Take off that gun and throw it over here,' the man commanded.

Anna obeyed, tossing it a few feet to his right. But he did not, as she had hoped he might, make any move to pick it up. 'Would I be addressing the famous Countess von Widerstand?'

Anna had been taking him in. He was not a big man, but looked very fit. He was also quite handsome in a dark fashion, with a little black moustache, and she also figured that in happier times he was something of a dandy, in that his clothes, if torn and dishevelled, had been very well cut and were obviously of good material.

And he was clearly not a Russian. Therefore... 'You would be correct,' she agreed. 'And you are from the Ravanellis.'

'I am Luis Ravanelli,' he announced proudly. 'You have sunk my ship, and destroyed my people.'

'The fortunes of war,' Anna said, sympathetically. 'It was very silly of you to put to sea with a hurricane about.'

'Ha! The storm was supposed to give us cover, Solly said.'

'Well, whoever Solly is, or was, he was a twit.'

'You have courage. I was told this. And you are as beautiful as they said.'

'You say the sweetest things,' Anna said.

'But I have come here to kill you. You know that.'

'I thought it might be likely.' Her brain was racing, but as long as he held his pistol to Johann's head – her father was looking petrified – there was nothing she could do save keep things going until either she saw an opportunity or he made a mistake ... as he was already doing by preferring to look at her than merely shoot her. 'May I ask, is this something personal? I mean, I have never seen you before in my life.'

'Sure it's personal. Now. You've killed nineteen of my people, plus Lorna Strezzi. She was a good girl. Anyway, I'm being paid. Twenty grand. What do you think of that?'

'Not a lot,' Anna said. 'Twenty grand? I'm worth a lot more than that.'

Almost the pistol moved. 'To whom?'

'Put that gun down and we'll talk about it.'

'Oh, no. I'm not stupid. I know all about you.'

'Do you? How exciting. There's just one thing more, though. Have you given any thought to how you are going to leave the island? Now the storm is gone, my staff will be coming back this afternoon, and they're not going to take kindly to finding me dead.'

'You keep thinking I'm stupid,' Luis pointed out. 'You have a boat in that dock. I'll use that.'

'Silly me,' Anna commented. 'I never thought of that. But do you know how to helm a boat? How to navigate?'

'What's difficult about handling a boat?'

A chink of light. 'Nothing at all. Well, then, I suppose you'll need the keys. They're right here in my bag.'

She held her breath; anyone who really knew boats would know that whenever they were securely moored the keys remained in the ignition. But she suspected he knew absolutely nothing about it.

'So hand them over. Throw them on the ground, here.'

'Yes, sir.' She sighed, opened her bag and put her hand inside. 'Jupiter,' she said. 'Kill!'

Jupiter, who had been gazing at Luis with total hostility, dashed forward, teeth bared. Luis swung to face him, retaining his hold on Johann's neck but moving the pistol to fire at the dog. But before he could squeeze the trigger Anna had drawn her Walther. She had only the head to aim at, but she wanted nothing more. Brains and blood flew, and Luis went down, the pistol flying from his hand.

Johann fell to his knees, holding his neck. Jupiter, realizing the crisis was over, licked his face.

'Anna,' Johann said. 'My God, Anna!'

'He talked too much,' Anna said.

'Mr Ravanelli,' Botten said, 'Would you happen to have a head for me?'

Don Giovanni, chewing on a Rennie's, gazed at him with undisguised venom. 'You don't read the papers?'

'I read the *New York Times*.'

Don Giovanni gestured at a paper on his desk.

'That is last Monday's *Miami Herald.*' He picked it up. 'The headline says, "Yachting tragedy in the Bahamas". And then: "Fifty-foot motor yacht *Calypso* reported lost in Thursday's hurricane. The yacht, owned by Miami businessman Joe Solly, left the mainland on Wednesday on a trip to Eleuthera in the northern Bahamas. With Mr Sully were several friends, including Chicago millionaire Luis Ravanelli."'

Botten frowned.

Don Giovanni went on reading. '"It appears that Mr Solly, an experienced yachtsman, thought he would reach Nassau harbour before the storm broke, but when he realized he could not make it, he attempted to take shelter at Fair Cay, a small island owned by a Miss Anna Fitzjohn. Unfortunately, the yacht struck the reef south of the cay, and was lost with all hands. 'It was terrible,' said Miss Fitzjohn, an Irish lady, to our reporter. 'We could see what was happening, but there was nothing we could do about it in those conditions.' According to the Nassau police, Miss Fitzjohn, who lives on the island with her parents, behaved with great courage, actually putting to sea in her own boat the moment conditions improved, in an effort to find survivors. But there were none. Nineteen bodies have been recovered out of the twenty, and these have all been identified. The missing man would appear to be Mr Ravanelli, who is married and a father of two."'

He laid down the paper and stared at Botten.

'What a shitting mess,' Botten remarked. 'Still, look on the bright side. Your boy could have survived. I mean, if they haven't found his body, well, anything is possible.'

'My boy is dead.' Each word was a drip of vitriol from Don Giovanni's lips.

'You're being pessimistic.'

'He must've reached the shore,' Don Giovanni said, 'And he ran into this dame, and she put a bullet in him. What she did with the body I don't know, but there ain't no reason for the police to suspect foul play.'

'That has to be pure conjecture.'

'If everything you told us about this dame is right, it's facts.'

Botten's frown was back. 'You reckon this Fitzjohn is the Countess von Widerstand?'

'According to Strezzi, this woman Fitzjohn is the girl in the photo you gave me. And you say that was this countess.'

Botten's forehead cleared. 'Well, well. That *is* good news. Now we have a name and we have an address. That's great, Don Giovanni. Give me back my twenty grand, and we'll take it from here.'

'My son is dead.'

'Yeah. Well, that's the way the cookie crumbles. I'm inclined to go with the paper and reckon he was pretty ambitious putting to sea with that kind of storm knocking about.' He held out his hand. 'Give me my money, and we'll call it quits.'

'You mother-fucking son of a Communist bitch. My son is dead, and you talk about cookies crumbling.'

'You'll get over it. Money.'

Don Giovanni stared at him for several seconds, then opened his desk drawer, drew an automatic pistol, and shot him through the head.

EPILOGUE

'So there I was,' Anna said. 'The heroine of the hour. For two or three days.'

'And no one ever suspected the truth?'

'There was nothing for them to suspect. That morning Papa and I found all the discarded weapons and took them up to the house. That five bodies should have been washed ashore was perfectly natural.'

'But the yacht ... the bazooka damage.'

'She had been reduced to driftwood by the sea pounding her on the reef. One or two of the timbers appeared to have fire marks, but the police reckoned there could well have been an explosion where she hit.'

'And Luis' body?'

'As soon as the seas went down a little, Papa and I took him out in Fair Girl, *weighted his body, and sank him in deep water. We were just coming back from that trip when the police arrived, so we told them that we had been out trying to find any survivors. That made me even more of a heroine.'*

'But if the Ravanellis knew where you were, surely they would have passed that information to the Russians?'

'Do you know, that puzzled me as well, but for

some reason they never did anything about it.'

'So all ended well, and Clive...?'

'Was back in a week. And we were married the week after that.'

'With your carte blanche?'

'No. The bastards wouldn't give it to me.' She shrugged, an entrancing sight. 'As it happened, as I was in the clear, I didn't need it. Then.'

'But?'

Anna sighed. 'Life is full of buts. Nothing lasts forever. But...' She smiled. 'I was coming up to the happiest time of my life.'